To Suzie and John, Brendan and Jack

Acknowledgments

Our thanks to these top professionals, who shared with us their valuable time and expertise:

Captain Rich Conklin; Dr. Humphrey Germaniuk; Captain Neil Oswald, USMC; Elaine Pagliaro, MS, JD; Steve Bowen; Ken Zercies; Mark Bruno; and C. Peter Colomello.

And our special thanks to our researchers, Lynn Colomello and Lauren Sheftell, and of course Mary Jordan, who manages it all.

James
Patterson

WITH MAXINE PAETRO

PRIVATE

Century · London

Published by Century, 2010

2 4 6 8 10 9 7 5 3 1

First published in Great Britain in 2010 by
Century
Random House, 20 Vauxhall Bridge Road,
London SW1V 2SA

www.randomhouse.co.uk

Addresses for companies within The Random House Group Limited can be found at:
www.randomhouse.co.uk/offices.htm

The Random House Group Limited Reg. No. 954009

A CIP catalogue record for this book
is available from the British Library

Hardback ISBN 9781846057687
Trade paperback ISBN 9781846057694

The Random House Group Limited supports The Forest Stewardship
Council (FSC), the leading international forest certification organisation. All our
titles that are printed on Greenpeace approved FSC certified paper carry the FSC logo.
Our paper procurement policy can be found at:
www.rbooks.co.uk/environment

Mixed Sources
Product group from well-managed
forests and other controlled sources
www.fsc.org Cert no. TT-COC-2139
FSC © 1996 Forest Stewardship Council

Printed and bound in the UK by
CPI Mackays, Chatham ME5 8TD

Prologue

"YOU'RE DEAD, JACK"

One

TO THE BEST OF my understandably shaky recollection, the first time I died it went something like this.

Mortar rounds were thumping all around me, releasing what sounded like a shower of razor blades. I was carrying Marine Corporal Danny Young over my shoulder, and I loved this guy. He was the toughest soldier I'd ever fought beside, funny as hell, and best of all, he was *hopeful* — his wife back in West Texas was pregnant with their fourth kid.

Now his blood bubbled down my flight suit, splashing on my boots like water from a drainpipe.

I ran across rocky ground in the dark, and I choked out to Danny, "I've got you; I've got you. Just stay with me, *you hear me?*"

I lowered him to the ground a few yards away from the helicopter, and suddenly there was a concussive explosion, as though the ground had blown up around me. I felt a stunning hammer strike to my chest, and that was the end.

I died. I passed to the other side. I don't even know how long I was gone.

Del Rio told me later that my heart had stopped.

I just remember swimming up to the light, and the pain, and the awful reek of aviation fuel.

My eyes flashed open and there was Del Rio in my face, his hands pressing down on my chest. He laughed when my eyes opened—and at the same time tears ran down his cheeks. He said, "Jack, you son of a bitch, you're back."

A dense curtain of oily black smoke rolled over us. Danny Young lay right there beside me, his legs splayed at weird angles, and behind Del Rio was the helicopter, burning bright white, getting ready to blow.

My buddies were still in there. My friends. Guys who had risked their lives for me.

I choked out a few words. "We've got to get them out of there."

Del Rio tried his best to hold me down, but I used an elbow to swing at his jaw, and connected. He fell back and I got away from him, started running toward the fallen bird just as its magnesium skin caught fire.

There were Marines in there, and I had to get them out.

The fearsome *chunk-a chunk-a chunk* of fifty-caliber machine gun ammo hammered. Ordnance exploded inside the aircraft. Del Rio shouted, *"Get down, asshole. Jack, get the hell down!"*

I felt all of his hundred and ninety pounds as he tackled me to the ground, and the helicopter disappeared in white-hot flames. I wasn't dead, but a lot of my friends were. I swear to God, I would have traded myself for them.

I guess that says a lot about me, and I'm not so sure that all of it is good. You'll see, and you can be the judge.

Sit back; it's a long story but a good one.

Two

IT WAS TWO YEARS after I got back from Afghanistan and the war. I hadn't seen my father in over a year, had no reason or desire to see him again. But when he called, he said he had something important to tell me. He said it was urgent and that it was going to change my life.

My father was a manipulative, lying bastard, but he'd hooked me, so there I was, walking through the forbidding visitors' gate of California State Prison at Corcoran.

Ten minutes later, I took a seat at the Plexiglas partition as he came into the cubicle on the other side and grinned at me, showing his gappy teeth. He had been handsome once; now he looked like Harrison Ford on meth.

He grabbed the phone, and I did the same on my side of the partition.

"You're looking good, Jack. Life must be agreeing with you."

I said, "You've lost weight."

"The food here is for rats, son."

My father picked up where he had left off the last time I'd seen him. Telling me how there were no gentleman crooks anymore, just punks. "They kill a clerk at a Stop-N-Go. Turn a robbery into a life sentence—for what? A hundred bucks?"

Listening to him made my head hurt and my back and neck stiffen. He ragged on blacks and Hispanics for being stupid, and here he was, serving life for extortion and murder. Same time, same place as the punks. I felt ashamed for all of the years I'd spent looking up to him, turning myself inside out to get an "Atta boy, Jack" instead of the back of his hand.

"Tell you what, Tom," I said. "I'll have a chat with the warden. See if I can get you transferred to the Bel-Air or the Beverly Wilshire."

He laughed. "I'll make it worth your while."

I finally smiled. "You never change."

He shrugged and grinned back at me. "Why should I, Jack?"

I noticed new tats on my father's knuckles. My name was on his left hand, my brother's name on the right. He used to knock us around with those fists, what he called "the old one-two." I drummed my fingers on the ledge.

"Am I boring you?" he asked.

"Hell, no. I parked my car in front of a hydrant."

My father laughed again, said, "I look at you, I see myself. When I was an idealist."

Narcissistic SOB. He still thought he was my idol, which couldn't have been further from the truth.

"Jack, let me ask you a serious question. You like working for that useless, pathetic hack Pinkus PI?"

"Prentiss. I've learned a lot from him. I'm happy. It's a job I'm good at."

"You're wasting your time, Jack. And I've got a better offer." He made sure he had my attention, then said, "I want you to take over Private."

I guess he'd gotten to the part that was supposed to change my life.

"Dad. Remember? All that's left of Private are a lot of file cabinets in a storage unit."

"You're going to get a package tomorrow," my father continued, as if I hadn't spoken. "It's a list of all my clients—and the dirt I had on them. There's also a document putting your name on my bank account in the Caymans," he said. "Fifteen million dollars, Jack. All yours. Do with it what you will."

I raised my eyebrows. Private had once done first-class investigation for movie stars, politicians, multimillionaires, even the White House. My dad had charged the maximum for his services. But fifteen *million*? How had he earned that much, and did I really want to know?

"What's the catch, right?" he said. "Simple. Don't tell your twin about the money. Anything I ever gave him he snorted or gambled. This is your birthright, Jack. I'm trying to do the right thing for once in my life."

"Did you hear me say that I'm happy at Prentiss?" I said.

"I wish you could see your face, Jack. Listen to me. Stop being the 'good twin' for half a frickin' second and think this through. There's no such thing as good money and bad money. It's all the same. Just a medium of exchange. And this is an opportunity, a big one. Fifteen million dollars' worth of opportunity.

"I want Private to be remembered as the best. You're a smart, good-looking kid, and on top of that, you're a frickin' war hero. Bring Private back to life. Do it for me, and more important, do it for yourself. Don't talk yourself out of a really good thing. Make Private the best in the world. You have the money, the talent—and the compassion—so do it."

A guard put a hand on my dad's shoulder. He hung on to the phone, looked at me with a kind of tenderness I hadn't seen since I was five or six, and said, "Have the life you deserve, Jack. Do great things." He touched the glass with his palm, then turned away.

A week after my visit to Corcoran, Tom Morgan took a shank to the liver. Three days later, my father was dead.

Part One

FIVE YEARS LATER, AND ALL GOING ACCORDING TO PLAN

Chapter 1

PEOPLE TRUST ME with their secrets, and I'm not exactly sure why. It must be something in my face, probably my eyes. Guinevere Scott-Evans had taken a chance and trusted me with her life and career a couple of months back.

Now she gripped my hand as I helped her out of my dark blue Lamborghini. She moved her narrow hips demurely, straightening out the black dress that fit her perfectly. She was gorgeous, an A-list movie star who was also genuinely funny and smart enough to have graduated from Vanderbilt.

I was Guin's date tonight for the Golden Globe Awards, her way of thanking me for tailing her rocker husband, who, it turned out, had been cheating on her with another man.

Guin was grieving, I knew, but she had her game face on for the Globes. She wanted to be seen tonight with a *hunk*—her word—and I could tell she also wanted to feel desirable.

"This'll be fun, Jack," she said, squeezing my fingers. "We're at a great table. Everybody from Columbia Pictures, plus Matt, of course."

Guin was up for best supporting actress for a love story she'd made with Matt Damon. I thought she had a chance to win; I certainly hoped so. I liked Guin a lot.

The fans out front of the Beverly Hilton were enjoying the pregame warm-up, calling out Guin's name as we headed up the rope line, cameras snapping away. A fan pointed her phone at me, asking me if I was somebody.

I laughed. "Are you kidding? I'm just arm candy."

Guin let go of my hand to embrace Ryan Seacrest, who pulled her into the spotlight. The fans wanted *her*, but she put her arm around my waist and brought me into the shot at her side.

Seacrest went with it, admired the cut of my tux and asked my name. His brow wrinkled as he tried to figure out if he knew me—and then Scarlett Johansson arrived, said "Hi, Jack"—and Guin and I were shooed along the red carpet that ran through the gauntlet of bleachers up to the entrance of the Beverly Hilton.

Wrong time for my cell phone to ring.

"Don't take it, Jack," Guin said. "You're off duty. You're mine for tonight, okay?" Her smile dimmed, and worry shadowed her beautiful features. "Okay, Jack?"

I glanced at the caller ID. "This'll just take a second."

The caller was Andy Cushman, and I couldn't believe it. Andy was a rock, but the voice on the phone was strained to breaking with tears.

"Jack. I need you to come to the house. I need you here right now."

"Andy, this is not a good time. Trust me, it isn't. What's wrong?"

"It's Shelby. *She's dead, Jack.*"

Chapter 2

DEAD? HOW COULD Shelby be dead? There had to be some mistake. But how could there be?

I was the one who had introduced Shelby to Andy. I was best man at their wedding less than six months ago. I'd had dinner with them last week at Musso and Frank. Andy told me they were going to name their first kid Jack. Not John or Jackson, just Jack.

Had Shelby suffered a heart attack—at her age? Had there been a car accident? Andy hadn't said, but he was devastated. And what hurt Andy hurt me.

I stuffed a wad of bills into the valet's hand, escorted a visibly upset Guin to the ballroom with apologies, and handed her over to Matt Damon. When I got back out to the street, my car was waiting.

I was in shock as I sped toward the Cushmans' home in my over-the-top sports car. The car was a gift from a client whose terrible secret I kept. When it wasn't in the shop for repairs, it was a cop magnet.

I slowed as I entered the Bluffs section of Pacific Palisades, the heavily patrolled village of small shops and homes within walking distance of the ocean. Ten minutes later, I braked in Andy's circular driveway.

Dusk was coming on. There were no lights on in the house, and the front door was wide open, the frame splintered.

Was an intruder in the house? I doubted it, but I took my gun out of the glove box before I went in through the open door.

Three years in the pilot's seat of a CH-46 during wartime had sharpened my visual acuity. I was adept at doing vigilant instrument scans, and then, in the next second, checking the ground for movement, dust, smoke, reflections, human outlines, or flashes of light.

As an investigator, I had another practical application for my somewhat unusual ability to pick out anomalies. I could look at a scene and almost instantly see what was out of place: a random speck of blood, a ding on a painted wall, a hair on a shag carpet.

As I entered the Cushmans' house, I scanned the living room for any signs of disturbance. The cushions were neat. Rugs were straight. Books and paintings were all in place.

I called Andy's name and he answered, "Jack? *Jack*. I'm in the bedroom. Please come."

I kept my gun, a custom Kimber .45, drawn as I went through the airy rooms to the master bedroom in its own wing in back.

I felt for the switches by the doorway and threw on the lights. Andy was sitting on the side of the bed, hunched over, holding his head in bloodstained hands.

Jesus Christ! What had happened here?

Unlike the living room, the bedroom looked as though it had been tossed by a tornado. Lamps and picture frames were smashed. The television had been ripped from the wall, but the cord was still plugged in.

Shelby's clothes, shoes, and underwear had been flung haphazardly around the room. *Oh, Jesus. Jesus Christ!*

Shelby was lying naked and very dead, face-up, in the center of the bed.

I tried to take it all in, but it was impossible to comprehend. Shelby had been shot through the forehead. From where her blood had pooled on the pale satin sheets, it looked like she'd taken a second shot in the chest.

Shock made my knees weak. I fought my impulse to go to Andy, to go to *Shelby*. I couldn't, mustn't do that. Stepping foot into that room would contaminate the crime scene.

So I called out to my friend, "Andy. What happened here?"

Andy looked up at me, his round face pasty white, his eyes bloodshot, his wire glasses askew. His face and hands were bloody. His voice was tremulous when he said, "Some-one killed Shelby. Shot her just like that. You've got to find out who did this, Jack. You've got to find the bastard who killed Shelby."

With that, my best friend broke down and cried like a little boy. The tough thing—I'd seen Andy cry as a little boy too.

Chapter 3

I FELT THE floor shifting under me, but I knew Andy was counting on me to think straight for both of us. Having a clear head in an emergency, that was supposed to be my calling card. I was Jack Morgan, right?

I told Andy to stay put, made my way back out to the car, and returned with an MD 80, the best camera ever made for shooting crime scenes. It had night vision, GPS, and spoke in a dozen languages — should I ever need to be told I'd left my lens cap on in Farsi or Mandarin.

I snapped off a dozen shots from the bedroom doorway, captured every detail I could think to cover.

While I took the photos, I tried to imagine what could have gone on here during the actual murder.

Apart from the blood on the bed and on Shelby, there was no other obvious trace around: no spray or prints on the walls, or drag marks or drips on the floor. She had almost definitely been killed in her bed. I pictured Shelby cowering against the headboard as the intruder busted up the room. He'd forced her to lie still, hadn't he? Then he shot her twice — in the chest and forehead. She had bled profusely from the terrible wounds, and then she had died.

Whatever the intruder's twisted motive, it clearly couldn't have been robbery. Shelby was still wearing her engagement ring, and an even bigger diamond was hanging from a chain around her neck. Her Hermès handbag was on the dresser, clipped shut.

So if this wasn't a burglary, what was it?

A thought occurred to me, the same one a homicide detective would have. Had Andy killed his wife? Was that why he had called me here? Because I was probably the best person in LA to handle this, to make it go away.

I talked calmly to my friend, telling him how sorry I was and how shocked. Then I asked him to leave Shelby where she was and come with me.

"We have to talk this through, Andy. We need to do it right now."

He came to the doorway, moaned, and sagged against me.

I held Andy up as I guided him to a chair in the living room. I took a seat on the sofa, separating myself from Andy on purpose. The next ten minutes or so were going to be bad — for both of us.

I asked the easy questions first. "Did you call nine one one?"

"I — I didn't want the cops here until I called you. No, I didn't call the police."

"Andy, do you own a gun? Do you have a gun in the house?"

He shook his head. "No. And I never have. Guns scare the crap out of me. You know that."

"Okay. Good. Did you notice—was anything taken?"

"The safe is in my study. I came in through the garage. I'd been at the office, and I put my briefcase in the study before I went into the bedroom....Everything looked okay. I don't know, Jack. I wasn't thinking about a robbery. I can't concentrate right now...."

I peppered Andy with more questions, and he answered them while looking at me as though I were a lifeboat and he a man overboard in a turbulent sea. He said he'd last seen Shelby that morning when he left for work, that he'd spoken to her from the car an hour ago. She'd sounded great.

"This is a tough question," I said. "Was she seeing anyone? Or were you?"

Andy looked at me as if I'd lost my mind and said, "Me, Jack? No. Her? She loved me. There was no reason to do that. We were both in love, totally in love. I never thought I could feel the way I felt about Shelby. We were trying to have a baby."

I took a controlled breath, then I pushed on. "Has anyone threatened your life, or Shelby's?"

"C'mon, I'm basically a glorified bean counter, Jack. And who'd want to kill Shelby? She's a sweetie. Everyone loved her...."

Apparently not.

I had to ask him. "You have to tell me the truth, Andy. Did you have anything to do with this?"

In about five seconds, Andy's expression went from grief to shock to fury.

"You're asking me *that*? You *know* how much I loved her. I'm telling you now and I never want to have to say it again. *I didn't kill her, Jack.* And I don't know who did. I can't imagine this happening. I can't, Jack."

Night was falling. I reached up and turned on a light. Andy was looking at me as though I'd punched him in the face.

Christ, I was his best friend.

"I believe you," I said. "The cops are going to grill you, though. Do you understand? The husband is always suspect number one."

He nodded his head and started crying again.

I got up and went into the foyer. I called Chief of Police Michael Fescoe at his home. Fescoe and I had become friends in the past couple of years. He was depressed due to his crap job, but he was a good man, and I trusted him.

I gave Fescoe the rundown, told him that Andy and I had been childhood friends and frat brothers at Brown and that I could vouch for his character a hundred percent.

I stayed with Andy as the cops and the CSU arrived. I heard him tell a detective that Shelby didn't have an enemy in the world.

And yet, whoever killed her had made a point.

This was not only an execution.

It was personal.

Chapter 4

JUSTINE SMITH was an elegant, serious-minded, academically brilliant brunette in her midthirties. She was a shrink by trade, a forensic profiler, and Jack Morgan's number two at Private. Clients trusted her almost as much as they trusted Jack. They also adored her; everyone did.

That evening, she was having dinner with LA's district attorney, Bobby Petino. Bobby was her best friend and her lover. He was a transplanted New Yorker, a connoisseur of Italian food. He had surprised Justine by picking her up as she was leaving work and driving her to one of their favorite places, Giorgio Baldi's in Santa Monica.

The restaurant was cozy, casual, family owned; the candlelit tables were close together, comfortably intimate. Several of the customers in the dining room were A-list celebrities, but Bobby's eyes were on Justine and no one else. Not even Johnny Depp and Denzel Washington, when they walked in laughing and joking as though life were just a big fun movie for them.

Bobby touched his wineglass to hers as Giorgio brought the steaming homemade pasta to the table. *There was nobody here but the two of them.*

"You know what?" Justine said. "I just love a surprise that puts a truly awful day into reverse. This is perfect. Thank you."

"All work, no play makes Justine a sad girl," he said. "And that just won't do."

"It's official. My awful day is in the rearview mirror. I've been helping out on a nasty case out of our San Diego office, but it's done for the day. Yahoo."

Justine smiled, but Bobby ducked her gaze a little. As if there was something he didn't want to tell her. They were usually good at reading each other's minds, but right now Justine didn't have a clue.

"What is it? Please. Don't make me guess."

"I got a call from the chief of police. I was going to tell you *after* dinner, I swear. Another schoolgirl was killed. They just found her."

Justine's mind skidded and spun out of control. She knocked over her wineglass and didn't move to stop the flow. Her glow was gone, her thoughts shooting back to very bad days in the recent past.

Morgue shots flooded her mind: teenage girls who'd been murdered over the past two years. The poor girls had all been in high school, lived throughout Los Angeles, but most had been from the neighborhoods of East LA. The last girl had been found dead just a month ago.

There had been so much police and media attention on that girl's death, Justine had almost come to believe that the killer had retreated or even quit. Maybe he was in jail. Or maybe he had died. Wouldn't that be nice?

But now Bobby had shattered that fantasy, and at least one other she had had about tonight and the possibilities it held for the two of them.

Chapter 5

"I HAVE TO call Jack right now," Justine said to Bobby. "I have to. Damn it. *Damn it!*"

He reached over and squeezed her hand. "I already called him. Your ride will be here in twenty minutes. You're going to be up most of the night, Justine. Have some pasta. Please, honey? You're going to thank me for making you eat."

A waiter put a clean cloth on the table and refilled Justine's wineglass, but she was no longer aware of her surroundings. She picked up her fork and stabbed a tortellini to satisfy Bobby and so she wouldn't have to speak while she mentally reviewed the case.

All eleven of the girls had been killed by different methods. That was *highly* unusual. The murder weapons had been removed from the crime scenes as had the victims' handbags and backpacks. The killer had always taken trophies: a hank of hair, a contact lens, a pair of panties, a class ring. What law enforcement people called "murderabilia."

Then, in a bizarre and audacious twist, the killer had claimed credit for one of the murders in an untraceable e-mail to the mayor.

He wrote that he had buried his trophies from the most recent murder in a planter outside an office building on the corner of Sunset and Doheny. He signed the note "Steem-cleena," a name that revealed nothing, then or now.

It took time for the e-mail to work its way through the system, and more time before it was taken seriously.

But three days after that encrypted e-mail was sent, the planter was dug up. A plastic bag was recovered. Inside were items taken from the latest victim. There was no DNA on the objects, no prints, no trace; the police were left with nothing but the humiliation of the killer's last laugh.

Justine had volunteered to consult with the LAPD, and they invited her in. She remembered now how seeing the girl's personal effects made her physically ill. The killer had handled them, buffed them up, and sent them back to the police with a meaningless signature and a dare.

Then Justine had come up with a plan. To make it work, she got Jack Morgan and Bobby Petino together.

And in a controversial arrangement that had outraged the homicide division of the LAPD, the district attorney's office approved Private Investigations to work the case as a public service — pro bono.

And now another girl was dead.

Bobby was answering his cell phone, trying to get her attention. "Justine. *Justine.* Your ride is here."

Chapter 6

DAMN IT! JUSTINE gripped the armrest of the sleek black, ridiculously fast Mercedes S65 as Emilio Cruz, her "ride" and fellow investigator at Private, took a hard right turn onto Hyperion Avenue in the Silver Lake area of East LA.

The four-lane road was lined with strip malls and fast-food restaurants of every kind, all within easy walking distance of the John Marshall High School, which two of the murdered girls had attended.

"What do you know about the victim?" Justine finally asked Emilio, glancing his way.

Emilio Cruz didn't even have to try to look good. He bunched his black hair back with a rubber band, put his ancient leather jacket over anything, and generally looked like a movie star just waiting to break out.

Cruz's voice was as soft as butter. "Her name is Connie

28

Yu. She was a bright light. In the eleventh grade, only sixteen years old."

"She's so smart," said Justine, "why was she walking on this street alone?"

"These girls, Justine, are being killed in *my* neighborhood. They're too tough to act scared."

"Sorry, Emilio. That's my frustration talking. I feel desperate and even guilty. Why can't I get a decent handle on this fucker?"

"Tell me about it. I'm here with you, right? *Pro bono.* I hate pro bono."

Cruz hated to lose too, really hated it. Maybe even more than Jack did. He had once been a ranked prizefighter, then a cop, then a special investigator for the DA's office under Bobby Petino. Three years later, Bobby Petino introduced him to Jack, who hired him as a Private investigator. Justine was in awe of Cruz's bulldog-like tenacity when it came to getting to the truth. This and his natural charm made Cruz a gifted investigator. Only the gifted made it at Private.

"What else, if anything, do we know about Connie Yu?" Justine asked.

"Hey, listen, I apologize, Justine. You're right. The girl was smart, so what's wrong with this fucked-up picture? Especially after you went to all these schools to warn the kids. You shouldn't feel guilty—you're doing more than anybody."

Cruz slowed the powerful car and pulled up to the curb between cruisers blocking off an alley a couple of blocks from the Hyperion Bridge.

Justine got out, shoved her hands into her jacket pockets, and headed toward the crime scene tape that cordoned off the alley. Ahead she saw the LAPD's lead investigator on the Schoolgirl case, Lieutenant Nora Cronin.

Cronin was feisty, a smart cop with maybe too much attitude. She had a crazy crush on Cruz and glowered at Justine. Her entire body, all two hundred pounds, radiated with just how much she hated Private's involvement in her case.

"The DA sent us," Justine said, biting off the line.

"Uh-huh. Your boyfriend calls, you go to a murder scene. That's kinky."

Justine walked away from the pissy lieutenant, signed the log for herself and for Cruz. Then she ducked under the tape and called out to the medical examiner, Dr. Madeleine Calder, a good friend.

"Hey, Madeleine. We need to take a look at the victim."

"Howya doin', Justine? Cruz?" said Calder. The ME was small boned and petite, but strong enough to flip the body of a homicide victim when necessary. She stepped aside, giving Justine a full-on view of the girl lying between bags of trash and the cruddy back door of a Taco Bell restaurant.

Justine stooped beside Connie Yu, saw the dark pool of blood around the girl's head. And also a gold stud glinting from the girl's left ear.

Madeleine Calder said, "Justine, check this out."

There was no earring in the victim's right ear.

There wasn't even an ear.

Dr. Calder said, "The ear's gone, Justine. Restaurant Dumpsters have been tossed. The crew has been up and down the street looking for it. Nowhere to be found. I guess the perp will tell us where it is in a couple of days."

Agonized screams at the police cordon caught Justine's attention. She looked up at Cruz. "Connie Yu's family has arrived. Let's get out of here, Emilio. We can't help those poor people. Not here, anyway."

Chapter 7

JUSTINE HAD GONE to the morgue with the girl's body, and it was past two a.m. when she called Private's chief criminalist, Seymour Kloppenberg, nicknamed Dr. Science — Sci for short — and said she needed him right away.

Sci told his girlfriend, Kit-Kat, he had to go in to the Private offices, made a snack for his rather unusual pet, Trixie, and left the apartment with his helmet under one arm.

His lovingly restored World War II courier bike with sidecar was in the garage under Sci's apartment building. He kick-started the motor and floored it up the ramp onto Hauser, then took Sixth all the way to Private's offices in downtown LA.

Flashing his ID at security, he took the elevator to the basement level, where his lab was located.

Justine was already waiting for him.

"This is about schoolgirl number twelve?" he asked,

unlocking his door, immediately switching on music—the theme from *Sweeney Todd*.

"Yes," Justine said. "And it's enough to turn your stomach. Well, maybe not yours."

Sci gave her a jokey fanged-monster face. Then he escorted Justine through the negative-pressure chamber into the lab, his "playground."

Accredited by the International Organization for Standardization, Sci's multimillion-dollar lab was the heart of Private's operations, as well as a profit center. It was used by several West Coast law enforcement agencies, since it was better equipped and faster than anything at the LAPD or the FBI.

Sci's crew of twelve technicians worked in several areas of forensic science: analysis, serology, forensic identification, and print and latent-print identification. Sci's latest pride and joy was the new holographic-manipulation technology that he used to tease apart cells with a microlaser under a high-powered microscope.

His people had been the first to test real-time use of a satellite, a method called teleforensics. Using a tiny camera, Private's investigators could bounce streaming images from a crime scene straight back to the lab, saving time and resources, preventing scene contamination.

Justine followed Sci across the vast underground space to his hub of an office and personal control center. Horror movie posters adorned the walls: *Shaun of the Dead, Carrie, Hostel, Zombieland.*

Sci dragged up a stool for Justine, then dropped into his chair and swiveled around like a little kid in an ice cream store.

"Sorry to take you away from Kit-Kat," Justine said, smiling, "but I need you to look at what we've got *before* I turn it over to the LAPD in the morning."

She brought Sci up to date on the details of the crime as she knew them: the location, the mutilation, the cause of death.

She handed him Connie Yu's backpack. "Found not too far from the crime scene by Emilio. The sonofabitch finally made a mistake...unless he *wanted* us to find this."

"You've got the victim's blood and tissue?" Sci asked.

"In the bag, along with her personal items. You'll see."

Sci opened the bag. Looked at the articles inside. He'd already started thinking about running the blood, deconstructing the wallet, frisking the phone. If there was anything there, he would have it in time for the staff meeting at nine.

"I'm on it," he said, and turned up the *Sweeney Todd* soundtrack to an almost deafening level.

Chapter 8

JUSTINE WALKED ACROSS the vast clipped lawn with its stunning canyon view—a very pretty picture in pearly light and sharp shadow *at 5:15 in the goddamn morning.*

She stripped down to her bra and panties, then quietly opened the gate to the tennis court.

She picked a racket off the bench and practiced her serve, powering balls over the net, taking out most of her frustration on the lime green hairballs.

Ten minutes into her workout she did a double take. She spun around and saw Bobby's silhouetted form standing at the fence, his fingers laced into the chain links.

"You okay, Justine? It's, like, five in the morning. What's going on, sweetie?"

"I'm working off my aggression so I don't act out," she said to Bobby, hauling back, grunting as she tossed up another ball and smacked it hard.

"Put the racket down and come over here. Please."

Justine did, walking through the gate into Bobby's arms. He held her for a good long few minutes, the feel of his strong hands on her back almost putting her into a trance.

Then Bobby said, "What would you like? Hot tub, breakfast, or bed?"

"All three—in that order."

Bobby took off his robe, draped it around Justine's shoulders, and walked with her toward the lanai. "Did you find anything interesting?"

"Apart from this murder being another freakin' *tragedy?*"

"Yes."

"Nothing I can tell you. Not yet."

"Let me put it this way, then, Justine. Have you got a new theory? Anything at all? Where are you on the case?"

Justine walked up the teak steps to the hot tub, dropped the robe and her underthings. Then she took Bobby's hand as she stepped into the steaming water.

She sat down on the seat and leaned back as his arm went around her. She closed her eyes and exhaled, letting the water do its work.

"You must have a theory," Bobby said.

"Here it is. The killer has multiple personality disorder." Justine sighed. "And every one of his personalities is psychopathic."

Chapter 9

MY DREAMS WEREN'T exactly identical, but they were all variations on the same disturbing theme. There was an explosion: sometimes a house blew up, or a car, or a helicopter. I was always carrying someone away from the fire toward safety: Danny Young, or Rick Del Rio, or my father, or my twin brother—or maybe the person in my arms was myself.

I never made it out of the fire zone alive. Not once.

My cell phone vibrating on the night table woke me from this morning's nightmare, as it had done almost daily for about three years.

Already, I was swamped with dread, that sickening falling sensation that hits you before you even know why.

And then my brain caught up with my gut, and I knew if I didn't pick up the phone, it would ring again and again until I answered.

This was my real-life nightmare.

I opened the clamshell, put it to my ear.

"You're *dead*," he said.

The voice came through an electronic filter. I called it "he," but it could have been a she or even an it. Sometimes he called in the morning: a wake-up call. Sometimes he called in the middle of the night, or he might skip a day just to keep me off balance, which he, she, or it did.

Every time my cell phone rang, I was shocked by a fresh jolt of anxiety. When it was my hate caller, I sometimes asked, "What the fuck do you want?" Sometimes I tried reason and said calmly, "Just tell me what you want."

This morning when the voice said "You're dead," I said *"Not yet."*

I snapped the phone closed.

I'd narrowed the list of my enemies to about a hundred, maybe a hundred and ten.

Whoever my caller was, he reached me from pay phones. That's right. *Pay phones.* They're still in hotel lobbies and train stations and on just about every block in every city. Each year or so, I'd change my phone number, but I couldn't keep my cell phone number a secret. My staff, my friends, my clients at Private, all had to be able to reach me. Especially the clients. I was always there for them.

I wondered again who my death threat caller was.

Did I know him? Was he in my inner circle? Or was he one of the crooks or deadbeats I'd brought down in my career as a PI?

I wondered if the threat was even *real*.

Was he watching me, tailing me, planning to kill me someday? Or was he just laughing his ass off at my expense?

Of course I had called the cops, but they'd lost interest years ago. After all, I'd never been physically attacked, never even seen my tormentor.

And then my thoughts went to Shelby Cushman again.

I imagined the horror of her last moments and pressed my palms to my eyes. I wanted to remember Shelby alive. I'd once dated her. I used to spend late nights in grungy little improv theaters where she did stand-up, then leave with Shelby by the back door. We broke up because I was me — and Shelby was getting closer to forty. She wanted a family and kids. And so did Andy. To hear them tell it, they were in love from their first date.

Now Shelby was dead and Andy was bereft and alone, and soon to be a murder suspect in the eyes of the LAPD.

I sat up in bed. *What the hell was this? Where was I?*

The sheets were flowered; there was a fluffy rug beside the bed, and the walls were painted a leafy green. Okay, I got it. I was fine.

I was at Colleen Molloy's house.

It was a good place to be.

Chapter 10

I WALKED OUT of the bedroom. Colleen was sitting at the kitchen table, her back to me, her head bent over her laptop, studying for her citizenship exam. She'd already drained her mug of tea down to the dregs. *Yep, this was a good place to be.*

I moved her long, dark, very lovely braid aside and kissed the nape of her neck. She turned, closed her morning glory blue eyes, and lifted her face. I kissed her again. I loved kissing Colleen Molloy, never tired of it.

But did I love Colleen? Truly love her? Sometimes I was sure that I did. But then I wondered if I could love anyone, really love them. Or was I too self-centered, too bruised and battered by my father?

She said, "You could get another hour's beauty sleep, boy-o."

I took in the Irish lilt in her voice, the black Irish coloring, and how she smelled of rosewater.

"I'm going to be late for my power coffee with Chief Fescoe." I gave Colleen another kiss and took her mug to the sink. I rinsed it out with hot water and poured her a fresh "cuppa" from the teapot. I hadn't completely put the murder out of my mind. But I needed to.

"Watch that someone doesn't knock seven kinds of lightning out of you," she said.

"And why would they do that?"

"Because a' you standing there as naked as a miley goat, telling me you're leaving to go to work, work, work."

I laughed, and Colleen finally came into my arms, put her small hands on my ass. I wanted to try and go with it.

"I'm going to bar the door," she said, giving my cheeks a squeeze. "Seriously, Jack."

She'd gotten to me already. How did she do that? Zero to rock hard in five seconds.

"You're a witch," I said, pulling her robe down from her shoulders. I hoisted her into my arms so that her legs wrapped around my waist, and I pressed her back against the refrigerator door. She squealed at the touch of the cold metal.

Colleen had once told me a joke: "What's Irish foreplay?"

I gave her the punch line now. "Brace yourself, darlin'."

She sucked in her breath, the two of us panting as the limited contents of the refrigerator rattled and danced to our beat.

"Sorry I made you late," she said when we were done. Her sweet, toothy grin said she wasn't sorry at all.

I smacked her bottom. "As long as I didn't make *you* late."

I left her standing under a hot shower, rosy cheeked and humming an old rock song she loved, "Come on, Eileen."

I set her burglar alarm, locked the door behind me, and ran down the stairs. Getting seven kinds of lightning knocked out of me hadn't felt too bad, actually. But now I needed to work, work, work.

Chapter 11

I STOPPED AT police headquarters on my way to Private. So far, there were no charges against Andy Cushman. I was already behind schedule, so I hurried to the office.

The "war room" at Private is octagonal in shape and features a round ink-black lacquered table, the only item there that once belonged to my father and the *old* Private. Padded swivel chairs are clustered around the table and jumbo flat-screens are mounted wall to wall.

Everyone was waiting for me when I walked in twenty minutes late. I was met with a stunned hush, pretty much what I expected.

"Sorry about Shelby," said Del Rio. "She was such a sweetheart. I just can't fucking believe it, Jack. None of us can."

Condolences were echoed by the others at the table as Colleen Molloy came in with a Red Bull for me and my call sheet. I'm not sure what it says about me, but apart from

Andy, the people I cared about most in the world were all there. They included half a dozen of my investigators, plus our criminalist, Sci, and a fiftyish computer genius, Maureen Roth, whom everybody called Mo-bot.

"Need me for anything else?" Colleen asked. She'd been my assistant for two years, which was how we met, and then it got more complicated than that, a lot more complicated.

"No, thanks, Molloy. I'm good."

I scanned the call sheet and saw that Andy had phoned twice since I'd left LAPD headquarters a half hour ago. Andy was worried, and for good reason. The cops had only one suspect, and he was it.

I booted up my laptop and punched in the photos I'd taken of the Cushman crime scene. They filled the screens wrapping around the conference room. "I took these last night."

There were extreme close-ups of the splintered door frame, the trashed bedroom, Shelby's wounds, and even a shot of Andy sobbing into his bloody hands that was worthy of a newspaper front page.

"I've got to tell you all something," I said to the group. "Shelby and I were once close. This was before she and Andy met. So, whatever you hear out there, Shelby was my friend, a good one."

The room stayed very somber and silent. Justine stared at me and through me. I knew she was trying to fit Shelby into the time sequence of my checkered past. She had good reason to.

"Take a look at these photos," I went on. "I've studied the images myself, but I'm not seeing much but the obvious so far."

Justine spoke up. "I assume *not,* but was anything taken from the house?"

"Only Shelby's life."

"Were either of them dealing?" Del Rio asked. "Sorry, Jack. The questions have to be asked. You know that."

I told him no. The Cushmans didn't use drugs and they certainly didn't sell. I knew that Andy made enough money as a hedge fund manager to keep him and Shelby very comfortable. I was certain of that much. Andy ran some of my money, and his investing had helped me open offices all around the world, including New York and, most recently, our shop in San Diego.

"Okay, assuming Shelby's jewelry is real, the room was trashed for effect," Justine said. "The shot to the breasts would appear to be the mark of a sexual sadist. The other shot says 'execution.' So why was Shelby a target?"

"Maybe the whole point was to set Andy up as the killer," Emilio Cruz said.

I nodded. "If that's what the killer was trying to do, it worked."

I told the group what Chief Fescoe had told me. The LAPD's working theory was that Shelby's death was a crime of passion, that Andy shot her and then called me as a cover story—a pretty good one, I had to admit.

"You're sure he didn't do it?" Emilio asked.

"I'm sure. I know some of you have no sympathy for Andy, but he was in love with Shelby. And now he's our client. LAPD says there's no match to the slugs the ME removed from Shelby's body, and before the killer left the premises he polished the surfaces to a high shine."

I asked Sci to reach out to the LAPD crime lab and report back on anything he could get out of them. I told Cruz to take another investigator with him to the Cushman house, canvass the neighbors, see if anything had been overlooked by the police. We were a lot better than they were, and we didn't have to follow their procedures and rules. Plus, I could put more people on the case.

I turned to Rick Del Rio, my blood brother. After he came back from Afghanistan, Rick had made some bad decisions. He paid for them with four years at Chino—which made him very valuable to Private. While doing his stretch, Del Rio had become a student of criminal law, first to help himself, but then he became a jailhouse lawyer, made friends in low places.

"Tap your sources," I said. "I'm pretty sure the shooter knew the Cushmans' habits. For one thing, he kicked in the door *knowing* that Shelby never set the alarm. He probably knew when Andy was due home too. And he wiped that place clean.

"As of right now, finding Shelby Cushman's killer is our most important case," I said. "Everyone's on it. That's all I've got at the moment."

I stood up and closed the lid on my laptop.

"Hang on, Jack," Justine said. "I've got news on Schoolgirl."

Chapter 12

JUSTINE KNOWS ME better than anyone, including Del Rio and even my brother. She and I lived together for two years, and after we broke up, we stayed close. Confidants, best friends. I've told Justine about my daily hate calls. She's the only one who knows. *You're dead, Jack.*

Now she reached under her chair, pulled out a blue knapsack, and put it on the conference table.

I asked, "Is that Connie Yu's bag?"

Justine nodded and said, "I'm handing it over to LAPD as soon as we're done with it here. We can do more with it than they can. We don't know if the killer made a mistake or if he's baiting us."

Then she described the young victim and the crime scene in excruciating detail, getting more worked up with every word. She stopped speaking as her throat tightened. She shook her head and swallowed hard, apologized before going on.

But on she went.

It killed me to see how much this case hurt her, and for that reason alone, I wanted to nail the killer almost as badly as she did. We all did.

"Jack, to repeat, whoever this psycho-killer is, he's not the first to use 'different means,' but it's rare. Most killers of this type have a pattern and stick with it. The pattern describes the killer's mood and maybe their personality too. These murders are all different. That's wacked out, and it's something I haven't seen before.

"Shooting someone is remote. Setting fire is a sexual crime. Strangling is personal. We've got those three methods and more.

"I don't see this killer evolving, and I still can't picture him. He doesn't fit any profile I know. The only good news," she continued, "is that Cruz found this sad little bag."

"It was lying on the riverbank in the shadows under the bridge," said Cruz. "Maybe the killer panicked for some reason and threw it away. Maybe there's a witness we haven't heard about yet."

Dr. Sci picked up where Cruz left off. He was wearing a red Hawaiian shirt, khaki shorts, and flip-flops, one of his standard outfits.

"I printed every fricking item in the girl's bag," Sci said. "There were smudges on Connie's wallet and a clear partial print, but it didn't ring any bells in the database. That print could belong to anyone, a friend of Connie's or her killer, but whoever left it for us has never been arrested, or taught school, or been in law enforcement or the military."

"Too bad," said Cruz. "I was hoping for something better than that."

Sci went on. "All is not lost. The cell phone is the jackpot, my friends. Mo-bot came in at four a.m.," he said, "and she pulled the data."

"Mo, you found something?" Justine asked.

"There were a slew of text messages," said Maureen Roth, aka Mo-bot, computer geek extraordinaire, self-appointed mom to the Private family. She was fifty-something but didn't look it, with her tattoos, ultrahip clothes, spiky hair—and then there were *the bifocals*, which looked like they ought to belong to somebody's grandmother in Boca Raton, Florida.

"I found hundreds of messages, all traceable to IP addresses and cell phones except for the last one, which came from a prepaid phone. I know. What a shock. But still, you'll all want to see this."

Mo-bot inserted a flash drive into a laptop and poked some keys. Messages scrolled up on the center wall screen.

I read the text message at the top of the list, time dated yesterday afternoon.

connie, it's linda. my mom took away my cell. i'm in massive trouble and i have to talk to you. meet me behind the taco bell? pleeeeze. don't tell anyone!

Mo said, "Let's assume that Connie gets the message that her friend Linda is in trouble. She has no reason to be cautious so far. She goes to meet Linda. Just like that, the trap is sprung."

"So the text message was a fake? A lure?"

"Exactly. Anyone could have known the name of one of Connie's friends, bought a no-name phone, and lured her to her death. But twelve girls have been killed now. They went to different schools, and none of the victims knew one another. That's why I find it probable, even a certainty, that each dead girl was tricked by a fake text. It's simple, even ingenious."

Justine said, "So a hacker gets into the girl's phone, figures out who she trusts, and takes on a friend's identity by texting from a no-name phone."

Sci said, "That's what I'm thinking. A ghost in the machine. But that still doesn't lead us to the killer. We hit a wall after that."

Chapter 13

JUSTINE GOT TO her feet, quickly changed places with Mo-bot, and put her fingers on the computer keyboard. *"I don't believe in ghosts,"* she said. "If the Schoolgirl psycho walks and breathes, he's got fingerprints and hair and skin cells. The more times he kills, the more likely he is to make a mistake."

She hit a couple of keys and projected a summary of the Schoolgirl case up on the flat-screens.

The time line placed the murders at roughly every two months for the past two years, except that recently the pace was accelerating. Next to the time line was a map of East LA with electronic flags representing the victims' locations.

The faces of the victims took up another screen.

The girls were of all descriptions. Light. Dark. Some pretty. Some fairly plain. Scholars. Athletes. Some thin. Some not. All high school girls. All unreasonably, tragically dead.

"We should put out the word about these no-name phone calls," said Mo. "Talk to the school principals again. Do a TV campaign about fake text messages with personal info."

"Saying we're right about this," Justine countered, "as soon as we broadcast a warning about texts from unlisted phones, the killer is going to change his pattern. And then we'll be nowhere again. He might even accelerate the murders further. We know he likes publicity."

"About what you said, Justine," Sci said in his usual nasal monotone. "The different profiles. How could a man who would set a girl on fire do it only once? How could that same person shoot someone from fifty yards away?"

"What are you thinking, Sci?"

"What if it's more than one piece of shit? What if it's more than one killer?"

Chapter 14

RUDOLPH CROCKER was hiding out in a toilet stall in the eighth-floor men's room at Wilshire Pacific Partners, a private equity firm, when his cell phone vibrated. He had been fantasizing about a new temp, Carmen Rodriguez, who had a perfect rack, beautiful brown eyes, and was practically brain-dead. He was thinking about asking her out on a date, preferably an all-nighter.

He fished the phone out of his jacket pocket, saw that the call was being forwarded from his direct line. It was Franklin Dale, senior partner, one of "the ancients." Crocker answered, and Dale invited him to have a drink after work.

Crocker had been an equities analyst for over a year. He'd done his work diligently while at the same time keeping his head down. His concept was to be one of those bright young men with a huge future in number crunching, a dull and steady sort of worker who kept the portfolio safe, the profits flowing, and his light hidden safely under a bushel.

Now he had to have a drink with pesky Franklin Dale.

At seven p.m., Crocker locked his office door and met Dale at the elevator bank. They took the car downstairs together, and Crocker wondered if maybe the old fuck was gay and going to make a move on him.

Two drinks and a bowl of cashews later, Crocker had been told that he was doing extremely well, and that dinosaur Franklin Dale was highly impressed with his work. Dale said that he thought Crocker was an outlier, a guy with hidden talents who would be rewarded the longer he stayed at this fine old firm.

As if that would bake his fucking cake. As if he cared what Franklin Dale thought about him or his work.

By the time Crocker got home, it was half past nine. The rest of the night was his, and this was going to be great.

He dressed for his run, and ten minutes later he was jogging around the Marina del Rey, his mind on the recent outing when his group had taken Connie Yu down for the count.

Sweating and panting, Crocker slowed outside one of the slips in the marina. He put his hands on his knees and caught his breath.

When he was sure he was alone, he took a pint-sized ziplock bag out of his pocket and began to bury it under a heavy coil of rope.

When he was done, he calmly finished his run. He came through the entrance to his apartment building, waved to the doorman, and went upstairs.

Private

After his shower he took a prepaid phone from the charger base.

He texted a message to LA's mayor, Thomas Hefferon, telling him where he could find Connie Yu's ear.

He signed it "Steemcleena."

Chapter 15

THREE DAYS HAD passed since Shelby Cushman had been murdered. Still no charges had been filed, and I couldn't get a peep one way or the other out of the DA's office.

I had breakfast with Andy in his office, a corner in a smart new office building on Avenue of the Stars.

Andy told his assistant not to put through any calls. Then he eased shut his office door. I could barely recognize his drawn face. There were bags under his eyes, and he'd obviously stopped shaving.

"I'm not sleeping," he said. "In case you missed that, Jack."

He gulped down his coffee as he unlocked his file cabinets, pulled folders, and explained to me what a very successful hedge fund manager did to keep his edge in Los Angeles.

"These people out here, actors, agents, studio heads, lawyers to the stars," he said, waving his arm so it took in the whole of Hollywood, "they make tens of millions. They don't know what to do with it, so they give it to me. I invest it for them. I get a percentage of whatever I invest for my clients," he said. "Five percent, usually."

"And if the investments tank?" I said, thinking of the housing meltdown, the credit crunch, money swirling down the drain, taking with it the well-heeled and struggling alike.

"People hold it against you if you lose their money, even if it's not your fault."

"So you've got disgruntled clients."

Andy sighed.

"You want the truth, Jack?"

"No, for Christ's sake. Please lie to me, Andy. The more you lie, the more likely it is that you're going to go to trial. I know the DA. He's going to sic one of his young sharks on you, and they're going to tear you into great bloody chunks—"

"Stop," he said.

"If someone wants to hurt you, I have to know about it. C'mon, Andy. You have to tell me everything. This is Jack."

"I was skimming," Andy said. It came out just like that— with no preface or warning. "I'm no Bernie Madoff, so don't look at me like that. I'd charge a fee, then I'd take a little of the principal off the top and ride the investment for myself. I was careful. But shit happens, and you can't let the clients know, of course."

"I'm listening."

"My investments dove in the first wave. You remember

when Lehman went under? I doubled down, tried to recoup my losses, and lost even more. A couple of my clients got burned to the ground."

"Give me the files, Andy. I want to see your biggest losers. I want to know exactly who they are. No more secrets."

Chapter 16

WHEN A DOOR says *Private,* you want to know what's on the other side.

When an envelope says *Private,* you immediately want to open it.

I entered Private through the reception area, waved to Joanie behind the desk, and climbed the grand spiral staircase that wraps around the open core of the atrium. The staircase always gives me a lift. Reminds me of the cross section of a nautilus shell.

I was on my way into my office on the fifth floor when Colleen stopped me.

"You've got company," she said. "Lots of it. Suits. Expensive ones."

I went to the threshold and saw three men lounging in my seating area, a corner furnished with upholstered armchairs, a deep blue sofa, and a chunk of polished sequoia I use as a coffee table. *This was where people came with their secrets, and where those secrets were always kept in confidence.*

Two of my unscheduled visitors were smoking like tobacco company CEOs. Colleen said, "The gentlemen said they didn't want to be seen in reception. What a surprise."

The third man turned to face us, and with a start, I realized I was looking at my uncle Fred. Fred Kreutzer is my mom's brother, the one who always told me to call him any time I needed an ear. He taught Tommy and me to play football when we were kids and encouraged me to play in high school and then college.

In short, Uncle Fred was the stand-in good dad for the man who'd sired me. Fred had gone further in football than I had—much further. He was a general partner of the Oakland Raiders.

The big florid-faced man stood, gave me a crushing bear hug, then introduced me to his associates, men I now recognized.

Evan Newman was as refined as Fred Kreutzer was rough. His suit was hand tailored. His hair had been sprayed into place, and his fingernails were as gleaming as his handmade shoes. He owned the San Francisco 49ers.

The third man was David Dix, a legendary entrepreneur, the kind of guy they write about in business school. Dix had made a killing in Detroit during the eighties, got out of auto parts before the meltdown in '08, and bought the Minnesota Vikings. I remembered something I'd read about him, that his apparent happiness masked his fundamental heartlessness. Sounded like an epitaph to me.

Evan Newman stood up and came toward me with a convincing smile and outstretched hand. "Sorry to barge in like this," he said. "Fred said you would see us."

"We have a problem," Uncle Fred said. "It's urgent, Jack. A screaming five-alarm emergency, actually."

"We'd like to be wrong," said Dix. "In fact, I have to say, if we're right, this could cripple the game of professional football."

Dix beckoned to me to sit. "We've got money," he said. "You've got the best people for this. Sit down so we can lay out a nightmare for you."

Chapter 17

EVAN NEWMAN BRUSHED invisible ashes off his trousers and said, "We have reason to suspect a gambling fix in our league, Jack, something that could be as bad for football as the Black Sox scandal was for baseball."

I was bothered by this intrusion into my office, but also intrigued. Andy's inventory of former clients was calling to me from my briefcase, Justine needed me on the Schoolgirl murders, and I had a conference call meeting with our London office in twenty minutes—a scandal in the House of Lords no one knew about yet.

I looked at my watch and said, "Give me the highlights. Please. I'll help if I can."

Fred spoke up. "Jack, we think this thing may have started about two years ago—in a wildcard play-off game. On paper, winning should have been no problem for the Giants. Their opponent, Carolina, was good, but a couple of defensive backs were out. Their quarterback had a hairline fracture in the index finger on his throwing hand. This game shouldn't have been close. But you may remember this, Tommy—"

"Jack."

"Jack, I'm sorry. *Jesus.* Anyway, in the third quarter, Cartwright's touchdown run, into a hole you could've driven a Brinks truck through, was called back. The ref said it was a holding penalty, and in the fourth quarter, as New York was trying for the kick that would've sent the game into overtime, there was another penalty that took them out of field goal range."

Fred went on, his face getting redder. "New York lost by three. At the time, the calls just looked bad. There was the usual talk in the sports press that eventually faded as the play-offs moved ahead."

"Okay, Jack." Dix spoke next. "Fast-forward to the third game of last season between the Vikings and the Cowboys. Different set of circumstances but basically the same scenario."

My uncle jumped in again. He wanted to tell the story play-by-play. "This time the Vikings get a forty-yard pass called back at the end of the second quarter that would've sent them into the locker room ahead by seventeen points."

Fred was gesticulating angrily, telling me that another questionable holding penalty wiped the pass off the board. "As they lined up at the end of the fourth quarter for what would've been the winning field goal, the Vikings get called for an illegal shift which nobody, *nobody* saw except the referee.

"Again it takes them out of field goal range, the game goes into overtime, and they lose."

I saw where these stories were going, of course. Bad calls happen in football and people scream about the officials and then they get over it. For Fred Kreutzer, Evan Newman, and David Dix to come to me, it meant they had more to go on than alleged bad calls in a couple of games.

Newman said, "We've looked at the tapes ad nauseam, Jack, including last Sunday's game in San Francisco. We see a pattern. All told, eleven games stink badly over two and a half years. Nine of the losing teams had winning records and seven of them made the play-offs."

My uncle said, "A lot of people lost a lot of money on these games. They're starting to wonder if there's something funny going on."

"Why come to me?" I asked. "Why not take this to the commissioner first?"

"We don't have any proof," said Dix. "And frankly, Jack, if something *did* happen, we don't want the commissioner and the press *and the public* to hear about it. *Ever.*"

Chapter 18

EMILIO CRUZ CAME through my office door first, and Del Rio arrived maybe five minutes after the owners had left. I waved them both into chairs. "We've been tapped by three NFL team owners," I said, "and they could be representing a dozen more. One of them is Fred Kreutzer. Fred is my mother's brother."

Cruz lifted his eyebrows. "Fred Kreutzer is your uncle?"

"He is. He and some other owners think that games are being fixed. They see a pattern of long-odds underdogs winning too often, and based on questionable calls."

"That's nuts." Cruz frowned. "You can't cheat at football. You can't predict a game-changing play, and even if you could, there are cameras on every move. Every second is under a microscope."

"If that turns out to be the case, we've got happy clients," I said, "and nice paychecks. We've been guaranteed double our rate for fast, thorough, and very confidential work."

"They're saying the players are rigging the games?" Del Rio asked.

Del Rio is my age, but the years he spent at Chino aged his face and shattered his faith in people. I think the sanctity of football is one of the few things he still believes in.

"Fred says that they didn't find any player infractions, just calls that may have been crooked. Or else the refs were seeing optical illusions.

"Before we make any decisions on this, let's talk about the Cushmans. I saw Andy this morning," I said. "The press is all over him. He hasn't been charged, and he wants to get out of town. I told him to check in to a hotel and not tell anyone but me where he's staying."

"He's got good reason to worry," said Del Rio. "Whoever killed Shelby got in and out of the house with the skill of a Beverly Hills proctologist. I'm looking into contract killers. I've got a couple of leads. We're going to break this one, Jack."

I asked Cruz and Del Rio if they could work both cases, and they said they could. That was the usual response at Private—we hired the best, at very high pay, and they expected long days and challenging cases.

"I want you to do thorough background checks on Shelby *and* Andy," I said.

"What are we looking for that you don't already know, Jack?"

"The answer to one simple question: Why would anyone kill Shelby Cushman?"

"No problem," said Del Rio. "Two cases for the price of three? I can go with that." We all laughed, then Cruz and Del Rio left and went to work.

I had been alone in my office for about sixty seconds when Colleen stepped in and closed the door.

"Your eleven o'clocks are here, Jack. I don't like the looks a' them."

"No? They're just lawyers," I said.

Colleen grinned. "Just lawyers. Sure thing. Smirky lawyers. Sweaty lawyers."

A minute later, she showed the two men in. I knew them by reputation.

Their names were Ferrara and Reilly, and they represented Ray Noccia, head of the Noccia crime family.

Chapter 19

I SHOOK HANDS with the men coming through the door and offered them seats.

Attorney Ed Ferrara was wearing a dark three-piece suit. His associate, John Reilly, wore black jeans and a black cashmere sweater. Reilly searched my office with his eyes, checking for hidden cameras in the bookshelves. *I don't think he spotted them.*

Ferrara said, "It's nice to meet you, Jack. You come highly recommended by several sources."

"Always good to hear," I said. "How can I help you?"

Reilly dug into a pocket and pulled out a photograph of a very pretty blond woman in her early twenties. I thought I recognized her, Elizabeth something, an actress. I'd seen her on Craig Ferguson once or twice.

"This is a picture of Beth Anderson. She's a film actress," Ferrara said, "and she's also Mr. Noccia's good friend."

Ray Noccia was at least seventy years old. After waiting for two generations, he had just taken over the top job from his uncle Antonio, deceased. And he was "good friends" with twenty-something Beth Anderson.

Reilly was saying, "Beth hasn't been seen in a week. She doesn't return Mr. Noccia's calls. He wants to make sure nothing untoward happened to her."

"Sounds like a job for LAPD," I said. "You should give them a shout. I highly recommend them."

Ferrara smiled and said, "We want to keep this quiet. We don't want publicity that could hurt Beth's career. Which brings us to you, Jack. We'd like a quote with a ceiling."

I wondered if Beth Anderson had left town or if she was dead. Either way, I didn't want Noccia's business at Private.

"Sorry, I don't do quotes," I said. "I don't do ceilings either. And I don't do business with the Mob."

There was a moment of thick silence, then Reilly and Ferrara got to their feet as one.

"You're doing Andy Cushman," said Ferrara. "And if I'm any judge of degenerate womanizers, you're doing the little piece of Killarney sitting outside your office too."

Reilly paused on the threshold to launch his parting shot. "And let's not forget your father was doing life for murder when he passed. You've got a lot of nerve, Jack-off."

I guess I did, but that was part of the reason Private was doing so well.

Chapter 20

AT THREE THAT afternoon, Jason Pilser was in his office at Howard Public Relations, waiting for the advisory board meeting to start, when he got a text message that catapulted his mood.

The message was from Steemcleena himself, posting particulars of the next "night on the town." The notice addressed him by his screen name, "Scylla," and said, "Get ready. You're IT."

Holy crap, it was actually happening, his baptism by fire. He'd been thinking about this night for weeks. In fact, he'd thought of little else. He'd originally met "Morbid" on Commandos of Doom, an online real-time war game. As allies, they had fought dozens of successful battles over the past two years.

But when Morbid recruited him into a much more select group of gamers, it had floored him. His introduction to

Steemcleena had been virtual, and he'd had to wait until Morbid locked it up. Now Steemcleena was on board. And soon Jason as Scylla would step out from behind the computer screen and see some real-life action.

Pilser worked like a robot for the next three hours. He didn't flinch when the head bitch blamed him for screwing up a proposal he hadn't even compiled. Screw her. At six, he put on his jacket and left for the day.

He drove straight to a hardware store in West Hollywood.

He walked the narrow stocked-to-the-ceiling aisles and picked out a six-foot-long extension cord, a roll of duct tape, and a pair of cotton jersey gloves. Nothing very unusual. He paid cash for his purchases, keeping his head down so the security camera over the cash register didn't catch his face.

He was so pumped that his hands were sweating.

The big night was only three days away. And he was "it." On Saturday he was going to kill a girl somewhere in LA.

Chapter 21

THIS WASN'T REALLY sleep, was it? It was more like going to war every night and getting bombed back into reality in the morning.

In my dream this time, I ran across the burning battlefield, Colleen in my arms, blood splashing on my shoes. My heart hammered against my rib cage as she said, "Save me, Jack. I'm the mother of your children."

The thumping explosion of mortar rounds threw me to the ground. My eyes flew open, and for an instant I had a strong sense that I was still on the battlefield on my last day in Afghanistan.

I remembered most of it, but some crucial recollection was missing, a gap in my memory from the time the helicopter went down and the moment when I died.

I had pushed the missing memory so far into my subconscious, it was subterranean.

I had to dig it up. Had to find out the truth about that day.

If I could retrieve the memory, maybe I could finally sleep.

I was still grasping at wisps of dream and memory when my cell phone vibrated on the nightstand.

I looked at the caller ID, read "out of area."

I left the phone on the table, sprang out of bed, and flipped on the house security monitors.

I scrutinized the six monitors and saw nothing out of place, so I left them and did an eyeball check of the grounds. Cars streamed by on the Pacific Coast Highway beyond my front gate. There are high fences between my house and my neighbors' on both sides. The beach was empty at the back of my house.

I was alone.

The phone finally stopped ringing. Light streamed through the glass, and the Pacific crashed outside my bedroom window.

This was the house I'd bought with Justine.

Talk about memories that can haunt you. I still saw Justine in this room, her dark hair fanned out on the white pillow, looking at me with love in her eyes. And you know what? I looked back at her the same way.

I showered and dressed in chinos and a blue oxford shirt, and then the phone started ringing again. I took the damned thing to the dining table I used as a desk and opened it.

"You're *dead*," said the mechanical voice.

"Not *yet*," I said.

I made very strong coffee, then spent the next hour and a half making phone calls, confirming appointments.

By the time I met Del Rio at Santa Monica Airport, it was almost ten.

Time to fly.

Chapter 22

WE BOARDED a Cessna Skyhawk SP, a spiffy and reliable single-engine aircraft, and Del Rio took his place beside me. Just like old times.

I looked at Rick. He looked back, our thoughts on the same track: Afghanistan, our friends who'd been killed in the helicopter, the fact that Del Rio had jump-started my heart and I owed him my life.

I wondered if he could tell me more about what happened that last day in Gardez. I'd gotten a medal for carrying Danny Young out of that burning helicopter. But I couldn't ignore the nagging dreams. Was my mind doing a head-fake: protecting me from an unbearable memory and at the same time prodding me to remember?

"Rick, that last day in Gardez?"

"The helicopter? *Why,* Jack?"

"Tell me about it again."

"I've told you everything I can remember."

"It still isn't clear for me. Something is missing, something I'm forgetting."

Del Rio sighed. "We were moving troops to Kandahar. It was night. You were the section leader and I was copilot. We couldn't see some raghead with his ground-to-air missile in the back of a truck. No one saw him. We took a hit to the belly. Nobody's fault, Jack.

"You brought the Phrog down," Del Rio said. "The bird was burning from the inside out—remember that? I got out the side door, and you went through the back. Guys from the dash two were running all over the field. I started looking for you. I found you with Danny Young in your arms. Always the hero, Jack, always the stand-up guy. Then the mortar hit."

"I see snapshots, not the whole movie."

"*You were dead,* that's why. I pounded on your chest until you came back. That's all I've got for you."

The pictures just didn't flow in consecutive order and wouldn't make a whole. I saw the crash. I remembered running with Danny Young over my shoulder. I woke up.

Something was missing.

What didn't I know? What else had happened on that battlefield?

I was still staring at Del Rio. He grinned at me. "Sweetheart. You gonna tell me you love me?"

"I do, asshole. I do love you."

Del Rio laughed like hell and pulled his sunglasses down from the top of his cap. I busied myself with the checklist.

I got clearance from the tower, advanced the throttle, and taxied the Cessna down the runway. Gave it some right rudder to keep it rolling along the center line. When the airspeed indicator read sixty, I came back a touch on the yoke and the plane gently lifted, practically flew itself into the blue and sunny skies over Los Angeles.

Smooth as cream.

For the next hundred minutes I flew the plane as if it were a part of my body. Flying is procedure, procedure, procedure, and I knew it all by heart. I listened to the radio chatter in my headset, and it erased my tormenting thoughts.

I forgot the dream and lost myself in the wonder of flight.

Chapter 23

JUST AFTER NOON, we landed at Metropolitan Airport on San Francisco Bay.

We rented a car and hit some heavy traffic on the Harbor Bay Parkway, arriving at the Oakland Raiders' practice field half an hour late for our appointment with Fred.

I gave my card to the security guard at the main gate, and Del Rio and I were waved through to the natural-grass practice field where professional football players were running pass patterns and pursuit drills. On the far end, two place-kickers took turns booting field goal tries from the forty-yard line.

Fred was standing on the sideline at midfield and came over to greet us. I introduced Del Rio, saying that he would be working with me on the case.

My uncle waved in a few of the Raiders' high-profile

players—Brancusi, Lipscomb, and tailback Muhammed Ruggins—guys who were earning millions a year. Jeez, were they big. We talked about the upcoming game with Seattle and then turned our attention to the Raiders' talented quarterback Jermayne Jarvis, who was out there taking snaps.

I said, "I can't get over his timing on those square outs. It's like he knows precisely when the receiver will turn."

Fred said, "You did good at Brown, Jack. You could throw it on a rope. You're better off that you didn't try and go pro, though."

I couldn't have. I didn't have the size for it, or probably the arm. Plus the Ivy League isn't exactly the Big Ten or the SEC.

I saw a light go on behind Fred's eyes. "So, Jack, maybe you and Rick want to toss the ball around with some of my guys?"

I protested, said, "Are you crazy? I thought you cared about me." But Del Rio looked like a kid who'd just won a video store sweepstakes.

He and I went out to the field and took turns running ten-yard crossing patterns as Jermayne Jarvis fired strikes at us.

Having warmed up, I found myself getting into it. But as I reached for one of Jarvis's precision darts, I ran into Del Rio, knocking us both down. Fred trotted over, put his hands on his knees, and while laughing at me, said, "That was beautiful, Jack. Poetry in motion. Now I've got something to show you that's not so funny."

We walked off the field through a long concrete hallway and a series of locked doors until we got to Fred's office. He opened a locked cabinet and took out a banker's box full of what he said were DVDs of the past twenty-eight months of NFL games.

"I flagged those eleven games that raised real questions. Check them out, and let's compare notes."

Then he told me where I should start looking for the crooks who were threatening to shut down professional football.

"I've never asked you for anything before, Jack, but this time I'm asking. I need your help."

Chapter 24

IT WAS DARK when I got back to my house. A waxing moon spotlighted the roof, which was just visible over the high steel-reinforced gate.

I was pulling the Lamborghini into my garage when I saw headlights in the rearview mirror.

The lights followed right on my tail, flashing, someone signaling to me. I braked, turned off the engine, and got out. I saw a black sedan easing into my driveway. Who the hell was it?

I waited by the side of my car until a front door of the sedan opened. The driver got out. He unbuttoned his jacket as he came striding toward me. "Mr. Jack Morgan?"

When I said that I was, he said, "Mr. Noccia wants to speak to you. It's important."

"I don't want to talk to anybody right now," I said without

pause. "Please be careful backing out. You don't want to get T-boned on the highway."

"You're sure that's what you want me to tell him?"

I was pretty sure. I stood my ground as the driver went back to the Town Car. I waited for it to leave, but instead the passenger-side door opened. A second man got out, and he opened the rear door for a third man. And then the three of them closed the distance between us.

I recognized Ray Noccia.

He was wearing a gray sport jacket and had gray hair, gray skin, and a nose that cast a shadow on his cheek. Reality hit me. A Mafia don, a made man who had ordered dozens of executions, was standing in my driveway. It was nighttime. Nobody had seen him come. Nobody would see him leave.

He stuck out his hand. "Ray Noccia," he said. "Good to meet you."

I kept my hand in my jacket until he put his down. A dark look passed over his face, as though I'd slapped him or pissed on his shoes.

Then Noccia smiled. "Your father and I did some business," he said. "That's why I sent my attorneys to talk with you. Apparently they offended you in some way. I owe you an apology, and I make my apologies in person."

"No apology needed," I said.

There was no humor in his smile.

"Good. So you'll look for Beth for me? I understand the rules. No quote. No ceiling. I'll pay your rate plus a bonus when you find her. That's because you're the best."

It was time that I ended this, now and for the future.

"Your men know where they buried her. Save your money. Drill down on them."

There was a leaden pause. Noccia didn't take his eyes away from mine, and when he spoke, his words were almost drowned out by the rush of traffic and the Pacific surf.

"You're much better educated than your father, but you're not half as smart," said Noccia. "And look how he ended up." He turned and walked back to his car.

I had probably gone beyond the realm of bravado, but I didn't care. Ray Noccia had already said the worst thing he could to me — that he and my father had worked together.

My hand was shaking when I put my key in the lock of the front door. I hoped I'd never see or hear from Ray Noccia again.

Fat chance.

Part Two

NUMBER THIRTEEN

Chapter 25

MORNING LIGHT FLATTERED the trash dunes with a rosy glow, and seagulls screamed bloody murder as they swooped over the acres of garbage at the Sunshine Canyon landfill. Breakfast was served.

Justine pulled her Jag over to the side of the road and stared out at the landscape. I twirled the dial on her police band radio until the signal was clear. She opened her thermos, passed it over to me. I took a sip.

The coffee was black, unsugared. That's the way Justine liked just about everything: straight up, no bullshit.

We hadn't exchanged an intimate touch in more than two years, but sitting next to her in the close confines of the car, I found it tough not to reach over and take her hand. It had always been confusing, even when we were together.

"How's it going?" she asked me.

Cops were picking over the dump across the road. We could hear them talking to base over the police band.

I said, "Andy Cushman has about twenty pissed-off former clients, any one of whom has the means, the opportunity, and especially the motive to kill him. So why kill Shelby instead? I'm not getting anywhere on it."

"Sorry to hear that, Jack. But what I meant was, how's it going for you?"

Actually, what she meant was, how was it going for me and Colleen—and I didn't want to get into that with her. Instead I said, "I have a new case to work on. It's heavy-duty and personal. You remember me telling you about my uncle Fred."

"Football guy."

"Yeah. He's worried that some of the games are being fixed. Could result in a huge scandal, the biggest since the Black Sox in baseball."

"Wow," Justine said.

"I'm having dreams again," I said.

Justine's eyebrows lifted. I had wanted to talk to her, but now I was going to have to *really* talk. Tell a shrink you're having dreams, it's like dangling string for a kitten.

"Dreams about what?" she asked. "The same ones?"

So I told her. I described the vivid explosions, running across the field with someone I love over my shoulder, never making it to safety.

"Could be survivor's guilt, I guess. What do you think, Jack?"

"I wish the dreams would stop."

"You're still funny," she said, "with the one-liners."

Private

I opened the folder I had wedged under the armrest and looked at the photo that Bobby Petino had e-mailed to Justine this morning. It was a school portrait of a pretty sixteen-year-old girl named Serena Moses. She'd been reported missing last night. Serena lived in Echo Park, a section of East LA that Justine called "the red zone," *the Schoolgirl killing field.*

Two hours after Serena's parents called the police, an anonymous and untraceable call had come in to 911 saying that Serena's body was here in the landfill.

Just then, voices came over the police radio, one sharper and louder than the others.

"I've got something. Could be human. Oh, Christ…"

"Let's go," I said, opening the car door on my side.

"No, Jack. I've got to do this alone. If you come with me, I'll lose my street creds. Just hang tight."

I said okay. Then I watched Justine cross the empty street and head toward where the police were already taping off a section of the stinking terrain.

Chapter 26

JUSTINE LIFTED HER hand in a wave to Lieutenant Nora Cronin, who gave her the customary dirty look before turning back to the black construction-grade trash bag lying like a crashed balloon at her feet.

Justine's chest tightened as she remembered another schoolgirl who'd been dumped here a year ago encased in a similar black plastic bag. Her name was Laura Lee Branco, and she had been knifed through the heart.

Cronin cut the tie with a pocketknife, and the bag fell open.

An arm tumbled out, almost in slow motion, the palm and fingers outstretched. It took Justine a long, heart-stopping moment to understand what she was seeing.

"What the hell?" Cronin said, pulling back the edges of the bag to reveal a department store dummy. Two other cops tugged the mannequin out of the bag.

Cronin turned over the female form and inspected it. There was no writing on the dummy, no note inside the black bag.

"So what's the big message?" Cronin asked the air. "You're the shrink, right?"

"The medium is the message," Justine said. "It's a dummy, get it? The implication is that we're being played."

Cronin said, "Why, thank you, Justine. That's very astute. It's a frickin' waste of time, that's what it is. And it definitely isn't Serena Moses."

Justine reeled from a wave of relief that was immediately followed by sadness. Serena Moses was still missing, wasn't she? They still didn't know where she was, or whether she was alive or dead.

She glared back at Cronin. "So where is Serena, Lieutenant? I guess you're going to have to keep looking. I hope you're as good as you think you are."

Chapter 27

JUSTINE THANKED PRINCIPAL Barbara Hatfield for her introduction and then she took the stage of the auditorium.

The newly refurbished Roybal High School had five thousand students, but only the junior and senior girls were permitted to attend her talk that afternoon. The principal had told Justine that her presentation was just too graphic and scary for the younger girls.

Justine thought she understood, but frightening the girls was a necessary by-product of informing them. And most of the girls who'd been killed were in the lower grades. The principal hadn't budged, though.

"I'm a psychologist," Justine told the students in the auditorium. "But I'm also investigating the murders of the high school girls that you've all read about on the Internet and seen on TV."

Someone sneezed up front. There was nervous laughter, and Justine waited it out.

"First, I want you to know that Serena Moses is *safe*. She was hit by a car and taken to a hospital. When she woke up this morning, she told the doctors her name. Serena has a broken arm, but she's fine and she'll be back at school soon."

The kids broke out into applause. Justine smiled. But Serena's being safe had raised a question for her: How did the killer know to fake an e-mail about her? Had he been watching the girl? Had *they* been watching her?

"It's a big relief," she said, feeling her eyes get moist. "But we have to talk about the girls in this area who weren't so lucky."

Justine nodded to the teacher's assistant who was running her PowerPoint presentation.

The lights went down, and the sweet, smiling face of a teenage girl came onto the screen.

"This is Kayla Brooks. She was a junior at John Marshall. She wanted to be a doctor, but before she even graduated from high school, she was shot four times for no reason at all.

"Her life, her future, the children she might have had, the doctor she might have become—all of that is over."

The pictures of Kayla's body came up on the screen, and the sound of girls crying out almost tore Justine apart. She had to keep going. Bethany's picture was next, then Jenny, a student at this school, and then the rest of the names and pictures and stories, including that of Connie Yu, who had died only five days ago.

"We know that whoever killed these girls had information about them that he used to gain their trust."

Justine explained about Connie's recovered cell phone and the text message from an unlisted phone.

"Girls, Connie's friend did *not* text her. This was a fake message, a trick—and it worked. So how can you know if someone is trying to fake you out?

"If anyone, anyone at all, asks you to go somewhere alone, don't go. Tell the girls in the lower grades, don't go anywhere alone. Do you understand?"

There was a sibilant chorus of girls' voices saying yes.

"I want everyone to stand up," Justine said. "And I want you to repeat something after me."

There was the shuffling sound of a thousand kids getting to their feet, seats slapping against the chair backs, books ringing as they hit the floor.

The voices sang out in ragged unison, following Justine's words. *"I promise. I won't go anywhere. Alone."*

Justine hoped that she'd reached the girls. But she was still afraid. That one of these girls was thinking she was special, that she knew better than Justine, that she was the one who would never die.

Chapter 28

JUSTINE STEPPED OUT of the high school and onto West Second Street. She had just opened her phone when a black car swept up to the curb. The window buzzed down.

"Need a lift, lady?"

"Bobby. What are you doing here?"

"Just looking after my girl. Get in, Justine. I'll drive you to your office."

"I was just calling a Town Car. What timing. Thanks."

She went around to the passenger side of his Beemer and got inside. She leaned over for Bobby's kiss.

"How did it go with the kids?" he asked, pulling the car into the stream of traffic.

"Pretty good, I think. If they ever listen to anyone over thirty."

"You don't look over thirty, sweetie. Not a day, not a minute."

"What do you want, Bobby? What *else* do you want?"

"Yeah. There is something. Uh, Justine, I wanted to tell you before this gets out. I'm thinking of running for governor. I've been approached by the DNC. Financial backing is there for me if I want it. It would be a hard race but worth it if I won. The powers that be think I have a good chance. Bill Clinton called me."

"This is kind of sudden, isn't it?"

"I've been thinking about it for a while. I didn't want to say anything until I'd made up my mind to take the idea seriously."

She didn't show it, but Justine was stunned by the announcement. She told Bobby he'd make a great governor, and she believed he would—but her heart was sinking. She had feelings for Bobby. He was the first man she'd been able to trust since she and Jack had broken up. If Bobby became governor, he'd move to Sacramento. Then what would happen? Where would she be?

"It would be great if we could find the dirtbag who's killing the schoolgirls," Bobby was saying. "In fact, it's got to be done. A conviction would really help me right now."

"Sure," Justine said. She felt a chill coming off the air-conditioning and dialed it down. Bobby seemed to be telling her something with a lot of subtext. So what was the real message?

If he was elected governor, did he want her to go with him to Sacramento? If so, as Diane Keaton had famously asked Warren Beatty in *Reds*, "As what?" Justine remembered that Bobby had taken a lot of heat from the police commissioner when he'd hired Private to work the Schoolgirl case. She hadn't questioned his motive for a second. If anything, she thought Bobby had brought in Private because the case was so important to *her*.

But now it seemed like maybe he was intensely involved in this case because it was important to *him*.

Bobby braked at a light and said, "You're quiet, Justine."

"I'm thinking about you as Governor Petino. You'd be good. That's all it is."

Bobby reached for her and kissed her. "You're wonderful, you know that? You're a wonderful woman, and I'm a lucky guy."

"I can't argue with any of that," said Justine.

Chapter 29

WE WERE WORKING late, Colleen and I, sorting though Andy Cushman's files and financial statements, many of them red-flagged for further investigation.

Colleen was wearing a blue silk cardigan over a lacy camisole and man-tailored pants. Her black hair swung around her face when she bent to put another stack of papers on the coffee table.

"Why don't you go home?" I said. "It's almost nine. I can do this."

"Let's get it done, Jack. It'll just be worse tomorrow."

"Sit down," I said, patting the cushion next to me on the couch.

She dropped onto the couch, threw herself against the back of it, and yawned. "Another hour should do it," she said.

I put my arm around her and drew her close to me.

"Don't be messing about, Jack. There'll be caps on the green and no one to fetch them."

"What the hell does that mean?"

"Trouble."

She was telling me "hands off," but without much conviction. Finally, she rested her head on my chest. She smelled like rosewater, her favorite. I put my hand in her hair, and she lifted her face.

I kissed her and she kissed me back. "Okay, Jack. Have your way with me. *Please.*"

"Hang on," I said. I got up and locked my office door, turned off the overhead lights, went back to the sofa. I said, "Stand up, Molloy. Please."

"I can do that."

I unbuttoned her sweater, unzipped her pants, and when she was in her underwear, I returned her to the sofa and undressed myself.

She watched me take off my clothes, then covered her face with her arm as I touched her and made her moan. Colleen cried out as I made love to her...but then she cried tears when we were done.

I wrapped her in my arms, held her between my body and the back of the couch so that she wouldn't get chilled. "What is it, sweetie? What's wrong?"

"I'm twenty-five," she said in a whisper.

"You don't mean — today?"

She nodded, sang, "Happy birthday to me."

"Why didn't you tell me it was your birthday?"

"I did," she said.

"No. I forgot."

"It doesn't mean anything, really. I'm not a birthday person."

"It does," I said. I tilted up her chin. "It does. I'll make it up to you."

She shrugged, then pushed me aside, swung her bare legs over the side of the couch, and picked her clothes up off the floor.

"I shouldn't say this, Jack, so I won't."

I already knew. No birthday present, no flowers, no dinner. Sex on the couch. I said, "Go ahead and say it. You deserve better than this."

"Anyone would," said Colleen.

Chapter 30

NOT ONE, but two celebrity couples were waiting for me in reception as I came through on the way to my office that morning. Their money manager had called ahead for them.

The most visually arresting of the four was Jane Hawke, the rock idol who was pierced, tattooed, and dressed in five shades of purple. Her husband, action movie star Ethan Tau, sat to her right. He was wearing cowboy garb down to his Lucchese boots.

Sitting across from them were tennis stars Jeanette Colton and Lars Lundstrom: fair-haired, tanned and toned, Euro-LA all the way.

When I got settled, Colleen showed the couples into my office, asked if they'd like coffee or tea. Then she gave me a tepid smile and said, "Is there anything else, Jack?"

"We're good," I said. But were *we*?

She closed the door behind her. It made an almost imperceptible click.

"How can I help you?" I said. Then I sat back to listen.

Jeanette Colton spoke first. "It's a little difficult to talk about," she said. Her stolid-looking husband, the Swedish tennis champ, folded his hands in his lap.

Jane Hawke sugared her coffee and said, "Go ahead, Jeanette. Of all of us, you're the one who'll get the story straight the first time out."

A look of pain flashed across Jeanette Colton's face. For the life of me, I couldn't imagine what she was going to say. What were the four of them doing at Private?

"Ethan and I are in love," she said of Jane Hawke's husband.

I looked at the rock star, who was sipping her coffee with a steady hand. I tried to avoid divorce cases. There were plenty of private investigators who liked them and were much better at snooping than I was.

Lars Lundstrom spoke next. "That's only part of the story, Mr. Morgan. Here's where it gets interesting. Jane and I want to be together as well." His accent was strong, but I was pretty sure I'd gotten it right.

Jane Hawke's eyes sparkled under purple shadow. "We've been neighbors for years. Now we want to switch."

Ethan Tau hadn't spoken yet. He smiled broadly, then said, "You don't shock easily, Mr. Morgan. I like that."

"Not often, anyway."

Tau continued. "We're all on board with changing partners," he said. "Jane will go live with Lars, and Jeanette will come live with me. But we're not as stupid as this might sound to you. We want you to investigate all four of us. We want everything out in the open. No surprises. Kids are involved."

"I see," I said. "I'm sorry to have to say this, but our case-load is so full we wouldn't be able to help you for weeks, if then. I'm sorry."

I *was* sorry. I would've loved to take on a plum job like this: no blood, no guts, no gunfire, just background checks and surveillance. A *lot* of surveillance. Could keep four operatives busy and on the meter 24/7.

I gave the interesting foursome Haywood Prentiss's phone number and told them that I'd not only worked for Prentiss, he'd taught me everything I knew. Then I showed them out.

I had another appointment, and I didn't want to be late.

Chapter 31

I WALKED SIX blocks to an address in downtown LA that Uncle Fred had given me. The building was three stories high, pink paint flaking off the stucco and a sun-bleached green awning over the front door.

To the left was a bike shop and to the right was a bodega. There was a locked metal gate barring the stairs to the second floor.

I spoke into an intercom, said my name, a code number, and that Fred Kreutzer had sent me. A voice told me to hang on, he'd be right down.

A minute later, a wiry man with dark skin and a face shaped like a weasel's opened the gate and said, "Barney Sapok. Pleased to meet you, Mr. Morgan."

I followed Sapok up the stairs to the third floor, where he opened a freshly painted door and showed me into a space filled with cubicles, about twenty of them, each occupied by a man or woman with a telephone headset, a scratch pad, and a computer.

They were taking bets.

The place looked like a police command center or a telemarketing office, but in fact it was a bookmaking operation that brought in tens of millions a year. Just this branch.

Sports wagering is illegal in every state but Nevada. As a result, it's become a cash cow for organized crime. Barney Sapok was either a family associate or he was forking over a substantial amount of money to the Mob for collection and enforcement and writing it off as a cost of doing business.

Sapok's office was in a corner, overlooking the street. He said, "Mr. Kreutzer told me to trust you. He told me to show you some things. But nothing can leave this office."

"I understand," I said.

He opened a drawer, removed a spreadsheet from a file, and put it on his desk.

"I pulled this data off the encrypted network. Bettors have code names and numbers, so I spent last night decoding it for you."

"I'm sure that will help, Barney. Thank you."

I dragged a chair up to the desk and began to scan the list. Familiar names jumped out at me immediately, players on a dozen teams in both leagues.

"These are their bets over the past year," Sapok said, running his finger down the columns under the names. "Notice something?" he asked.

"I see some fifty-grand bets on a single game."

"Anything else?"

"None of the players are betting on their games."

Sapok nodded. "If the players are putting in a fix, I don't know about it." He dropped the spreadsheet into a bucket of water he kept next to his desk.

The spreadsheet and all other documents in the bookie's office were printed on rice paper. I watched the pages and the ink that was printed on them dissolve in the water.

Sapok asked, "Mr. Kreutzer is your uncle? Is that right?"

I nodded. "More like a father, actually."

"There's something else he thought you should see. We've got a certain client who's into us for over six hundred thousand dollars. He's in big trouble. Could have a fatal outcome."

"A football player?" I asked.

Sapok wrote block letters on a pad of paper, turned the pad so I could read it, then ripped off the top page, which followed the spreadsheet into the bucket of water.

The rice paper dissolved, but the afterimage of those block letters hung in front of my eyes.

Sapok had written down my brother's name.

Tom Morgan Jr.

Tommy owed over $600,000 to the Mob.

Chapter 32

I THANKED BARNEY Sapok and left his place of business in a fury. I wasn't mad at Sapok. That guy was trying to help by telling me about Tommy's $600,000 debt. Clearly, Uncle Fred wanted me to know that Tommy was in trouble, and that he couldn't help Tommy himself.

Fred and Tommy hadn't spoken in a dozen years. I'd never known what their fight was about, but Tommy held grudges and he had a big one against Uncle Fred. I guessed that Fred had tried to stop Tom from getting into a jam like the one he was in now, and of course my brother had resented it.

I was enraged at Tommy and I was disgusted with him. And I didn't know what to do next.

Through Tommy, I'd become familiar with the cycle of the sickness. Gamblers gamble for the rush. It goes from compulsion to addiction. They win and place another bet. They lose, which is far more likely, and the elation turns to deflation, and they bet again to cover the loss. Either way, they keep betting.

Small losses go onto their tab with their bookie. If the debt isn't paid, the Mob's loan sharks sometimes move in. The interest on the loan, the vigorish, is obscenely high and it's due weekly. Too often, the bettor can't gather enough money to pay back the principal, and when he falls behind on the vig, the threats start, and then the beatings. The next thing he knows, a Mob guy owns his business.

Tommy had a business. He was doing okay. But a weekly interest charge of 20 percent on a $600,000 loan? That was $12,000 a week before he ever put a dent in the principal.

Had Tommy borrowed against his house? His business? Was he hanging over the abyss by his fingertips, or was he already falling into a bottomless hole? Sapok had said the outcome could be fatal.

I ran up the winding stairway to my office and told Colleen that I couldn't be interrupted.

I spent a couple of hours making calls. And then I phoned Tommy at his office.

I told his assistant, "Don't give me any bull, Katherine. Put him on."

Tommy's voice came over the line. He sounded reluctant and irritated, but he agreed to have lunch with me at one o'clock.

Chapter 33

TOMMY, WHO HAD always been a control freak, picked the restaurant where we would meet. Crustacean is a popular Euro-Vietnamese place on Santa Monica, a few doors down from his office.

I told him I'd be there in twenty minutes, and twenty minutes later on the nose, I walked through the front door.

I gave my name to the hostess, who walked me across the glass-covered stream of live koi and settled me with a menu in "Mr. Tommy's booth" near the fountain.

I studied the menu, and when I looked up again, my brother was zigzagging across the floor, shaking hands along the way as if he were campaigning for office.

If anything was important in Beverly Hills, it was appearances, and Tommy was doing a fine job of keeping up his.

"Bro," he said, arriving at the table. I stood. We hugged warily. He clapped me on the back.

"How's it going?" I said.

"Fantastic," Tommy said, sliding into the booth. "I can't stay long. I'll order."

The waitress came over, cocked her hip, noted that we were identical twins, and flirted with Tommy. She took our lunch order from the "secret kitchen." Throughout it all, I was pacing in my mind, trying to figure out how best to approach Tommy with what I knew.

He said, "I hear your friend Cushman is looking good for killing his wife."

"He didn't do it."

"How much you want to bet?" he said.

Tommy's business, Private Security, was an agency that placed bodyguards with celebrities and businesspeople who were looking for protection or status or both. Tommy had benefited from Dad's contacts a lot more than I had. Tommy looked around the room, said, "As big a shit as Dad was, it would have taken us much longer to make it without him."

"So, you're really doing okay, Tommy? That's good to hear."

"Sure. Half the people in here are on my books, for Christ's sake."

Tommy leaned back from the table and glared at me suspiciously as the waitress set down dishes of cracked crab and garlic noodles, and asked if we needed anything else.

"We're good, sugar," he said to the waitress. To me, he said, "So what's this about?"

"I hear you're still wagering," I said to my brother.

"Who told you that? Annie, that little—"

"I didn't talk to her."

"—bitch," he said of his too patient, too forgiving wife and the mother of his son. "Why'd you call her, Jack?"

"I haven't spoken to Annie since Christmas."

"She should be grateful for the life I've given her," Tommy said, breaking a crab in half with his hands. "Clothes. Cars. Everywhere she goes, people treat her like royalty. I'm going to have to explain to her again about flapping her mouth."

"Does she know you're into the Mob for six hundred thousand bucks, Tommy? Because I'll *bet* you didn't tell her that part."

"It's none of her business, big shot. And it's none of yours either. Whatever I'm into, I can get out of. Trust me on that."

"I wish I could."

"Go to hell. Don't call me anymore, okay? A Christmas card will do fine. No Christmas card would be even better."

Tommy threw his napkin on the table and bolted for the front door.

Chapter 34

I DROPPED TWO hundred bucks on the table and followed Tommy out to Little Santa Monica Boulevard, a teeming thoroughfare that cuts through a canyon of office buildings and collateral businesses: a drugstore, an AT&T phone store, an assortment of trendy cafés and upscale banks.

"Tommy. Tom," I shouted after him. "Talk to me, okay? Let's talk. *Tom*."

He pulled up short and turned, a frown on his face, clenched fists at his sides. I'd been toe-to-toe with my brother before, but this seemed more serious.

"Stay out of my business, Jack. I said I can handle it. I know these guys."

"You have the money to pay off your debt? Because what I hear is the Mob is going to start breaking bones, *your* bones, Tom. That's just before they wire up your ignition and take over your business."

"If they kill me, they won't get paid, will they?" Tommy said with a smirk. "Stay out of it, Jack. Don't make me tell you again."

"As much fun as this is, I'm butting in because of what this is going to do to Annie and Ned."

"Yeah, I see your halo twinkling now. Doesn't that get a little old?"

"So rather than let me help you, you'd rather be a selfish, out-of-control son of a bitch with a colossal death wish, and destroy your family in the process. That's it, right?"

Tommy gave me a sour grin. "So what are you offering? A bridge loan if I never call my bookie again? You're out of your mind."

He turned and strode away from me, but I caught up with him and put my hand on his shoulder.

I had fought with Tommy so many times that I saw the roundhouse punch coming almost before he threw it.

I ducked, put my shoulder into his gut, and knocked him down. We both hit the pavement, but my fall was cushioned by the paunchy body of my well-fed twin.

He got an arm free and tried to get me into a headlock, but I rolled him over and hiked his right arm behind his back. Then I got his wrist up between his shoulder blades.

"Owww. *Listen, stupid*," he grunted. "Any of my guys see you doing this, they'll pound your head to a pulp. I won't stop 'em either."

"I'm taking you somewhere," I said. "And you're going to come with me and be a good sport about it."

"You're crazy. *Owww*."

"I'm the best chance you have, asshole. Always have been."

"Bastard," he grunted. "I wish you were dead."

It came to me in a flash. How had I not seen this—or had I just blocked out the obvious? "You've been calling me, haven't you, Tommy? Day and night, calling me and wishing me dead."

"What? Ow, *damn it*. Never. I *never* fucking call you, you fuck." And then the starch went out of him and he started to cry. "The bastards killed my dog."

"Who? Who did that? Your dog? *Ned's* dog?"

"Boys from the Mob."

I said, "Okay. I'm sorry, Tom. I'm letting you up now. Don't fight me, okay?"

"You want me to say thank you? Don't hold your breath."

"I want you to come with me—and don't give me any trouble."

"Fine. Whatever you want."

I didn't let him up just yet.

"Pinkie swear?" I said, looping my left pinkie around his. It took a couple of seconds, but then he squeezed my finger.

"Pinkie fucking swear," he said.

Chapter 35

MARGUERITE ESPERANZA TOLD her grandmama she'd be back in a few minutes, *all right?* She let the screen door slam behind her as she left the small brown stucco house with the red tile roof on St. George Street, a five-minute walk to the video store, where she'd gone a hundred thousand times before.

She was listening to her iPod as she turned onto Rowena. The four-laner was bright with storefronts: Pizza Hut, Blockbuster, Sushi-to-Go. Busy and totally safe.

No problems on the horizon. Besides—Marguerite could handle problems. *For sure.*

Marguerite waved to a couple of kids she knew and kept going toward the Best Buy sign blinking at the end of the next block. Her phone buzzed, signaling that she had a text message.

She didn't recognize the number, but only one person

called her Tigerpuss. That would be Lamar Rindell. Lamar was a supercute senior, a basketball player who'd been flirting with Marg both in person and on the phone. She'd hung out with him and a bunch of other kids after school, but Marg was hoping for more.

Lam: Wassup Tigerpuss.
Marg: getting a video. New Moon. I ♥ vampires.
Lam: Video World?
Marg: yeh. ☺ it's close, right?
Lam: want to get pizza after?
Marg: I can't.
Lam: ok. Never mind.

Marguerite leaned against a mailbox while she weighed her options. It was Grandmama versus Lamar, and she shouldn't have to choose. Pizza Hut was only one block down. It wasn't even dark out yet.

She typed to Lamar: "OK. C U soon."

Then she called home, said, "I'm stopping for a slice and a Coke. You can practically see the place from the kitchen window. I'll have Lamar walk me home, okay?"

Marg rehearsed her attitude, her mind focused on how she'd remember everything she and Lamar said to each other so she could tell her BFF Tonya all about it when she got home. She grinned to herself just thinking about that.

She headed to get her vampire movie. She started off walking, but then she began to skip.

Chapter 36

A BLACK HYUNDAI van with a cable TV logo on the side cruised the streets of Los Feliz.

"I've got your pigeon on the grid," Morbid said to the guy sitting next to him in the back. "She just left her house. She's going to bite. She's going down."

"I'm ready," said Jason Pilser in his role as Scylla. A freakin' Greek monster. Six heads. "Let me do this. She's all mine, right?"

Morbid gave the keyboard to Scylla, who watched the tracking icon that stood for Marguerite Esperanza as it traveled across the GPS map.

Scylla tapped on the keys, sending a text message to Marguerite using the name of this guy, Lamar, who'd been texting Marguerite for a couple of weeks.

And Marguerite was answering.

After some dialogue and a change of mind, she said yes. She'd meet "Lamar" at Pizza Hut.

Scylla felt the sweat gather at his hairline. He patted his jacket pocket, put on his fresh gloves.

He listened in on Marguerite's call to her grandma over the speaker, and when she'd told her good-bye, Steemcleena parked the van on Rowena. Maybe twenty yards from the pizzeria. No more than that.

Scylla watched Marguerite's icon on the GPS grid close in on the icon for the van. He looked through the dark glass of the side window as the girl came up the sidewalk past the stationery store.

"She's a babe," he said.

"And she's all yours, Scylla. She's *your* babe. Think you can handle her?"

For a few seconds Marguerite would be between the dry cleaner and the van, like an eclipse of the moon.

"Scylla. Go," Morbid said. "Go now."

Scylla pulled open the van door and got his first good look at the target. The girl was bigger than he'd thought.

She was at least five ten and looked ripped. With only seconds to make his decision, Scylla leaped to the sidewalk, came up behind her, and threw a cloth bag over her head, cinching the drawstring.

She screamed incredibly loud, and she fought back too.

Scylla clapped his hand over her mouth. He was so filled with adrenaline, it took nothing for him and Morbid to lift her off the sidewalk and throw her into the back of the van.

Morbid slammed the doors closed and slapped the divider

to signal Steem to go, *go*. Then he and Scylla threw their bodies on top of the struggling girl.

"Gotcha," Scylla said. "Now be a good girl."

Morbid yelled at her, "If you shut the hell up, we'll give you a chance to win."

Scylla's mouth was dry. He was so pumped. Even if he wanted to, there was no backing out now.

"What do you mean?" she asked. "Give me a chance to win what?"

Chapter 37

THERE WAS A screech of brakes as the black van jerked to a halt. The doors ground open, and Scylla and Morbid hoisted the girl out by her long arms and legs. They carried her quickly away from the street and tossed her to the ground.

Suddenly she was a blur as she pulled off the hood and got to her feet in one startlingly fast movement. She lashed out to clear the space around her and faced Scylla, who was in a wrestling crouch only a body's length away.

He grinned, a ski mask covering most of his face. She was nothing like the combatants he'd faced on Commandos of Doom. Her *reality* was startling and exciting, but most of all, it was a challenge.

"Hey, Tigerpuss. Here, kitty kitty," he said to the girl.

"Who are you?" Marguerite screamed back at him.

"I'm the one who's going to test you," Scylla said. "It's me against you, Marguerite."

Private

The girl looked around, and Scylla saw her take in the scene. They were on Rowena, past the strip malls and stores, right on the bank of the reservoir, a place as desolate as the dark side of the moon. Cars zoomed by beyond the fence that walled off the reservoir from the road.

Morbid and Steem danced around Marguerite, executing martial feints that Scylla had used innumerable times on Commandos of Doom. It not only kept the target off balance, it blocked her escape.

But where some girls would have begged and cried, this one lunged. She shot out the heel of her hand and connected with a cracking sound, square on Scylla's nose.

He fell back with a howl of agony and held his face with both hands. He saw the girl turn to run, dodging the others as if she were weaving through defenders for a layup in a playground basketball game.

Steem reached out with a long arm, grabbed the girl's hair, and yanked her right off her feet.

Then he let go of her and stepped back. This wasn't his turn.

Scylla thought he knew what to do now. He went straight for the girl, visualizing throwing her to the ground and choking her with a headlock—but she was much faster than he was.

She spun around, chopped at him in some kind of judo move, then followed the chop with a kick to his groin. He saw the kick coming and deflected it so that it connected with his thigh, but it still hurt like hell. Another hard blow landed on his forearm. Had she cracked a bone?

He dodged several more of her blows, and when she

connected, he didn't go down. The pain was actually feeding him now, real pain, a real life-and-death game. It stoked his fury as he danced around her. Morbid and Steem were taunting her, crowding her, waving their arms.

"I'll remember you," she shouted at them, a fierce warrior and opponent. "You. You. And especially *you*, asshole!"

As Scylla watched, Marguerite spun and missed. He saw his chance and chopped the back of her neck with the side of his hand. Then he kicked her legs out from under her.

She was down, crying now, *"Why ... why?"* But then she bounced right up again.

She went at Scylla and smashed a foot into his throat. He went down—and the girl saw a hole to run through, to get away from them.

Steem called to Morbid, "She's too good for him." Then he started to laugh. She was getting away, though. So he pulled a gun from his waistband. He shot her in the chest. That knocked her straight back, and she fell over Scylla.

She lay there, and Steem stood over her.

"You were great," he said. Then he shot her in the face. Twice to be sure.

Morbid stepped up beside him over the dead girl. "That was kind of cool. She *was* great."

Chapter 38

JASON PILSER—Scylla—wanted to lift his chin and howl. The pain started at his nose, radiated out and along every nerve in his body, pounded in his left thigh and right forearm, which was probably broken. If pain could be seen, he would have been blazing like a fucking light show.

But there was justice too. The bitch was dead. Now he was in charge of staging the body.

He taped the free end of an electric cord to her hand and positioned it over her head; the other end, he tightly knotted around her neck, so it looked as though she had hanged herself.

Gallows humor—and the original plan before Steem had had to shoot her.

If he hadn't been in such agony, it would actually have been pretty damn funny. He took off the bitch's athletic shoes and threw them into the van. His trophy. The shoes were so big, he could probably wear them himself. That would be a hell of a thing, wouldn't it?

He was about to say so as he looked up at Morbid and Steem. Objectively, they were savages. He was sure they killed for the same reason he had. For the unparalleled thrill. It was like a drug. And they were smart enough, disciplined enough, to pull it off in populated areas, like here.

Shit. He'd just killed a woman with traffic racing by on the other side of a fence.

Steemcleena finally spoke. "Scylla. That was a very poor showing, man."

Jason didn't like the expression on Steem's face. Getting injured had cost him points. Hell, she had knocked him down. Jason said, "You're kidding, right? She's some kind of judo expert."

"You guys, get into the van," Steemcleena said. "Scylla, you'll get another shot at this. Maybe next time you'll even win."

Chapter 39

DEL RIO AND CRUZ left the fleet Mercedes with the valet at the Beverly Hills Hotel and headed through the lobby to the Polo Lounge. The maître d' said that Ms. Rollins was on the patio. Cruz rolled up his jacket sleeves and followed Del Rio out into the bright sunshine.

Cruz thought that Sherry Rollins looked about thirty, although it was getting harder to tell women's ages in this town. She was wearing a floppy hat and a skinny black dress with white detailing; she looked like a young executive at one of the studios.

Both men shook hands with her, said their names, and the blond-haired woman moved her dog from a chair and invited them to sit down.

"Are you hungry?" she asked. "The lobster salad is quite good."

"Something to drink, maybe," Del Rio said.

The waitress trotted over and took an order of beer for Del Rio, tea for Cruz. Then Cruz took the lead.

"Ms. Rollins."

"Sherry," she said.

"Sherry. We're investigating the death of Shelby Cushman. I'm sure you've heard about it."

"A break-in, wasn't it? A burglar broke into the house and shot her."

"Actually, that's not right," Del Rio said. "All the indications are that Shelby Cushman was murdered with premeditation. Nothing was taken. Not a thing."

"That's insane," said the woman. "I'm sure I heard it was a robbery. Why else would someone kill Shelby?"

"How well did you know her?" Cruz asked.

"I've known her a few years," she said. "I wouldn't say I was a close friend."

"But she used to work for you, didn't she? She was one of your escorts."

Sherry Rollins didn't miss a beat. "Not since she got married. Last few months, she was working for someone else. That's what I heard, anyway. I'm sorry—this is very upsetting."

"It would really help if you'd tell us all about it," said Cruz. "And don't leave anything out. Try to hold in your grief."

"I don't know any more than what I've told you."

"You do, Sherry," said Del Rio, his voice all business, no kidding around now. "You know a lot more. And I'll tell you what. Help us out here, and we won't go to the police. We won't tell them why we think you're a suspect in Shelby Cushman's murder."

126

"Suspect? That is absurd. Why would I want to kill Shelby?"

"I don't know why, but the police might like to question you about that—and any number of other things."

The woman in the hat gave him an icy look, but he had her, and he knew it.

Sometimes Del Rio really liked his job.

So far, he was giving this day five stars.

Chapter 40

AT JUST AFTER FOUR, the sun was a dull white disk glowing in a pewter gray sky. The reservoir was covered with algae, and the trees were large humps, massed like woolly mammoths, making the whole place seem prehistoric.

If you squinted, you couldn't see the city of Los Angeles at all. You could pretend the rush of traffic on Rowena was just a bitter wind.

Justine Smith's heels sank into the ground as she walked down the slope toward the cordon of crime scene tape that stretched from tree to tree, a bright yellow ring in the smog and the gloom.

Lieutenant Nora Cronin lifted the tape for Justine, but instead of making a snarky remark, she just said hi. Something had changed, and Justine had an idea what it might be. Cronin now felt so desperate about the case, she would accept any help.

Even from Private. Even from Justine.

"Chief Fescoe has been looking for you," Cronin said. "He's *here*."

Justine nodded, then continued on toward the scrum of cops huddled around the body. At six-foot-three, Mickey Fescoe stood a bit above the others. It was rare to see the chief of police at a crime scene, but she guessed that Fescoe too was feeling the heat.

Thirteen girls had died in just over two years. Fescoe had been promoted in the middle of this murder spree, but now the bad news had caught up with him and threatened to swamp him. The parents of the murdered girls had formed an action committee and were on the television news every night. The public was scared and inflamed.

Justine put her hand on the police chief's arm.

Fescoe turned and said, "Justine. I'm glad you're here. Take a look." He handed her a pair of latex gloves. "It's escalating, getting worse."

Justine stooped beside the body of Marguerite Esperanza. There was an extension cord knotted into a noose and pulled tightly around the seventeen-year-old girl's neck.

The loose end of the cord was taped to her left hand, which was positioned at an odd angle above her head. The really weird part was that the girl had been shot at least twice — in the chest and in the face.

The scene had been made to look as though the girl had hanged herself. What the hell was that supposed to mean? Once again, this felt like a different killer.

Justine asked, "Any witnesses? Any anything?"

"It looks like she was killed right here," Fescoe told her.

"The ground is all chewed up, like there was some kind of scuffle. We found blood on a pile of leaves. Hers or her killer's. Maybe she managed to rake the scum with her fingernails. Let's hope so. Give the good guys a break for a change."

"What about her handbag? Was it found?"

"No, it's gone, along with her shoes. So there's your signature. A couple of kids found her and called it in. They said the place was empty when they got here almost an hour ago."

Justine touched the girl's cold cheek. Marguerite had been pretty, and more than that, she looked strong. There were bruises on her arms and face. She'd taken an awful beating before she'd gone down.

"The pose is obviously theatrical," Justine said to Fescoe. "This MO is different than the other kills, which, unfortunately, is *the hallmark* of this string of killings. I wonder why was she killed so soon after Connie Yu? And why shoot her, then pose her as if she had been hanged?"

Chapter 41

SCYLLA'S LUXURY APARTMENT was on Burton Way. His building was one of four high-end residences in a row, each about six stories tall.

Jason's place was on the top floor, with a wraparound terrace. It had a wide view of the hills. He had never had real friends, but the apartment helped to get him superficial ones and even dates.

Jason stood on the terrace now and watched the city lights merge seamlessly with the city sky and the whole of the universe. The view was the shits, but for once, its beauty failed to engage his sense of awe.

He went back inside, turned on the TV, watched the Boston Celtics get pounded by the Lakers. He didn't give a damn who won the stupid game so adored by men without any imagination or flair in their humdrum lives.

Jason had a lot on his mind, but he was so high on

painkillers, he doubted his ability to reason. He'd have to explain to his coworkers about the tape across his nose, the black eyes, his arm bandaged. He wondered what he was going to say, how he would spin it.

Meanwhile, Morbid was coming over to talk to him about a second chance. They'd texted back and forth, Morbid explaining to Scylla how embarrassed he was, since he was the one who'd recruited him.

There was an unspecified threat, but clearly an offer of redemption. As a favor to Scylla, Morbid had convinced Steem to agree to an unscheduled night on the town so that Scylla could erase the black mark against him.

Morbid had told him that they had a pretty little pigeon already picked out, and Scylla would have to take care of her this very night.

"So soon?" Jason had said.

"You have a problem with it?" Morbid asked.

"No. Tonight's good."

The doorbell rang, and Jason got up off the sofa. He hobbled to the foyer and pressed the intercom button.

"It's me," said Morbid. "And Steem."

"Come on up."

He was going to kill another girl—only this time it didn't seem like such fun and games.

Chapter 42

SCYLLA OPENED HIS front door, and Steemcleena entered, Morbid right behind him. They seemed purposeful and serious, and Jason got the feeling that the two of them had been longtime buddies, maybe even outside the game. Actually, it was cool that they were letting him in at all.

"How's the nose?" Morbid asked, taking a leather lounge chair, sprawling in it, as Steem looked over the bookshelves.

"It's okay. You guys want a beer?" Jason asked.

"Not for me, thanks. Nice place, Scylla. The view is great from here," Steem said as he headed toward the sliding door that led out to the terrace.

"Let me get that," Jason said, limping after him. He unlatched the door and pulled it open. "It's the shits—like a thirty-mile view," he said.

Steemcleena whistled. "Hey, Morbid. You should see this. Come out here, man. It's like a movie. *Cinematic.*"

Jason moved aside the metal bistro chairs so that all three of them could line up at the terrace wall and share Los Angeles.

Steemcleena said to Jason, "See that?" He pointed to a van across the street, the one with the Comcast logo. "That's redemption for you, partner. Tonight's ride. You believe you're getting a second chance?"

"Sure I do," said Scylla.

"*Well, you're not, asshole*. You're tonight's pigeon."

Steemcleena bent quickly. He grabbed Scylla by the knees. At the same time, Morbid pushed his shoulders so that Jason was lying across the wall, head and chest over the sheer cliff of the terrace. Below him was sixty feet of air.

"Don't," Jason cried out. "Please, just put me down. Please?"

"Don't whine, you little twerp. Just spread your wings and fly."

Jason's belly scraped concrete as he was shoved a few more inches over the wall. Cars sped by on the street below. Blood rushed to his brain, and his mind spun. What could he say? That this was the most incredible game of all?

Jason's mind kicked off disconnected images. His father's hand holding a pen. The priest who gave him first communion. The look on Marguerite Esperanza's face while she fought for her life.

His own voice was loud inside his head.

I'm not supposed to die this way.

I'm not supposed to die at all.

He was too scared to scream as he dropped over the rail, and he clearly heard Steem yell, *"Pigeon!"*

Chapter 43

TO BE HONEST, my recurring dream was sometimes more real than reality. More focused, more magnified, and usually in high-definition color.

I ran across the broken landscape toward the back ramp of the CH-46. The powerful helicopter was actually the easiest for the Afghans to bring down—their heat-seeking missiles would rather lock on to its engines than the sun. Men screamed in pain, and the *crump* sound of mortars exploding rang in my ears. I stood at the lip of the ramp, felt horror as I looked inside and saw—

Jesus, I was ripped from the dream, from some kind of closure, by a loud humming noise.

My eyes flashed open, and I saw my cell phone vibrating less than two feet from my face.

I palmed the phone and stared at it, my heart still thudding. The time was 9:35. The caller ID read "R. Del Rio."

I put the phone to my ear.

"Rick. I overslept. I never do that."

"That's all right. I have to tell you something, buddy. You're not going to like it."

I swung my legs over the side of the bed. My knees felt shaky, as if I'd really been running over rock and rubble. My mouth tasted like gunpowder.

"Go ahead. I'm listening."

"It's about Shelby," Rick said. "She wasn't exactly who you thought she was."

Now I was wide fucking awake. "What does *that* mean? What did you find out? Let me have it, Rick."

"She was a hooker," Del Rio blurted. "More of a high-class party girl. Whatever. And Jack, she went back to work *after* she married Cushman."

"That's crazy. Who said that about Shelby?"

"Jack. Jack, calm down. I wouldn't lie to you. Cruz and I talked to some credible sources. Get dressed. I'll be out front of your house in fifteen minutes. We've got a witness to interview."

Ten minutes later, I threw my briefcase into the backseat of one of the fleet cars, a Mercedes S class. Rick was at the wheel. He handed me a container of coffee.

"Shelby was not a hooker. I'm sure she wasn't. That's bullshit," I said.

"You think I'm lying? Why would I lie to you, Jack?"

"I didn't say that."

"Buckle up," he said. "Let's get to the bottom of this. Let's find out who murdered her and why they did it."

Del Rio drove the car through the smog-gray morning up into the hills. The neighborhood got richer as we climbed.

Mansions worth millions were set on lush grounds with staggering views. Del Rio slowed the car and pulled up to the high wrought-iron gates in front of one of the great houses in Beverly Hills.

Since the early 1940s, this mansion on Benedict Canyon Road had been owned by a notorious gossip columnist, an Oscar-winning film director, and a Saudi prince.

Now the sprawling Mediterranean-style villa was masquerading as "the Benedict Spa."

But I knew, the LAPD knew, and men of means from all over the world knew it too—this cliff-hanging spread was a glorified whorehouse, currently occupied by Glenda Treat, madam to the stars and star makers. The landlord was none other than Ray Noccia.

I heard myself say to Rick, "You're not telling me that Shelby worked *here?*"

Rick nodded once.

"Ms. Treat isn't expecting us," he said. "We have to ask her about Shelby, let it come from the horse's mouth. I suggest you turn on that charm thing you do so well."

"I don't feel too charming this morning."

"Just work it," Del Rio said.

Chapter 44

THERE WAS AN unlocked gate maybe twenty yards down a hill from the so-called spa's main entrance, and I opened it. With Del Rio behind me, I bushwhacked through Glenda Treat's side yard, batting away branches as I made my way toward the pool in back.

I stopped at the edge of a flagstone terrace to let Rick catch up, and at the same time, I took in the scene.

An assortment of slender, very pretty young women lay in powder blue chaises, their feet pointing toward a circular swimming pool. I was reminded of an hors d'oeuvres platter. Chicks and dips.

"That's her," said Del Rio, jutting his chin toward a forty-something woman with a white-blond ponytail. The visor shading her eyes made her look like a dealer in Vegas.

The moment I fastened my eyes on Glenda Treat, she looked up and saw the two of us.

Ms. Treat had hardly aged since she'd been in the news as "the Don's Madam" several years back. Arrested for pandering, she had threatened to open her little black book to the media: a long list of leading men, power brokers, and politicians. In the end, she had backed away from the tabloids and quietly done her five-year stretch. When she got out, the story goes, Ray Noccia had presented her with the keys to this place in appreciation for her stiff upper lip.

I tried to imagine Shelby with Ray Noccia and Glenda Treat, and it just didn't compute. Shelby wasn't hard and she wasn't sleazy, not the Shelby I knew, anyway. The Shelby I knew had a funny line for every occasion and would give you the shirt off her back. So maybe that was the problem.

Glenda Treat uncurled gracefully from her lounge chair and came toward me and Rick, sizing us up—and I did the same to her. She obviously liked her cosmetic surgery: green eyes stretched tight, Hollywood thin, pillowy breasts. I wondered if she could actually swim in her pool, or if those artificial flotation devices kept her bobbing at the surface.

She smiled her famously winning smile, which had always seemed a little forlorn to me.

She thought we were johns, of course.

I introduced Rick and myself, then handed her my card.

"I'm not wearing my glasses," she said.

I told her I was with Private. She knew the firm. Everybody does. She had even heard of me.

"What can I do for you gentlemen, then?" Glenda said. Her smile had lost some of its gleam. "Manicure? Seaweed wrap?"

"I need some information on Shelby Cushman."

The remnants of her welcoming smile faded to a distant memory.

"I hear she's dead," said the madam. "Excuse me."

She showed me her back and a long stretch of thigh as she bent at the waist to whisper into the ear of a twenty-something brunette at poolside. The brunette picked up a cell phone, then walked away to make the call.

Glenda returned to say, "I have to ask you to leave my property. It's private as well."

"Give me one minute, okay?" I said. "This is strictly personal for me. I'm working for Shelby's husband. She was a friend of mine."

"Mr. Morgan, Shelby was a fine masseuse. She could do four or five massages a day and make every one feel special. She started working here after her marriage. I recall that she said she was bored being home alone all day. About what happened to her? All I know is what I read in the *LA Times*. Of course, we all know what a rag that is."

"Did anyone want to hurt Shelby?" I asked. "Anyone make any threats?"

"She was popular," Glenda said. "Miss Congeniality. Everybody liked her, and she thought she was their friend."

She addressed her last remark over my right shoulder. I turned to see three men coming through French doors out to the patio.

They were casually dressed, with bulges under their armpits. I recognized two of them from the night I met Ray Noccia in my driveway.

One of them, the guy in the lead, was wearing a black

shirt, black pants, black jacket, no tie. He locked eyes with me, and I saw that he remembered me too.

"What are you doing here, Morgan? You have an appointment for a massage?"

I held up my palms to show that I wasn't looking for trouble. But it didn't matter. Trouble had found me.

"Do I look like I have to pay for a massage?" I said.

Chapter 45

THE MAN WEARING all black had mostly been a shadowy presence in my driveway, standing behind Ray Noccia when the don paid me a call. He was muscle, and I could see him better now: in his late thirties, handsome if you like his type, bulked up, and heavily armed.

Glenda smiled in his direction. "Do you know Francis Mosconi, Mr. Morgan? He's in a related line of work," she said.

"We've met," I said. *"Francis."* I nodded his way.

I also recognized the man directly behind Mosconi. He was Noccia's driver, the fifty-something gentleman who'd maybe wisely advised me not to refuse a conversation with the boss. I placed him now. He was Joseph Ricci, the don's cousin, I believed.

A third man followed Ricci and Mosconi out onto the patio. He was young, blond, tanned, and looked like a lifeguard in his yellow polo shirt and khakis.

Mosconi patted me down. A few feet away, Lifeguard was doing the same to Del Rio, who pushed his hands away and said, "Get your hands off of me. Right *now*."

Lifeguard paid no attention, spun Rick around, and pushed him against the wall. I didn't think that was a good idea.

The kid was younger and possibly more fit than Del Rio, but it didn't matter. Rick hit him square in the nose with a jab and followed with a terrifying uppercut. The blond was out on his feet, and I felt like I ought to applaud.

But then Ricci lunged for Rick and hugged him from behind, pinning his arms to his sides while Mosconi put a nine-mil Beretta to Rick's temple.

"Stop," I called out. "We're done."

I raised my hands. Kept them high and in sight as Mosconi walked my way. Then he hit me hard with the Beretta. I guess we *weren't* done.

I went down. Then we were done.

Chapter 46

A FEW SECONDS LATER, Mosconi stood over me, eclipsing the weak sun. I tasted sour bile. Meanwhile, I was thinking that no one knew where we were. Del Rio and I were outnumbered and outgunned. It was Dodge City at high noon, and the smart odds were with the black hats.

Mosconi spoke softly, even kindly. "That one's for the way you talked to Mr. Noccia," he said. "Now get the hell up, Morgan."

I struggled to my feet, and as soon as I was upright, Mosconi hit me with a hard right to the chin. I staggered back and fell again, crushing a lounge chair, breaking a table. Spots blinked in front of my eyes.

"*That's* for trespassing," Mosconi said. "And calling me Francis."

I felt cold metal as he screwed his gun down into my ear.

The other two were working Rick over, cursing and scream-ing as they pounded him.

"You've got to learn some respect, Morgan. You and your friend."

"I understand," I said. "I do. I apologize. Help me up."

Mosconi laughed at me. He reached his hand down, and I grabbed it and twisted his wrist until Mosconi shrieked and followed his pain to the ground.

The Beretta clattered to the flagstones. I grabbed it on the second bounce and jammed the muzzle into Mosconi's tem-ple. Fair is fair.

"Put your guns on the ground," I shouted to Ricci and Lifeguard. "Guns on the ground and step away."

Joe Ricci immediately put his gun on the ground. Then so did Lifeguard.

"Morgan," Mosconi said with a sneer. "It's over. You win this time."

"It's not over yet," I said.

I didn't want to be followed and I didn't want a bullet in the back, so I ordered the three of them into the pool.

Ricci took off his shoes and his watch and walked down the steps at the shallow end like a gentleman. Mosconi shed his jacket and did a cannonball. Del Rio stiff-armed Life-guard over the side.

"Don't forget these," I called to them.

I tossed their guns into the pool.

The call girls began to move in closer. One of them put her hands on her knees and glowered at Mosconi in disgust. She was a little thing with blazing eyes.

"Now how are we supposed to swim in there?" she asked.

"Flap your arms and kick your legs," Del Rio said to her.

Glenda Treat watched from a vine-draped window as Del Rio and I left her yard. I waved bye-bye, and predictably, she gave me the finger. Unfortunately, that was all I'd gotten at the Benedict Spa.

Chapter 47

"CONSIDER US EVEN," Del Rio said. He was holding a wad of paper towels to his bloody nose as I drove us back down the road toward the office.

"What are you talking about?"

"You saved my life back there. I've been waiting for this day."

"Not even close. They were just messing with us. You're delirious."

"Shit," Del Rio muttered.

"Why was Shelby working for Glenda Treat?" I said.

"She was your friend, Jack. I barely knew her."

A muted ring came from my briefcase in the backseat. I asked Del Rio to pass me the phone, and he did. I opened it, saw that I had a dozen missed calls. I said hello to Colleen.

"Where've you been, Jack? I've been calling and calling."

"I know that. I was at the spa. What's going on?" I asked

her. My jaw was throbbing, my skull was a ball of pain, my ego was messed up.

"Justine wants to speak with you."

"Put her on."

"I'll warn her that you're a wee bit cranky."

"Put Justine on, Colleen. My mood couldn't be better."

Justine's words came in an agitated rush. "The mayor got an e-mail from the son of a bitch," Justine told me. "He said that he left Marguerite Esperanza's running shoes in a mailbox on La Brea. The lab is going over the shoes now. Jack, where the hell are you?"

I said, "Hang on."

There was a gas station coming up on the corner of Sunset and Fairfax. I pulled in.

"We've got almost a full tank," Del Rio said.

"Use the restroom. Wash the blood off your face. Justine? You still there?"

"*Blood?* What happened to Rick? What's going on? Why aren't you in the office? What's this about a spa?"

I got out of the car and walked to a secluded part of the Chevron's concrete lot. I told Justine about the pool party at the "spa" and that Glenda Treat had confirmed that Shelby had worked there but not why.

"You're a shrink; explain this to me," I said. "Why was she a working girl?"

"Without knowing her, I don't think I can."

"Pretend you're doing a profile. Just starting one."

There was a pause. Then she said, "Shelby was a comic, right?"

"A good one."

"Okay. Well, if you combine equal parts narcissism and self-hatred, you might come up with a stand-up comic. You might also come up with a prostitute."

I must have groaned.

Justine said, "Was I too rough, Jack?"

"Shelby must have found out something she wasn't supposed to know. Maybe about the Noccias."

"I'm sorry."

"It's not over."

"I know. Jack?"

"Uh-huh."

"Are you coming to the office? Sci and I have two very different approaches to the Schoolgirl case. I need another opinion."

"Sounds like we're making progress," I said. "I'll be right there."

Chapter 48

FOUR PAIRS OF eyes looked up in dismay, and maybe even shock, when Del Rio and I entered the war room.

"No one died," I said.

"Because there were too many witnesses," Del Rio added as a charming note.

Colleen came in to take orders for lunch as I was winding up my theory of the Shelby Cushman–Noccia family connection. She looked at me, wide-eyed and stunned. My jaw was bruised pretty badly. I had a nice laceration on my cheekbone. And those were just the injuries she could see.

"We were outnumbered," I said.

"The usual?" she asked me.

"Extra fries," I said. "Extra ice."

When Colleen left, I turned the floor over to Dr. Sci.

"Jack, I've been over this with Mo. We agree. If the Schoolgirl killer is baiting his victims with fake messages, he has to have wireless access to their mobile phones *in real time*."

Mo-bot piped up. She was sleeveless, showing off a colorful mess of tattoos. It was hard to imagine her at Harvard, where she'd gone through her PhD. She took off her bifocals and said, "What Sci is implying is that we think the scum is waiting at a location, probably in a vehicle that won't call attention. We'd say a van.

"Scum grabs the signal out of the air and accesses the target's mobile unit and basically clones it. That's how he's able to send his own messages using a screen name from one of the victim's friends."

"If he can do that," Sci said, "he can block all other messages, incoming and outbound. As far as I know, there's no program that can hijack cell phone content wirelessly," Sci said.

"But it's imaginable. If you can imagine it, it can be done," added Mo-bot.

Chapter 49

"HOLD ON TO that thought. Justine?"

Justine had dark circles under her eyes, but she still looked good. On the other hand, I couldn't remember the last time I'd seen her smile. This case had a hook in her and wouldn't let go.

"Something's been nagging at me for a couple of days," she said, "and it finally crystallized this morning. Five years ago, another girl was left dead in the same alley where Connie Yu was found. I went through the *LA Times* archives and found the story.

"Her name was Wendy Borman. She was seventeen," Justine continued. "Like Connie Yu, she left her house to make a quick trip to Hyperion Avenue and didn't come back. Her body was found the next morning."

"Wendy Borman is an unsolved case?"

Justine nodded and said, "She was killed by manual strangulation. She had a bruise behind her ear that came from a concussive blow with a heavy object. There were no witnesses, no sexual assault, and no forensic evidence. Sound familiar to you?

"And how's this? Her handbag and cell phone were taken. Also, she'd been wearing a necklace, a hand-wrought gold star on a chain. It wasn't on her when they found the body. Her mother said she *always* wore the necklace."

"So obviously, it was made to look like a robbery-homicide."

"Makes me wonder how long these Schoolgirl killings have been going on. How many girls has this sick bastard killed? How many different ways? Was there somebody even before the Borman girl?"

We reviewed assignments and workloads over lunch. Everyone in the room was expensive, but I didn't much care. Obviously neither did Justine.

I said, "Everything basically goes on hold but Cushman, NFL, and Justine's case. That's all we do until all three cases are closed. And we will close them."

I limped up the stairs to my office, and Colleen followed me to my desk.

"You got a call this morning," she said. "Maybe it's a prank, but it's *evil*, Jack. You should listen to it. Seriously."

She picked up the receiver, got into voice mail, and switched over to speaker.

I was sorry Colleen had to hear the eerie electronic voice that came over the phone.

"You're dead," the caller said. Colleen looked shocked, and for good reason. Nothing about the voice sounded like a hoax.

I took Colleen into my arms and held her against my chest. She made a purring sound like a cat, then laughed at herself.

What was I going to do with this lovely, lovely woman?

I said to her, "Not yet, Colleen. I'm not dead yet."

Part Three

WHAT'S LOVE GOT TO DO WITH IT?

Chapter 50

I WAS STANDING next to Colleen at a horseshoe bar that smelled faintly of an honest day's labor. "I come here most nights after work," she said of Mike Donahue's Tavern. She was wearing a pink fitted jacket over a flowered dress, her long hair falling in waves around her shoulders. Colleen was working hard to become an American citizen, but I saw why this dark Irish pub with its stout on tap and olde Irish barflies made her feel at home.

I felt troubled about what was happening between us. Colleen and I had been seeing each other for about a year, and we took that fact two different ways. To Colleen, it meant "time to get off the stick."

While we waited for our table we drank black and tans and shot darts, a beginner's game called Round the Clock. My throwing hand was still messed up from the fight with Mosconi, and Colleen was beating the socks off me.

"You shouldn't *let* me win, Jack," she said. "I'm going to take a lot of guff for this."

"You don't think I'm losing on purpose, Molloy?"

"Try to hit the number eight," she said, patting my hip.

My next flight of darts missed the mark, but I was laughing at myself, enjoying Colleen as she stood poised to throw, showing a lovely angle from her fingertips to her heel. Her first dart landed on the twenty, ending the game.

"I guess this means dinner's on me," I said.

She laughed and kissed me as her friend Donahue came out of the kitchen. Donahue was thirty-six and bearded. Colleen had said he was already suffering from gout.

"So this is the man who robbed us of your heart," he said.

"Mike's a sweet talker," Colleen said, hanging an arm around my waist. We followed Donahue to a table in a snug corner of the back room. After we'd eaten, the waiter came out carrying a cake blazing with candles.

When all the clapping and whistling was over, I leaned across the table for a kiss. "Happy belated birthday, Molloy." I pushed a little gold-wrapped box toward her. Colleen's face brightened as she peeled back the tape and paper. She slowly lifted the lid on the box.

"Thank you, Jack. It's lovely," she said, taking out a gold wristwatch.

"It suits you, Colleen."

"Go on then, Jack. You don't have to say tha' when you mean sumthin' else," she said.

Message received loud and clear. *It's not a ring.*

Chapter 51

COLLEEN'S RENTED BUNGALOW was in Los Feliz, a homey, artistic community with low buildings and one-family dwellings packed together on charming streets. We sat in my car and I told her why I couldn't stay tonight, even though we were celebrating her birthday.

People walked dogs in the street; kids ran by, shouting to one another. Idyllic stuff. Colleen looked down at her folded hands and at the little gold watch that gleamed dully under the streetlight.

"Rick and I are flying to Las Vegas in an hour," I told her.

"You don't have to explain. I made the arrangements into McCarran, Jack."

"It's just business, Colleen. I'm not going to a casino."

"It's fine, Jack. I have to study tonight anyway. I wouldn't be much fun. Thanks again for the lovely birthday, and the present. It's the nicest watch I've ever owned by far."

She gave me a peck on the lips, then reached for the door handle.

"I'll walk you to the door."

She sat back until I opened the car door, then she stepped primly out. I marched alongside her, past the mop-head rose-bushes and lavender in the narrow garden bordering the walk. She fumbled for her keys. "Have a safe flight."

"I'll see you in the morning," I said. Then I went down the fragrant walk to my car. I felt terrible about leaving her tonight, but I had to go.

The lights went on inside the cottage.

I tracked Colleen's movements from the entryway to the kitchen to the little sitting room where soon she'd be doing her work with a cup of tea, the radio on to keep her company.

I imagined her looking at her new watch, thinking of all the things she might have said to me, and what she'd say to me tomorrow. I started up the car and pulled away from the curb. At a stoplight, I called Rick.

"How're you doing?" I asked him. He'd been in a black mood since the incident at Glenda Treat's. Del Rio is the toughest man I know, and he held a grudge about that beating.

"I'm just leaving," he said. "I should be at the airport in twenty minutes, traffic permitting."

"This is a reminder," I said. "Bring your gun."

"Yeah. And Jack, you bring yours."

Chapter 52

CARMINE NOCCIA'S HOME was a half hour from McCarran Airport, fifteen minutes from the Strip in Las Vegas. I braked the rental car outside the high gated entrance to a community populated by celebrities, sultans, casino moguls, and others of the mysterious über-rich who are often the clients of Private.

Del Rio got out of the car and spoke our names into an intercom. The gates swung open.

I drove along a twisting road to another gate, this one with Noccia's number worked into wrought iron next to the intercom. Del Rio buzzed, and then that gate too opened and admitted us.

I put the car in drive and almost immediately heard an impossible rush of water. We drove across a bridge over a man-made river, past tennis courts and stables, then we arrived in the forecourt of a Spanish-style house fronted by up-lit date palms.

It was a little hard to believe that this over-the-top oasis had been constructed on barren sand, but that's what had happened.

A man in jeans and an open-necked red shirt opened the massive front door, showed us into the foyer, and told us to put our hands on the walls. He took our guns and frisked us for listening devices.

I saw Del Rio's face darken. He was cranking up his anger, but I warned him with my eyes.

The mutt in the red shirt said, "This way," and led us through a series of archways and high-ceilinged rooms, past wiseguys shooting billiards, to a great room with glass doors leading out to a pool.

Carmine Noccia was sitting in a chair in front of a fireplace, reading a hardback book.

He was of medium build, and although he was only forty-six, his hair was going gray. He wore a gray silk sweater and slacks, casual but excellent fabric and cut. He certainly looked the part of a wealthy capo, scion of the last significant Mafia family on the West Coast, a man taking in several illegal millions a week.

I knew quite a lot about Carmine Noccia. He had graduated with honors from Stanford and got his master's in marketing at UCLA. After graduation, he'd proven himself to his father, and over the past ten years he'd run prostitution, and probably drugs, for the family business. The don's son had never been charged with murder, but prostitutes had been found in Dumpsters. A middleman who'd imported girls from the former Soviet Bloc had disappeared. And my gun and Del Rio's were on top of an antique cabinet in the foyer.

We crossed the threshold, and Noccia immediately got to his feet, putting his hands in his pockets. He asked us to have a seat, and Del Rio and I plopped onto the leather sofa at an angle to his chair.

Noccia said, "Did you bring the money to bail out your brother? I hope so. Otherwise, you understand, this is a waste of my time."

I patted a pocket of my jacket and said, "I need your help on something else. Someone killed Shelby Cushman. It looks professional, and that's how LAPD is taking it. If you know who shot her, I'd like to know. She was a friend of mine."

As I was talking, Del Rio got up and began strolling around the great room, examining photographs and the rifles hanging from hooks on the walls. He asked Noccia, "You ride those horses in the stable out there?"

"I don't know who killed Shelby," Noccia said, following Rick with his eyes. "I can tell you that we liked her. She was a good lady. Very smart, very funny."

I took the thin envelope out of my jacket and handed it to Noccia. He opened the flap, peered in at the cashier's check for $600,000.

Tommy's gambling debt was now paid in full.

"I'll get this to the right people," Noccia said. He put the envelope between the pages of the book he'd been reading: *The Audacity of Hope*. Interesting. I wondered if he was pro or con on Barack Obama.

"If I hear anything about Shelby, I'll give you a call," he said. "You impressed me tonight, Jack. You did the right thing by your brother."

Chapter 53

THE NEXT MORNING at Private, Andy Cushman sat in the chair across from my desk. His face was very red, with bright white circles where his shades had been, evidence of too much time spent out by the pool. His hair was combed. He had shaved, and his clothes were neat and clean. It didn't look as though Andy had hit absolute bottom, but I knew in the next few minutes, he'd be there.

"You've got news for me," he said.

Colleen brought in my Red Bull and Andy's espresso. We both thanked her.

"Andy, I have something to tell you. You're not going to like it."

"Don't worry, Jack. Whatever it is, I can take it. That's why I'm here."

I nodded as if I agreed. Then I told my old friend that we

had found out where Shelby had been working before she was killed: the Benedict Spa.

Andy jumped up, shouting as he stabbed the air with a forefinger. *"What the fuck are you telling me? She worked there? That's a hundred percent horseshit. It's a lie! Somebody's jerking your chain, Jack!"*

I waited for Andy to finish his rant and sit back down. I understood why he was upset. "I wouldn't tell you if we hadn't checked it out, Andy. I'm sorry. But it's true."

Andy's face was nearly purple with rage. His breathing was fast and shallow. I worried that he might have a heart attack in my office, maybe a fatal one.

"Then tell me *why,* Jack. Tell me *why.* She had everything she wanted. Jesus, we had a very active sex life." He pushed away from the desk. "I want proof; I need it. That's your business, isn't it? *Proving things?* Proof, Jack, proof."

"Del Rio and I went to Las Vegas last night and met with Carmine Noccia."

Andy did a double take. "What's he got to do with it? This doesn't make any sense, Jack. None at all."

"He owns the Benedict Spa. He knew Shelby, and doesn't dispute that she worked for him. But he has no information on who killed her. So he says."

"You're telling me that my wife was a whore and a liar, and on top of that, she was working for the Mob? *Why,* Jack? She didn't need money."

I said again, "I'm very sorry, Andy."

"So any crummy dick with a gun could've killed her? Is that what you've found out?"

"We're working on it right now. We're all working on it. We're going to find the guy who did this."

Andy slammed his fist down on my desk. "Guess what? I no longer care who killed her," he said. "I don't want to spend another nickel on her. Fuck it, Jack. Fuck it."

I shook my head. "Please think this through. If we don't find Shelby's killer, the police will continue to focus on you."

"Let them. They have nothing on me and they'll get nothing. You just put yourself out of a job, Jack. You're fired."

Andy knocked his chair over as he got to his feet, then he steamed out of my office. He almost ran Colleen down as she came through the door.

"Did I hear right?" Colleen asked, putting a hand on her hip. I saw that she was wearing her new watch. "He fired us?"

"No. Well, yeah. He's upset, but he's my friend. I'm moving the Cushman case to the pro bono list," I said. "We're still working it. Only now we're doing it for free."

"I'll take care of it, Jack," Colleen said. Then she shut the door to my office. "Am I still your friend, Jack?"

Chapter 54

CRUZ PARKED HIS car outside the Benedict Spa and watched as an absolutely stunning young blond woman came out the front gates and strolled down the hill toward where he sat watching her promenade.

She was about five-foot-one, small boned, with a short boyish haircut, wearing black bicycle pants, a green spandex top, and flat shoes. She disarmed her Lexus convertible alarm as Cruz approached.

"Hi, could you wait up a second?" he said, walking toward her. She got into her car and locked the door.

Cruz took his badge out of his back pocket. He flashed it and made the universal motion to ask her to roll down her window.

"What are you?" she asked. "FBI?"

"Private investigator," he said, smiling at her. "I just need a moment. You work at the spa, right? This won't be hard, I promise."

"I can't talk to you. Please step back so I don't run over your toes."

"My name is Emilio Cruz. What's yours?"

"I'm Carla. Make an appointment, okay? I can talk to you *at the spa* all you want. For hours, if you like."

"Carla, stay right there in your car. Keep the door locked. I have two or three questions, that's it."

Carla, last name unknown, put her key into the ignition and started the car. Cruz crossed in front of the hood around to the passenger side. Carla reached across the seat and pushed the lock button down, but the window was half open.

Cruz reached in, pulled up the door handle, and got into the car.

"Get out or I'll scream. I'll call the house and someone will come out here and beat the hell out of you, buddy. They can get real ugly in a hurry."

"I come in peace. I'm not trying to upset you," Cruz said. "I just want to ask you about Shelby Cushman."

"Let me see that badge again."

Cruz held it up. "I'm licensed," he said. "But I'm not a cop. I'm here for Shelby."

Tears suddenly formed in the woman's eyes. That surprised the hell out of Cruz.

"I loved her," she said.

"I've heard terrific things about her."

"She would cry for you when you were upset. She'd give you the shirt off her back—even if you didn't want it. And she was so funny."

"So what happened to her?"

"What I heard? I don't know if this is the truth or not. She was in her bedroom, and someone shot her. Shot her twice."

"How do you know where she was when she was shot, Carla?"

"There was talk around the pool. Wait. I think Glenda said it."

"Who told Glenda? This is important."

"I don't know. And I don't know anyone who would've done anything to Shelby," Carla said. "But I'm glad you're trying to find out who killed her."

Cruz said, "Just between us, you think the Noccias had anything to do with this?"

Carla folded her arms and seemed to shrink into herself. "Is that what you think?"

"I'm asking you."

"Shelby was a moneymaker and absolutely no trouble. I just don't see it."

Carla was clearly getting restless, and nervous. Cruz smiled at her. "I'm almost done. Who were her regulars? Did anyone in particular strike you as volatile? Or possessive? Or vindictive?"

"Not really. But a couple of guys booked her a lot," Carla said. "Two of them came in a few times a week. Shelby only worked days."

"Who were they? This could really help. Did Shelby talk about them, her regulars?"

"Hollywood types. One is a film director. The other is an actor. A bad-boy type. I can't tell you who they are. But maybe you can figure it out. Do you like movies?"

"Sure, who doesn't?"

"You ever seen *Bat Out of Hell*?"

"Thanks, Carla. You're terrific."

"Don't mention it." She revved the engine. "Really. Don't tell anyone. And please don't be paying me any visits, in there or out here. I'm taking one hell of a chance as it is, sweetheart. I don't want to end up like Shelby."

Chapter 55

CRUZ AND DEL RIO trooped into my office. Cruz combed his hair back with his fingers, refastened his ponytail. Del Rio righted the chair Andy had knocked over and sat in it.

"Andy fired us? You've got to be kidding."

"I had to tell him about Shelby and the spa. He couldn't believe it."

"Ooof," Cruz said. "I feel for the guy."

"Me too," I said. "Ever wish you were wrong?"

"He fired us because you told him the truth, huh?" said Del Rio.

"He'll change his mind in a few days."

"You think?" Cruz said.

"So, how are you doing?" I asked them. "We're still working this case, right? We're going to find out who murdered Shelby."

Cruz put a hand in his inside pocket. He withdrew a

narrow notebook and started to report. He said that he'd interviewed a woman who worked at Glenda Treat's spa and that she'd given him the names of two clients who saw a lot of Shelby Cushman.

"They're both in the entertainment business," Cruz said. "I did some research. Also, I checked with the New York office. One of the guys, Bob Santangelo, came from Brooklyn. You know him?"

"I know his name. I think I've seen him in a couple of movies."

"Pugnacious type from back east. One of those actors who don't give TV interviews. Likes to throw his weight around."

"He saw Shelby a lot?"

"A few times a week, apparently. The other guy is Zev Martin, an A-list director, works for Warner Brothers a lot. People say the *A* stands for *asshole* in his case. Apparently, he's quite in love with himself."

"*Bat Out of Hell*," Del Rio said. "Horror classic, freakin' masterpiece. I saw it about six times. Martin directed it. Santangelo played the bad guy."

"Both of them are married," Cruz continued. "Neither has a record."

"License to carry?" I asked.

"Negative," said Cruz.

"You have a preference?"

"Nope."

"You take Santangelo," I said to Cruz. "Keep in touch."

Chapter 56

DEL RIO AND I drove to Warner Brothers studios out in Burbank. I showed my badge at security, then told them to check with the studio head, who was a client. A couple of minutes later, I drove down the wide, bright roadway through the lot, past the commissary and the soundstages, out to the bungalows that were laid out in a campus-like setting.

We found Zev Martin working on his motorcycle to the side of a white house with his name stenciled over the door. He was a small guy in his thirties with tightly clipped facial hair and a barbed-wire tattoo around his biceps.

I introduced Del Rio and myself while Martin squinted up at us suspiciously. "What?" he asked.

"We're investigating the death of Shelby Cushman," I said. So far, this line had proven to be a conversation stopper. This time was no different.

"You saw her several times a week," Del Rio said. "At the

Benedict Spa. Did she ever say anything to you about anyone giving her trouble there?"

Martin stood up, wiped his hands on a dirty rag, and said, "You don't go to see girls like that so you can listen to their problems. Pretty funny idea, actually. Is that what *you* do?" Martin said to Del Rio. "You pay women to talk about themselves? Why don't you just get married?"

Del Rio's bruises were still dark and plentiful. He looked like a pit bull who'd been matched with an equal—and won.

"I don't pay women," Del Rio said. "What kind of guy does that, I wonder."

"Rick," I said, "wait for me in the car, please."

But he didn't listen to me. He grabbed Martin by the shirt and pulled the collar tight at his throat. The bike went over, folded in on itself.

"We don't want any of your bullshit," Del Rio said into Martin's face. "Tell us about Shelby or after I beat your brains in, I'll personally tell your unfortunate wife about your unfortunate visits to the spa."

"Hey! What's with you?" Martin squealed.

I heard the bleeping of a security cart coming up the roadway in our direction.

Martin was going red in the face as Del Rio wrung the next few words out of him. "Shelby was in love with some guy. Not her husband, okay?"

"Rick," I said, grabbing him from behind, "let him go."

"Who was this guy she loved?" Del Rio said, shaking the director.

"I don't *know*. It was a rumor with a few of the other girls. Shelby never mentioned it herself."

I wrenched Rick off Zev Martin and apologized as Rick stalked off toward the car.

"Are you okay?" I asked Martin.

"Fuck no," he said, running his hand around his throat.

"Del Rio is a vet," I said, leaving out that he was also an ex-con. "He's suffering from PTSD. I'm very sorry."

"I should have him charged with assault," Martin said, as the studio cop cart parked at the curb.

"I could be wrong, but I don't think you want any more attention drawn to this situation," I said.

I avoided looking at the security cop and walked back to my car. I got in and slammed the door.

"It better not be that Shelby was in love with *you*, Jack," Del Rio muttered. "'Close friends,' I think you called it."

I started up the car and said to Rick, "What the hell is wrong with you? Did you take yourself off your meds?"

He was curled up against the passenger door. "Let me ask you something," he said. "Have you ever sleepwalked?"

"No, I haven't."

"I wake up, I'm behind the couch, or in the closet, or outside on the lawn. I have no idea how it happened. I have nightmares, bad ones."

"Take the rest of the day off, Rick. Go home and get some sleep before you get us killed."

Chapter 57

JUSTINE SIPPED room-temperature coffee from a cardboard cup.

The cop she'd tracked down, Lieutenant Mark Bruno, was sitting behind his desk in an office overlooking the homicide division bullpen. Bruno was somewhere around forty years old, stocky, thoughtful. Five years ago, he'd been one of the detectives working the Wendy Borman murder case in East LA.

"Wendy had been dead a day when she was found in that alley," Bruno was saying. "It had rained. That just added to the tragedy. Whatever trace might have been left on her body was washed right down the tubes."

"What's your theory of the case?" Justine asked.

"More than a theory. There was a witness," he said. "Somebody saw the abduction."

Justine started and sat up straight in her chair. "Wait. There were no witnesses."

"Yeah, there was. The papers didn't carry the story because, for one thing, the witness was eleven years old. A girl, Christine Castiglia. Her mother wouldn't let her talk to us for long, and what she saw didn't actually amount to much."

"I'm desperately seeking a lead," Justine said. "I need whatever you've got, however insignificant it may seem."

Bruno said, "Nobody ever put Wendy Borman together with the schoolgirls. You'd make a good cop—if you could afford the precipitous drop in pay."

"Thanks," Justine said. "But I could be wrong about this angle."

"Well, you just keep sticking your neck out," said Bruno. "I'm not one of the cops with a hate-on for you, Dr. Smith."

"Justine."

"Justine. I don't care who catches the son of a bitch. In fact, now I'm rooting for *you*. Obviously, we need all the help we can get."

Justine smiled. "Tell me about Christine Castiglia."

Bruno swiveled his chair a hundred eighty degrees, opened a file drawer behind him, and took out a spiral notebook with "Borman" written on the cover in thick caps. He swiveled back around and rubbed his forehead as he flipped through his notes, saying, "Uh-huh," from time to time before he looked up again.

"Okay, I remember most of this pretty well. Bottom line, Christine and her mother, Peggy Castiglia, were in a coffee shop on the corner of Rowena and Hyperion. The girl is facing Hyperion and she sees two guys throw a girl into a van—"

"*Two* guys?"

"That's what she said. She couldn't be sure that the abducted girl was Wendy Borman. And we couldn't establish Wendy's time of death close enough to say if she was killed within the time the Castiglias were eating."

Bruno sighed. "But she saw two guys. In effect, that was pretty much the beginning and end of our investigation. Nothing else was turned up."

"Was Christine able to give a description of the men? Of either of them?"

Bruno shuffled through the pages and came up with an Identi-Kit approximation of a young man with curly hair and glasses. His features were regular, almost bland. Not much help there.

He turned the book so Justine could see it.

"This drawing tells me Christine didn't get a good look at his face," Bruno said. "The perp had dark hair and glasses, and that's all she saw."

"Too damn bad, huh?"

"Yeah, but I'm remembering now. Christine also saw the back of the second guy. He was shorter and had longer, straighter hair than the first guy. Great news, huh? That eliminates all but a couple of million white males in LA."

"Did she look at mug shots?"

"No, we couldn't get her to. The mother rushed her daughter out of here like her hair was on fire. Nothing we could do to change her mind."

"She was eleven," Justine said. "So she'd be sixteen now, high school sophomore."

Private

"I never really stop thinking about Wendy Borman," said Bruno. "Here's the Castiglias' last known address."

Justine said, "Thanks, Mark. One more thing that might help me. I could use an introduction to the best cop you know in cold cases."

He nodded his head slowly. "Consider it done."

Chapter 58

IT TOOK CRUZ the rest of the day and into the night to get anywhere near the film star Bob Santangelo—and he only managed it by hanging outside Teddy's Lounge like some goofy groupie waiting for the actor to head out to the street with his entourage.

Cruz drifted a ways behind a bodyguard through the mob scene. He got to the pearly gray Mercedes at the curb as it started to roll. He pressed his badge up to the tinted glass of the windshield, and the car jerked to a stop.

The back door opened, and a bodyguard climbed out. Asian or Samoan. Big. "What do you want, sir?"

"I just have a couple of questions, then Mr. Santangelo can be on his way."

A voice came from inside. "It's all right."

Santangelo was in the backseat. He was tanned, with short brown hair and ten o'clock shadow. He sported a brown leather bomber jacket like the one he'd worn in *The Great Squall*. The actor slid over, and Cruz got in beside him.

Once again, the gray sedan moved off from the curb.

Cruz said, "My name is Emilio Cruz. I'm a private investigator."

"What the hell?" Santangelo said. "I thought you were a cop."

"Sorry to disappoint," Cruz said.

"So what is this? Is Ellen having me followed?"

"I don't know your wife."

"But you know her name is Ellen. Tell me what this is about and do it fast. When we get to Gower, that's the end of the ride."

"I'm investigating the death of Shelby Cushman."

"Jeez. Poor Shelby. I'm serious. I couldn't believe it when I heard."

"You knew her for a while? How long, Bob?"

"Just a couple of months. You ever meet Shelby? Well, she was one sweet lady. Plus she was hilarious. Here I am, married, have everything, and all I really wanted was to be with Shelby. I fell in love with her. I think I actually did."

"Where were you when she was killed? Sorry to have to ask."

"I was flying to New York with Xo," he said, indicating the muscle in the front seat. "I had dinner with Julia Roberts at Mercury that night. Check it out if you need to."

"I will. If you had to name someone who might have wanted to hurt Shelby, who would it be?"

"I don't know, man. Her dealer? Orlando something. She borrowed some money from me to pay him once. I never actually met the dirtbag. He set up a lot of girls at the spa."

The actor leaned toward the driver, told him to pull over. He said, "This is your stop, Mr., ah, Cruz."

Cruz smiled and shook his head. "Drive me back to Teddy's. That's where my car's parked. Now that we're such good friends."

"Teddy's," the actor said to his driver. "I don't want to see you again," he said to Cruz.

"Only at the movies, dude."

Emilio Cruz settled back into the plush leather. The case was starting to make some sense, at least. Shelby Cushman, the girl with the golden heart and a rich husband, also had a drug dealer. Maybe she was hooking to support her habit.

Andy wasn't going to like that, and neither was Jack. Nobody liked hearing that somebody they loved was a junkie.

Chapter 59

UNCLE FRED was on his mobile, leaning against a wall in a corner of my office with his back to the door when I walked in. It had been almost a week since he, David Dix, and Evan Newman had hooked me in with a major assignment and a big bonus sweetener. So far, I felt we had barely earned the retainer.

Fred had looked worried then. Now his forehead was so rumpled he reminded me of one of those Chinese dogs. Football was not only his livelihood, it was his passion, the one thing he'd found to love in life. He'd told me as much a dozen times or more, ever since I was a kid. If the game was fixed, his world would become a sinkhole.

Fred said into the phone, "He's just walking in now. I'll get back to you."

The big guy who used to tousle my hair when I was small came toward me with a limp that betrayed his bum knees.

He shook my hand with both of his, then sat down heavily in a chair.

"I thought we were supposed to meet on Friday," I said.

"I got a call last night, Jack. I didn't want to tell you about it over the phone."

He reached into his pocket, pulled out a pack of smokes, put them back, said, "I'm trying to cut down. This doesn't help one bit."

Colleen came in to say good night. "I put Mr. Moreno's phone number in your briefcase. You've got a phoner with the office in Rome at seven a.m. tomorrow. About the retainer for Fiat. Need anything else, Jack?"

"Thanks, I'm fine. Good night, Molloy."

She closed the office door.

"So how are you doing with our project?" Fred asked me. "Please tell me we're somewhere."

"We're making progress. I think Del Rio is onto something interesting. It's going to take a couple of days to check it out. Tell me about the phone call."

"Barney Sapok," Fred said. "I've known him for, I don't know, fifteen years. He's never called me at home before."

Fred reached for the cigarettes again, resisted. "He said our friends in the 'gaming industry' are poking around, coming to the same conclusions we did. Something's not kosher this season.

"I should've come to you earlier, Jack. I just didn't want to believe it. Now I've got mafiosi asking questions the commissioner should have asked. But didn't. Whatever's going on, I've got to know before they do."

"I'm not going to let you down. This whole operation is at your disposal."

"I know. You're my guy. You were always the smart one."

I walked my uncle to the elevator, then stepped back as the doors closed.

I stood for a moment and watched as the numbers above the elevator counted down. I thought about the Mob looking into those iffy plays that had sent final scores skidding sideways in the last moments of the games, moments that had probably cost organized crime multimillions. Someone would have to pay for that.

But who had been clever enough to fix pro games with dozens of cameras and millions of witnesses watching any suspicious move? For the life of me, I couldn't figure how it could be done.

Chapter 60

SCI'S APARTMENT WAS on the top floor of a run-down building that had once housed a printing press, back in the days when some people in Los Angeles actually read.

The space was open, with metal columns supporting the high ceilings. Photos were being projected onto white walls in a looping slide show: the Vatican at night, the Tatshenshini River in the wilds of Alaska, the quad at Harvard, an aurora borealis, the Wailing Wall in Jerusalem shot from a high floor at the King David Hotel. Some of Sci's favorite things to behold.

A twelve-foot-long tiger shark was suspended above the space by chains attached to a framing timber.

Trixie, Sci's lab monkey rescue, was perched atop her cage, greedily eating banana chips, while Sci, seated in front of his computer, chatted with his beloved Kit-Kat by webcam.

Her pretty face and large body filled the screen.

"You're very anxious tonight," she said. "This case has really upset you, hasn't it?"

"It's all about sick fantasies that have turned into real murders. Sound about right, Kat?"

"*Ja.* That's how these rotten killers operate. Happens all over the world."

"Only this time, there's no pattern we can see."

Sci knew that Kat was a biochemist. He also knew she was married and that she lived in Stockholm, but he didn't know Kit-Kat's actual name. They had no plans to meet, because that would ruin everything, wouldn't it?

"I called because I found something for you, Sci. It's just a whisper. I can't confirm it. Rumors of a wireless spy-bot program that originated in the US. It lets the user grab the signal of a particular cell phone and clone it. Undetected."

Sci felt his heart pumping pure liquid *hallelujah*. He'd often imagined such a program, and now Kat was telling him that it existed.

"Tell me everything, Kat, my sweet girl."

Trixie the monkey shrieked, threw down her snack, and ran across her rope line. She leaped to Sci's shoulder, where she squatted and chattered at Kat's image on the screen.

"Hello, beautiful Trixie. . . . Anyway, this program seemed a little familiar, Sci. So I chased down a different program that's a few years old but with a similar signature. That program was created by a gamer called Morbid. Don't take this for more than it is, darling, please. It's an educated guess, built on a rumor. I have been searching *everywhere*, though."

"Kat, I can't thank you enough. This is the closest thing I have to a lead yet."

"I have to go in a few minutes," Kat said. "I have just enough time..."

Kat unbuttoned her blouse, and techno music with a complex melody and a pounding beat came over the speakers. Sci's thoughts about a spy program moved to the back of his mind as he locked Trixie in her cage and turned to Kit-Kat.

The very large, very lovely woman took a clip out of her thick blond hair and began to slip out of her clothes. "Tell me what you like tonight, my lover," she said. "Then I will do the same."

Chapter 61

LATER THAT NIGHT, Sci sat in the shadow of the fearsome, wondrous shark, his fingers on the keyboard, his eyes on the screen.

Since signing off with Kit-Kat, he'd run the name Morbid through his browser, coming up with trash bands Morbid Angel and Morbid Death, and *morbidity* in every absurd category imaginable.

When he'd exhausted Google and Bing, he signed on to one geek message board after another, searching for references to a spy-bot that cloned cell phones wirelessly and to a programmer called Morbid.

He ransacked every board he subscribed to and came up dry. So Sci e-mailed his good friend Darren in India. Darren worked for a major Internet provider and he responded to Sci's e-mail with links to exclusive websites that were restricted to high-level tech professionals. Darren also sent Sci his IDs and passwords.

Sci made coffee and then prowled the back corridors of the Internet. He struck gold on a supergeek board he hadn't even known existed, and that in itself was news. He plucked the name Morbid from a recent thread and read a post saying: "Morbid-the-great has taken to the streets. Rumor has it he's a key player in a combat game IRL called Freek Night."

Sci was virtually bolted to his chair, both excited and afraid that this lead might run into a wall. *This* was why Private was the best—they had the best resources, and they weren't constrained in ways the police were. They operated with their own sense of justice.

Using his friend's ID, Sci posted a query about Freek Night, and he got an instant message from a member who believed Sci to be Darren.

"Darren, dude. What I can tell you. Freek Night is so sick, it's transcendent. It takes fantasy to a new level—real life."

"How do you know about this?"

"A gamer named Scylla posted a couple of times on Extreme Combat. He said he was recruited into the game. Could be bullshit tho. I tried to get in myself. Never got a reply."

"First I've heard of it," Sci replied as Darren.

"Because you live in a dungeon in Mumbai. LOL. In most places, murder is not a game. Even so, Scylla must've been high when he wrote that post."

Sci bookmarked the site, guessing that yes, Scylla *was* high. Like many addicted gamers, he no longer separated his real life from his virtual one—or even knew the difference. He'd *become* his screen name, invisible and invincible.

Private

Sci searched the gamer board Extreme Combat until he found a post from Scylla: "Our game is warriors vs. sluts," he had written. "Come Saturday night, think of me!"

A new thread was later started by a member called Trojan: "Saturday *plays*. Sunday *pays*. Scylla flew off his own terrace. Flying is easy. It's hitting the pavement that's hard."

Sci opened the site's user profile pages and found that Scylla had listed his name as Jason, his address as Los Angeles.

It was four a.m. in Los Angeles when a board administrator noticed that "Darren" was using an unapproved IP address and blocked Sci from the board.

Sci made fresh coffee. His fingers were stiff, and his hands were shaking.

He cupped his mug until his fingers relaxed, then he trawled a legitimate news blog for a man named Jason who had fallen from a terrace in Los Angeles the night Marguerite Esperanza was killed.

He found an article in the *Times* online, read it twice, then he called Mo-bot.

She growled at him, "Late-night phone calls are one of my least favorite things, Sci. Right behind having my tits in a mammogram sandwich."

Sci told her what he'd found, and she listened to all of it before saying, "So who is this Morbid? I'm out of rocks to turn over. I'm calling Jack."

"Let him sleep. I guess this will hold until morning."

Chapter 62

I PICKED UP the phone, yelled into it, *"Not yet!"* then I chucked it back onto the nightstand.

I'd been dreaming, actually peering into the downed CH-46, looking into the cargo bay. I could almost *see* my subconscious, and I'd made a decision about what to do next.

Now the dream was gone.

What was the question?

What had I decided?

The phone rang again. My annoying death threat caller had *never* called back once I'd answered and hung up.

This time, I looked at the faceplate. It was Sci.

He said, "I've got a lead on Schoolgirl."

Chapter 63

A HALF HOUR LATER, I was at Starbucks, drinking an orange-mango Vivanno with Sci. He was wearing blue pajama bottoms with smiley faces and a Life Is Good T-shirt with a pink heart in the center of his chest. His hair was flattened into a bowl shape from his motorcycle helmet. I would've ribbed him about his wardrobe, but I was still tired and he was so intensely, deadly serious.

I stirred my smoothie with a straw and tried to focus on what he had on his mind.

Sci said to me, "The thing is, some guy named Jason did go off his terrace right after the Esperanza girl was found dead. It was a suicide, according to LAPD."

"Jason is a programmer?"

"He's in public relations. *Was.*"

"I don't get it. Explain the connection to me again."

Sci sighed. He knew that I wasn't like him. I know my way around a computer, but I'm no geek.

"Look," Sci said, trying again. He grabbed a shaker of cinnamon and a shaker of chocolate powder, one in each hand.

"The cinnamon is a wireless program that can clone phones and send and receive messages, okay? The chocolate is a combat game—*in real life*. It's called Freek Night."

He clinked the two shakers together, said, "What these two items have in common is a gamer who uses the screen ID Morbid."

I said, "Explain to me the part about the computer games again."

"Most of the really popular ones are war games. Mo-bot plays one of them. World of Warcraft. It's an MMORPG, a massively multiplayer online role-playing game, that is ongoing twenty-four hours a day around the planet. It has eleven million players a month."

"War games on the computer. Trust me, that has to be better than the real thing."

"Most of these games concern big wars with armies. The gamers play to take over countries or planets, past, present, or future. It's addictive, seriously addictive. It feels real. Get that? You with me so far?"

"Yep," I said.

"A few games are one-on-one, where the players fight like old-time samurai or Roman warriors. Sometimes they have teammates or allies, like war buddies."

"I know this is going somewhere, Sci, or you wouldn't have called me at five thirty in the morning."

"Hang in, okay, Jack? I haven't slept at all."

"I'm with you. I'm here."

"Okay. Imagine a player whose screen name is Scylla bragging about playing a real live combat game called Freek Night. He describes it as 'warriors versus sluts.'"

"In real life."

"Bravo, Jack. And the night Marguerite Esperanza was killed, Scylla—who's actual name is Jason—took a swan dive off his terrace. I found a story in the *Times* online. A man named Jason Pilser suicided that night."

"To review," I said, "a programmer using the name Morbid created a wireless clone program to get into people's cell phones."

"Evidence suggests."

"And he is also a player in this offline combat game called Freek Night?"

"Offline. Very good," said Sci.

I picked up the cinnamon shaker and said, "And a guy going by the name of Scylla, actually Jason Pilser, the PR guy, was a player in this game. And he killed himself Saturday night—"

"That's what I've got, Jack. It hasn't all come together yet, but it's jellin'. There are too many connections to be coincidental. Even dead, Jason Pilser is a lead with legs. I think we're getting very close."

"So—*be careful?*"

"Be extremely careful."

Chapter 64

BEING EXTREMELY CAREFUL started *right here*, at Jason Pilser's apartment building on Burton Way in Beverly Hills. It's uncommon to find rows of high-end apartment buildings in Beverly Hills but this block was an exception.

The buildings on this side of Burton had terraces and extraordinary views of the hills.

I counted up to the sixth-floor balcony. The sliding doors were closed behind the terrace wall. I said to Sci, "Why would Jason Pilser jump?"

"Remorse, maybe? Nah, I doubt that."

I'd gathered some information about Pilser in the past few hours. He was twenty-four, an account executive in a notable public relations firm. He had probably earned fifty thousand a year, not bad for a young guy in these tough times, but not the kind of income that would make this address affordable. I smelled "trust fund" or maybe rich, divorced parents.

There was a *whoosh* of tires as Bobby Petino's car pulled up to the curb. He got out in his three-thousand-dollar black silk suit and put a card saying that he was here on official business under the windshield wiper.

He said hello to Sci and me, set the car alarm, and said, "A spanking-hot lead at long last. Nice work, Sci. Jack, what did Justine say about this?"

"She's working the case from another angle. We're covering it any way we can."

"Okay. I'm starting to feel cautiously optimistic," said Petino. "Getting a prickling sensation in my oversized ears."

We followed Bobby's ears through the lobby doors and across the black marble floor toward the security desk with its huge and twisted bouquet of exotic flowers. Petino introduced us all to the doorman, Sam Williams, an elderly man in uniform, and showed him the search warrant.

"Has anyone been inside Mr. Pilser's apartment except the police?" Petino asked Williams.

"Mrs. Costella in six-A took back her ficus tree. I was told to keep the door locked after that and to wait for Mr. Pilser's mother to arrive from Vancouver."

I asked, "Did you happen to see Jason Pilser the night he died?"

"Never did. He was home when I came on. I sent up a delivery guy from the drugstore, and at around eleven, Mr. Pilser called down to say he was expecting a few friends."

"Pilser's friends," I said. "Did he mention any names? Did you see them?"

"Nope. Just 'friends.' And they must've come after my shift

ended at midnight. No one is on duty until Ralph comes on at six in the a.m."

"You have security cameras?" I asked.

"That one there. It's on a forty-eight-hour loop. It's already recorded over Saturday night. What's this about, you mind telling me? You think it wasn't a suicide?"

"Thanks for your help," Bobby said to Williams. "We might want to talk to you again when we come back down."

The doorman nodded. "You know where to find me."

I thought of one more question. "Mr. Williams, what did you think of Jason Pilser? Just between us."

He nodded, then spoke in a low voice. "Asshole. Major."

I talked to Bobby as we walked to the elevator. "I suggest you clear the way for Private to search Pilser's place. If I turn Sci and his crew loose, we'll have everything processed by this time tomorrow, and you'll have a report in your hands by the end of the day."

"Consider it done," Bobby said. "Let's find out what this asshole was up to."

Chapter 65

I WAS TRAINED to have a sharp eye as a Marine helicopter pilot and I still had it. I snapped wide-angle and close-up pictures of Jason Pilser's apartment from the foyer, staying out of Sci's way and out of the evidence, in case a murder had been committed here.

Dr. Sci was quiet as he worked, he and his crew speaking to one another in shorthand as they used our state-of-the-art forensic equipment, worth every penny of the fortune it had cost. From where I stood, nothing looked disturbed—which might mean something.

When Sci told me it was okay, I followed him from room to room through the spare, modernly furnished one-bedroom apartment.

The sofa and armchair cushions were neat, there were no glasses in the sink, the bed was made, the bedroom closet in fastidious order. And I didn't see a suicide note.

I did make note of a suit jacket on a valet stand in the bed-room. A roll of bandages and iodine on the bathroom sink.

"The ME said he had mixed nuts, a couple of martinis, and painkillers in his stomach," Sci said. "Maybe he was going out to dinner with his friends. Or his killers," Sci said. "The scrape marks on his belly were consistent with the blood and skin on the terrace wall. He *slid* himself over the wall—which is improbable, or at least unusual."

"Or he was shoved across it in increments until he was airborne," I said. "Seems more likely to me."

"We've got some prints," lab assistant Karen Pasquale said to Sci from the hallway. "Three sets so far."

"Excellent," Sci said. "Now. Where's his computer?"

"What's that?" I said, pointing to the briefcase almost invisible in the shadows, wedged between the desk chair and the wall.

Sci picked up the case with his gloved hands, set it down on the desk, and unsnapped the locks.

The case sprang open.

There was a tie on top of a laptop. A sheaf of papers in the side pocket.

And a cell phone.

"This'll keep me busy," Sci said. "Another no-sleep night."

"Mind taking a look at the phone now?" I asked.

"Not at all."

Sci opened the phone and said, "His battery's almost gone, but I'll give it a shot."

I stood behind Sci, looking over his shoulder as he scrolled through messages. Suddenly he stopped as if he'd been turned to stone.

Private

"Sci?"

He showed me a text message on Pilser's phone that had been sent last Wednesday. It was short and to the point.

"Freek Night is on, Scylla. Get ready. You're IT."

It was signed by someone using the name Steemcleena.

I said to Sci, "Wait. Shouldn't this be from Morbid? He's the connection, right? Who is Steemcleena?"

Sci worked his jaw soundlessly a few times, then he said, "Who is Steemcleena? As brilliant as I am, I'm going to have to get back to you on that."

Chapter 66

THE EXCLUSIVE AND astronomically expensive rehab center where Tommy was staying was called Blue Skies—some marketing person's concept of hope, I guess.

The facility was in Brentwood, north of Sunset, spread out over a dozen acres and sited so it had a flat-out awesome view of the Santa Monica Mountains. You could stand at the administration office and look down into the canyon, see people trotting their horses on trails through their woodsy backyards.

I hadn't seen Tommy since I'd checked him in to Blue Skies, and now I felt duty bound to make sure he was doing okay there.

I found Tommy in a lounge chair at poolside. He was wearing peacock blue swim trunks under a fluffy white robe.

He looked healthy and tan. Somewhat at peace. The rest was doing him good. I hoped so, anyway.

When my shadow crossed him, he squinted up at me, made a visor with his hand, and said, "Don't think I'm thanking you for this, bro. I was just wondering how the hell to escape in a bathrobe."

I took a seat in the chaise longue next to him. "Want to thank me for going to Carmine Noccia and handing him a cashier's check for six hundred grand?"

"Sure. Thanks."

"It's a loan, Tommy. Just so you know. And I didn't tell Annie that the Mob was about to turn your car into a bomb. Or maybe blow up your house."

"Don't you ever get a headache? That halo up around your ears all the time."

"I do, actually. You ought to let me be the evil twin for once. I'd like that."

"Uncle Fred was here," Tommy said. "He told me there's something big waiting for me — if I clean up my act."

"So what's your problem with Fred? I never knew."

"He put his hand down my shorts when I was a kid. Rubbed my little joint."

"Fuck you, Tom."

"He did. I swear to God, Jack. On our mother's eyes."

I stood up, grabbed Tommy by the lapels of his robe, and gave him a shot to the jaw that made my hand bones grind. The chair flipped over as Tommy went down hard.

A husky dude in a white jumpsuit looked up from across the pool and started running toward us.

Tommy raised a hand, indicating the situation was over. He picked himself up, choking on his own laughter.

"You're so goddamn easy, Jack. It's like, dangle the bait

and you jump out of the water, right into the boat. Get off me. You'll get your wings all dirty."

"Take back what you said."

"O-kay. I take it back. Maybe it was Dad who molested me. Or was it you?"

"How can you stand yourself?" I asked him.

"It was Fat Fred who told you about my debt, though, am I right?"

My knuckles were throbbing.

"It's always good to see you, Tommy. Take care of yourself."

"Buh-bye, Jacko."

He was still laughing as he righted his chair.

I went back into the administration office and paid Tommy's bill for the rest of the month. The girl behind the desk was very nice, and she asked how my brother was doing. I couldn't say a word to her. Just gave her my credit card, and after she ran it through, I got the hell out of there.

It's a hard thing—hating your own brother.

Chapter 67

I STOPPED AT home to change my wings and buff my halo, then I drove to Beverly Hills.

I needed some quality time to myself, so I went to Mastro's, one of the best steak houses west of Kansas City. The vibe at Mastro's was retro crooner, and not just because someone was singing "My Way" at the piano.

I saw Joseph Ricci in the corner getting into something with Frank Mosconi. They didn't see me. I told the maître d' I wanted a quiet table on the second floor, and after I was seated, I ordered a highball and studied the menu of gonzo prime beef that the place is justly known for.

The liquor, also first-class, was settling me down. I had brought a book with me, a well-worn paperback of *Me Talk Pretty One Day,* by the humorist David Sedaris. He's brutally honest and laugh-out-loud funny, and his family life seems to have been almost as messy as mine.

I got a call from the head of our office in London. I told him my pick for deputy manager, then went back to my book.

I was starting to feel like a prince, one of the chosen few in LA. I didn't lift my eyes from the pages until the bone-in rib eye and broccoli rabe showed up at the table.

Once I put the book down, my mind started circling back to the real world.

I thought about my brother, older than me by three minutes, so much like my father that I disliked him just because of that. Tommy was easily as narcissistic as Dad had been, just as arrogant, felt just as entitled to have what he wanted his way; but I didn't think he had always been like that.

We'd been inseparable from pre-K through ninth grade. I remember we even had hand signals and secret words. We were total confidants, we stuck up for each other, we got our black belts the same day. And then our father started to pit us against each other. We got competitive, and everything changed.

Clearly, Dad had favored the son with his name and the same cynical view of the world. I gravitated to Uncle Fred. Tom became cruel to my mother, like my father was. I tried to protect her, and Tom and I became real enemies after that.

The waiter broke into my thoughts to ask if I wanted another drink, and I said that I did.

A couple came in and sat at the table next to mine. It was a first date; I could just tell. The two exchanged one long look that said everything they saw in each other was fascinating and that they were probably going to end the evening in bed.

I drank some more, and my thoughts turned to Colleen.

She would have liked this place. I thought about taking her home to the house that I'd once owned with Justine. I'd never brought Colleen there for the night. It just confused me too much. I liked Colleen an awful lot, and I didn't want to hurt her, though I knew I sometimes did.

I had told her that my place wasn't entirely safe, that I found it more relaxing to spend the night in her arms in her sweet nest of a house. She knew I was keeping her at arm's length, but she was taking what she could get, hoping I would change, which only multiplied my guilt and confusion about what should happen with the two of us.

My hand was on my phone. I started to dial Colleen's number, then I closed the phone gently and slugged down the rest of my drink. I wasn't being fair to her. I was going to have to end it, but I couldn't imagine causing her all that pain, and losing her too.

I paid the check, left a big tip, and took to the road, thinking, *Fuck you, Jack.*

Chapter 68

JUSTINE COULDN'T GET the Schoolgirl case out of her head, even when she desperately wanted to.

She walked down a long, cool corridor hung with fluorescent fixtures and pushed open the door marked 301. Detective Sergeant Charlotte Murphy's desk was one of four in the large water-stained room in a hidden wing of the police station, the place where cold cases lived and died.

"Charlotte," the detective introduced herself, shaking Justine's hand.

Charlotte Murphy was wearing navy blue man-tailored pants and a button-down collared shirt. A gold badge hung from a chain around her neck. Her expression was guarded, but its severity was offset by exceptionally pretty blue eyes and a welcoming smile.

Murphy introduced Justine to her colleagues, then offered her a chair. She said, "I had a few hours to get Wendy Borman's effects out of archives. Want to look at the murder book first? Take your time. I've got plenty of other hopeless work to do."

Detective Murphy pushed a thick three-hole-punched notebook toward Justine.

Justine couldn't open the notebook quickly enough, and then she wanted to pore over it slowly so that she didn't miss a thing.

The pages were glassine sleeves, the contents catalogued and in chronological order.

The first several pages were photos of Wendy Borman lying dead in the alley off Hyperion, yards from where Connie Yu's body had been found. She was fully dressed, her hair soaking wet, her left arm hidden under a pile of trash bags.

Following the photos were sketches of the crime scene and a photocopy of a seven-page report from the ME. Cause of death: manual strangulation.

Copies of Detective Bruno's case notes followed, the pages stapled together and stuffed into a single sleeve. After the notes were transcripts of the interview with the only witness, Christine Castiglia, eleven years old.

Next, Justine looked over the list of stolen property, an itemized account of the contents of Wendy Borman's backpack. A piece of handmade jewelry had also been taken, a gold chain necklace with a gold charm in the shape of a star.

Toward the back of the book was a photograph of Wendy Borman wearing that necklace while she was alive. She was posed standing between her parents. She was already taller than they were, and she had looped her arms over both their shoulders. Wendy had been a grinning, blond-haired girl with an athletic build. She didn't look like she should ever die. How sad was that?

"I'm ready for the contents of the evidence box," Justine said. "I think so, anyway."

Detective Murphy offered Justine latex gloves from a dispenser, then used a pocketknife to slit the red tape around a plain cardboard box. She removed the lid, lifted out a large paper bag, and sliced the seal on that.

Justine was hit with an adrenaline high, a rush of bright anticipation she couldn't control. This was precisely the feeling that had gotten her into forensics and made her good at it. Something here might open a window into the Schoolgirl case.

Maybe it would even reveal a killer.

She reached into the bag and pulled out a pair of stretch jeans, size six, and a baby blue jersey-knit top with a scoop neckline.

She plunged her hands into the bag again and brought out a pair of Nike cross-trainers and baby blue socks.

She spread out the clothing, examining where samples had been cut out of the fabric by the LA crime lab.

"I take it the blood belonged to the victim."

Murphy nodded yes.

"I need to borrow her clothes," Justine said.

"Chief Fescoe and DA Petino already okayed their release," said Murphy. "You're the man."

She pushed a form over to Justine and handed her a pen.

"Wendy's left arm," Murphy said. "It was under some garbage bags. The rain didn't soak the sleeve. I'd have your lab check it out. Technology is a lot better now. Especially at a lab like yours at Private."

"Let's keep some hope alive," said Justine.

"No, let's get this bastard," said Detective Murphy, smiling again, but also showing Justine just how tough and relentless she was.

Chapter 69

"YOU REMEMBER THE Wendy Borman case?" asked
Justine.

The air smelled of fried fish, fried onions, fried potatoes.
Justine sat across a small square table from Christine Castiglia in the Belmont High School cafeteria. The only witness
to Wendy Borman's abduction was sixteen now. She was
petite, hugging herself, looking up at Justine with big eyes
half hidden under thick brown bangs.

You didn't have to be a shrink to see that Christine was
afraid. Justine knew to tread carefully, and she wasn't feeling
so steady herself. She was desperate for this girl to tell her
something that could lead to the Schoolgirl killer *before he
killed again.*

"I was only eleven when it happened," Christine said.
"You know that, right?"

"I know." Justine swirled a straw in her plastic cup of ice

and Diet Coke. "Can you tell me what you saw anyway? I need to hear it from you."

"Are you thinking those same boys—I guess they're men now—might have killed the girls around here?"

Someone dropped a tub of dishes behind the steam tables. An awful, nerve-rending clatter.

Justine waited out the kids' applause before saying, "It's possible. There was a gap of three years between Wendy Borman and Kayla Brooks. That's why no one thought to connect them. It's why what you witnessed is so important. If Wendy Borman was their first killing, they might have made a mistake."

"It was a plain black van," Christine said. "It stopped in a cross street off Hyperion, and when I looked again, two guys had grabbed this girl. Like, it only took a second? And she was like having a fit or something. They swung her into the van, and then one of them got into the driver's seat and they drove off. I told the police what the driver looked like."

"Wendy Borman was zapped with a stun gun," Justine said. "That was the fit you saw. And your mom didn't see *anything?*"

Christine shook her head. "I wasn't sure what I'd seen myself. It could've been a commercial between my thoughts— that's how fast it was. I froze, and when my mom turned to see what I was looking at, the van was gone. She didn't believe me—or didn't want to.

"But when it was all over the TV, she finally called the police. My mother believed the TV but not me."

Kids were passing the table, staring at the woman in a business suit having a deep discussion with a kid at their school.

"Tell me about the boy—the one whose face you saw."

"In the drawing the police made, he looked kinda like Clark Kent in the Superman movie. But he didn't exactly look like that. His nose was a bit pointy? And his ears stuck out? I mean—they *definitely* stuck out."

"Did you see the license plate number on that van? Even one or two numbers would give us something to work with."

The girl paused, eyes flicking up and to the left, searching her memory.

A class bell rang then, loud, jangling. Kids got up en masse, and a couple of them brushed Justine's arm and knocked over her briefcase on their way to the trash bins and out the door.

Christine said, "There was a decal on the rear window. It said 'Gateway.' Like that computer company? But there weren't any cow spots."

"You told this to the police?"

"I think so. My mother was freaked out. She couldn't get me away from the police fast enough."

Justine looked at the girl, and for a moment, the girl held her gaze. "See if you can draw that decal," Justine said. She passed over her PDA and stylus.

The girl sucked hard on her lower lip as she sketched an oval shape and the word *Gateway* in graduated letters.

"I think this is it. I don't know why I remember so well, but I do."

Justine stared at the crude drawing. The logo looked like that of a private school in Santa Monica called Gateway. When she had worked for the city's psych ward, she used to drive past Gateway Prep when she did sessions at Stateside, aka the California State Hospital for the Criminally Insane.

She still vividly remembered her patients, the ones who burned down houses, killed their siblings, shotgunned their parents, and lit up schoolyards with explosives. It had been devastating and demoralizing work that had taught her about the mental workings of some of the most heinous humans on earth.

Justine had thought then about the contrast between Stateside and Gateway Prep, only a mile apart geographically, worlds apart in every other way. Now she thought about the Gateway decal.

There was no mention of a Gateway decal in the Wendy Borman murder book.

The decal was *news*. The facial characteristics were *news*. Maybe she was getting somewhere. *If* these were the same boys.

"Could you identify this boy if you saw him again?"

"I could never forget his face."

"Christine, thank you." Justine gave the teenager her card. "Call me if you think of anything else. The next time we meet, we won't be strangers."

Chapter 70

THIS WAS ANOTHER reason Private was the best place for Justine to work, or investigate a murder. Processing DNA took an eternity at the city lab because of the length of the line and the sheer volume of cases. At Private, it would take twenty-four hours from the git to the go because the forensic lab was Private's, and because Wendy Borman was job one.

The basement level was blazing with artificial light at four in the morning. Sci's crew had been working for twenty hours straight, running swabs over Wendy Borman's clothes, which had been stored in the LAPD evidence room for five years.

The clothing had been packaged correctly after Borman's body was discovered, but the rain and garbage had already contaminated the evidence. Still, more sensitive equipment and a new form of capturing trace had emerged since the murder. It was called "touch DNA."

Sci believed in happy endings, and his optimism drove

him across the desert of repetitive tasks, inconclusive results, and negative findings.

He had ordered the Borman clothing to be swabbed under the left arm of the jersey shirt and in the fold of a sock, places that hadn't been soaked by the rain.

After separating the DNA from the substrate and copying the DNA in a thermal cycler, Sci ran the samples through an instrument the size and shape of an office copy machine, a method called capillary electrophoresis. In this procedure, the material was sent through a long pathway, a capillary, that separated the DNA with attached dye by size and electrical charge. The output would be displayed as an electrophoretogram, ready to be matched against the national DNA database.

Kat's image was on one of Sci's desktop monitors. He glanced in her direction to tell her how the work was going.

"Still here with me, sweetheart?"

"You forget the time difference, Sci," she said. "There are other things I should be doing."

"Like what? Name something."

"*Anything* would be more productive, darling. Defragging my hard drive. Organizing my tax receipts. Having a nice lunch with Helga, whom I despise—*Sci*. Look at your integrator. You have something there!"

Sci looked at the printout. There was one set of peaks—and then *another*. It was a freaking miracle: *two* single-source samples had been identified, both with Y chromosomes.

This was a bombshell, actually.

Sci turned to Kit-Kat, his open mouth curling into a smile.

"Two males put their hands on Wendy Borman's clothes. You believe it, Kat? We've got evidence. Beautiful, solid evidence."

Kat was saying, "I must be bringing you the luck."

"Baby, baby, what a lucky charm you are."

"So, you are welcome, and I will be going now."

"Stick around while I run the profiles through the system."

"You are looking for a spindle in a haystack," said Kat. "And there are haystacks out to the horizon. As far as the eye can see."

"We can pass the time together, anyway," said Sci. "I like it when you're here with me."

Kat smiled. "Okay. Let's dance, good-looking."

Chapter 71

EVERYBODY AT PRIVATE was involved with Schoolgirl, and they all cared about the case. Mo-bot was in her pod in the lab down the hall from Sci. She'd personalized her windowless space with a recliner, scarves draped over her lamps, a slide show of her kids on the monitor to her left, an aquarium of utsuri to her right, and incense burning at all times.

Jason Pilser's laptop was open in front of her.

Mo used a unique program she'd developed. She called it her "master key." She had already begun to pick Pilser's passwords, frisk his hard drive, rifle through the remains of his electronic brain.

"I'm into his e-mail," she called out to Sci. "I'm the best. Right, Sci?"

"Motherboard of all geeks, Mo," he called back to her.

"You got that right. Watch me now."

Jason Pilser had been a pack rat when it came to

electronic communication. He deleted nothing, and he utilized several screen names. Mo easily cracked open his office account, skimmed the memos to and from his bosses and colleagues. They revealed nothing, meant nothing, led to nothing, so she moved on.

Pilser's Commandos of Doom mailbox was listed under the screen name Atticus. Mo-bot attacked the password and it fell. Then she ransacked the suspect's files. Pilser used "Atticus" to enter gamer message boards and send private messages while he pillaged kingdoms and slaughtered foes in the virtual netherworld of Quaraziz, circa 2409. *What a fricking dork this guy must have been.*

Mo made note of his friends and enemies in Quaraziz, then accessed Pilser's MyBook page with her electronic passkey.

Pilser had posted photos of himself on his page, blogged movie reviews, hailed and poked his MyBook "friends." But there was nothing on his web page more sinister than political vitriol. No screen names crossed over from Commandos of Doom to MyBook, and Mo found no indication that Jason Pilser had been depressed. *Though it sure was depressing to probe into his life.*

Closing his mail folders, Mo-bot clicked through the icons on Pilser's toolbar. One intrigued her—a graphic of lightning shooting from a pointed finger. It was captioned "Scylla."

Mo-bot clicked on the link and was taken to a new web page. Pilser had titled the page "Scylla Lives." It was a trapdoor to Pilser's personal journal—and it almost stopped Mo's heart.

She read quickly, clicked through links, then found a bridge between the real and virtual worlds.

She pushed away from her desk, and her chair rolled back. A moment later, she was standing in the doorway to Sci's office.

Sci stared as if he were looking through her.

What was wrong with him? Didn't he get it? She'd unlocked the whole damned murder plan. She was the female modern-day Sherlock Holmes.

"Less than a week from now," she said, "there's going to be a Freek Night. You hear me, Sci? That's what they call their killing game. Jason Pilser would've been part of it—if he'd lived."

"I'm sorry. I'm distracted. I'm running the DNA—"

Mo said, "Listen to the words coming out of my mouth. There are two of them. They call themselves Street Freeks. Their screen names are Morbid and Steemcleena, and they've already picked their target. She lives in Silver Lake, calls herself Lady D.

"*Sci*. Are you getting this? *In five days, they're going to kill this girl.*"

Chapter 72

JACK HAD CALLED ahead to Private's new East Coast office. A senior operative, Diana DiCarlo, was waiting at the gate when Emilio Cruz disembarked at Miami International Airport.

CIA trained, DiCarlo was very efficient. She handed Cruz a briefcase with everything he would need: gun, surveillance equipment, car keys, and phone numbers of Private sources throughout South Florida. And she told Cruz where his subjects were staying.

Cruz checked in to the Biltmore, the room directly above the men he was tailing. He set up his microphones and listened.

Later, he followed his subjects from the hotel to clubs and restaurants, even watched them place their bets at the dog track in Hialeah.

Now, three days into the job, he was in South Beach, the flashiest, sexiest part of old Miami.

Emilio Cruz was sitting on a coral-rock wall, the beach rolling out before him to the ocean's edge. He was dressed to blend in, wearing a wife beater under an open shirt, black wraparound shades, hair banded at his nape.

He appeared to be engrossed in the daily racing form, but it was a prop. He had a camera eye embedded in the frames of his sunglasses that was not just taping; the images were bouncing off a satellite a couple of miles overhead, sending pictures and sound back to the office in LA.

Directly ahead and maybe thirty feet away, three men sat on a bench facing away from him and toward Ocean Drive.

They were talking together, but their eyes were on the inked, half-naked girls skating by on the hot plum-colored sidewalk.

The two men Cruz had been following were Kenny Owen and Lance Richter. Both were NFL referees. Owen was bald and freckled. Richter was twenty years younger, with a lot of bushy brown hair, a fresh sunburn, and a gaudy Rolex watch that must have weighed a pound.

Five minutes ago, the refs had been joined by Victor Spano, a lieutenant in the Chicago-based Marzullo family.

Cruz had almost said it out loud.

Holy shit.

Chapter 73

SPANO LOOKED FRESHLY showered and wore a shoulder holster under his ice blue jacket. He was telling the refs about the good time he'd had last night at the Nautilus Hotel across the street. There was no sexier town in America than Miami, not even Vegas.

"The mother was a little hotter than her kid. But the kid was more enthusiastic."

Richter shrugged and said, "Mr. Spano, wasn't that, like, incest?"

"Nah," Spano said. "It was her stepmother. What do you think? I'm a pervert?"

Everyone laughed. The kid with the hair said, "But seriously, Mr. Spano. Back to the assignment we have this week. Tennessee by seventeen points at Oakland? Seventeen points is no walk in the park, and we could be under a lot of pressure here."

Spano said, "I follow your point, Lance, but you know what they say. Pressure is self-inflicted. You guys are pros. I don't see a problem."

A homeless teen with meth mouth and wearing a Speedo and a dirty green shirt came over to Cruz and asked for some spare change for his college fund.

Cruz said, "You're standing in my sun."

The kid—already a bum—said, "It's why they call it *spare change,* dude. You won't miss it."

By the time the fresh kid had pushed off, Spano and the refs had finished their meeting and split up, Spano returning to the art deco hotel across the street, the refs inside a cab heading downtown.

It didn't matter. Cruz had the whole story. The Titans were favored to mow the Raiders down. The refs had to prevent a massacre and protect that seventeen-point spread. If they did, someone was going to make a whole lot of millions.

Cruz tapped buttons on his iPhone, calling Jack.

"Good news, *very* good news. I recorded the fix. Do you receive me, captain?"

"Loud and clear. We got it all here. Audio and video. Who's that in the blue jacket?"

"Victor Spano. Out of Chicago. Marzullo family."

"Unreal," Jack said. "Good job, Emilio. Come home. We need you here."

Chapter 74

JUSTINE WAS AT BESO, the spectacular restaurant owned by Eva Longoria and Todd English. It was a huge vaulted space known for its Mexican cuisine with an original twist.

Justine's round booth gave her a wide view of the room, but she hadn't exactly been stargazing. That wasn't her style.

She'd been passing the time paging through a short stack of yearbooks from Gateway Prep. The waiter cleared the table and brought her check.

"Everything was good this evening, Dr. Smith? You enjoyed your lemon sole?"

"Yes, Raphael. I'm practically addicted to the lemon sole. Everything was perfect."

Actually, nothing was perfect, other than the fish. She'd tagged ten boys, Gateway graduates from the years 2004 through 2006, who somewhat matched Christine Castiglia's description. Some had pointy noses, some had sticking-out ears; none of them had a police record.

Justine paid her check, and as she waited for the valet to bring her car around, she switched on her phone and checked her messages. She saw that Bobby had called and so had Christine Castiglia's mother, Peggy.

Was it possible? Had Christine made a breakthrough? Justine tapped the button to return Peggy Castiglia's call. She muttered, "C'mon, c'mon," until the phone was answered on the fifth ring.

"Leave my daughter alone," Christine's mother told her. "She's an anxious child, and now she's got *you* to worry about. You can't rely on anything she says, do you understand? Because she doesn't want to disappoint you. She's in her room crying right now."

Justine blocked out the traffic, the pedestrians on the sidewalk. She stared at her blue pumps as she told Peggy Castiglia that she was sorry, she didn't want to upset Christine, but it was necessary to keep her involved.

"*Necessary?* Not for Christine," Peggy Castiglia said.

Justine's head throbbed. She clenched the phone and said, "Peggy. Someone has already *murdered thirteen girls*— that we know about. Christine is our only real lead so far. Do you seriously want to get in the way of bringing down a killer?"

"I can't afford to worry about other girls, Dr. Smith. If you had a daughter, maybe you'd understand. Just stay away from Chrissy. Don't make me call the authorities."

"I *am* the authorities. I can have her interrogated as a material witness," Justine said, her voice high, strained, getting away from her. "Please," she said to Peggy Castiglia. "Don't make me force her to talk to the cops."

"You just try it, Dr. Smith. I'll fight you to my last breath." And then Peggy Castiglia hung up the phone.

Chapter 75

JUSTINE WAS SEETHING as she headed toward home on the freeway. Sci had gotten viable DNA from Wendy Borman's clothes, but there were no matches in the database. Without a match, she couldn't put a name to the DNA left by Wendy Borman's killer.

They were so close — and they were nowhere.

And right now, the Street Freeks were planning another kill.

Justine saw a familiar exit sign and made a snap decision. She took the off-ramp and turned in the direction of Bobby's house.

Bobby had a way of quieting her anxiety. Maybe he could reason with Peggy Castiglia. If not, he could start legal proceedings to get her daughter's cooperation.

Okay, good.

Bobby's car was parked in the narrow one-car spot that

clung to the sloping roadway above his house. Justine parked on the verge of the hill, walked through the gate, and rang the bell. When Bobby didn't answer right away, she took the familiar stone path around to the vast back lawn with its extraordinary canyon view.

She slipped off her shoes and let her feet feel lush grass.

Then she saw him. Bobby was in the hot tub, so Justine called out, "Bob. I'm returning your call."

He stood up in a self-conscious crouch—and that's when Justine saw that a woman was in the hot tub with Bobby. She was naked.

Chapter 76

JUSTINE TOOK IT all in at once. The woman in the tub screamed, then covered her small breasts with both hands. Bobby's face contorted with anger as he called out, "Justine. Stay right there."

He patted the edge of the hot tub for his glasses while his "date," bright pink from the heat, shouted at him, "Get me my robe. Please, I need my robe!"

Justine recognized the naked woman now. She was Bobby's wife, Marissa, the woman he'd separated from over a year ago, the one he didn't love anymore, the one who had moved to Phoenix and was ready to sign the divorce papers any day.

Justine's guts liquefied, then froze. She was so disappointed and so hurt.

She wanted to run, but it would be better to do the hard thing. Face the truth. Get answers.

She had a pretty good idea why Marissa Petino was here, but she had to ask anyway.

Justine's feet carried her within speaking range of the hot tub. She said to Marissa Petino, "I'm Justine Smith. I'm sorry to interrupt. I thought Bobby would be alone."

Marissa clutched a robe to her chest, turned blazing eyes on her husband.

"Bobby, *who is this?*"

Justine said, "Bobby and I have been seeing each other for—what, Bobby? About a year?"

Bobby had tucked a towel around his waist. His glasses were perched at a cockeyed angle on his nose. He looked as though he'd lost his cool in the hot tub, and Bobby hated that. The man had to be in control.

"Justine, damn it. This is damned *crazy,* you know that? Let's go. I'll walk you to the gate."

Justine ignored Bobby and said to Marissa, "Just bear with me, please. Did Bobby tell you he's running for governor?"

"What do you mean? Of course he told me. You mean you're seeing him *now?*"

Bobby stood between Marissa and Justine, his face so red that Justine thought he was going to try and punch her.

"I wouldn't have told you this way," he said. "You shouldn't have come here without calling."

"I loved you," said Justine. "I trusted you."

"I never promised you anything. I never lied to you."

Justine slapped him and saw her handprint white against his cheek. "*Everything* was a lie," she said. "Don't you even understand that?"

Marissa Petino cinched her robe and faced her husband.

"I get it now, Bobby. Running for governor with your *wife* plays better than running with your *girlfriend*."

"Please, Marissa, please let's talk about this later," Bobby said.

"I don't want a 'later.' And thanks, Justine. I appreciate the reminder of what a snake my soon-to-be-ex husband is."

"My pleasure," said Justine.

"Can you give me a lift?" Marissa asked Justine. "My car is at the Beverly Hilton. I can be dressed in two minutes. Bobby, *I hope you freaking get leprosy and die.*"

"My car is parked on the side of the road," Justine said to Marissa. "Blue Jaguar. I'll be waiting for you." She turned back to Bobby. "Lots of luck in the gubernatorial race, Bob. Don't ever call me again."

Part Four

SHOOTER

Chapter 77

A "DO NOT DISTURB" card hung from the doorknob of Andy's third-floor suite at the famed, or perhaps infamous, Chateau Marmont off Sunset. It was almost eleven a.m. I pounded and pounded on the solid wood door.

"Andy. It's Jack. Let me in."

"Go away," Andy said from the other side of the door. "Whatever you're selling, I'm not buying it."

"Come on, bozo. I've already told the manager you're on a suicide watch. He's going to key me in if you don't open up."

The door finally opened.

Andy was in rumpled pajamas, holding a half-full bottle of Chivas by the neck. His hair was standing straight up, as if he hadn't combed or washed it in a while.

"I fired you, didn't I?"

"Yeah, you did, asshole. I'm not billing you anymore. I'm here because I'm your best friend."

I followed Andy into the sitting room. The room was dark, curtains pulled closed.

An old Harrison Ford movie was on the television, *Witness*. The suite looked like a set from the 1930s, or a West Side apartment in New York, except for the open pizza box lying on a chair next to the extralarge TV. I took the pizza box to the kitchenette and dumped it into the trash. Then I returned to the sitting room and sat down.

"How are you doing?" I asked.

"Fucking fine and dandy, can't you tell?"

"I'm sorry," I said.

Andy took a pull off the bottle and said, "So what now, Jack? Last time I saw you, you told me that my wife was a whore. What else have you got for me?"

"She was using."

"What? What did you say?"

"She was a crack addict. Maybe heroin too."

"Hey, fuck you, Jack. Oh, for God's sake. I mean, who cares, anyway? She's dead, Jack. Dead. And look what she left me. I got cops on my ass all day and night. Friends avoiding me, for good reason, I guess. And this fricking room is costing a bomb and a half. All because of my whore-junkie wife."

"The thing is, Andy, her being a user maybe explains a few things about Shelby. Why she had a secret life, for instance. Why she needed the money. Maybe why she couldn't tell you the truth."

Andy picked up the TV's remote control and surfed around while I talked. His eyes were vacant. He was already a lost soul.

"It's also a lead of sorts," I told him. "We already have a

line on her dealer. As I've been saying, if we find out who killed Shelby, you stop being a suspect."

Andy finally looked up at me. "Come here, Jack. I want to give you a big wet kiss."

I got up and took the remote out of his hand. Turned off the tube.

"I didn't do this to you. I'm trying to help you."

"Yuh-huh."

"Like you helped me in school. When that girl I was seeing turned out to be doing Artie Deville behind my back."

"Laurel...something."

"Right. You got me through Laurel Welky and kept me from killing that guy. Killing him, Andy. And how about when I ran my car through a phone booth in downtown Providence? You placated the dean and my old man."

Andy laughed. "Har-har. Your old man."

It was weak, but it was laughter. And I kind of recognized my friend Andy again.

"I'm going to nail this guy, Andy."

"I know. You're good, Jack. Private is good, better than it ever was under your father."

"I'll take you out to dinner tonight," I said. "Cool place. Up the coast."

"Thanks." His eyes watered up.

We hugged at the doorway, thumped each other's backs a couple of times.

"I fucking feel sorry for her," he said, and started to cry. "She was in hell, and she couldn't tell me. Why couldn't she tell me? I was her husband. I was her *husband*, Jack."

Chapter 78

ACCORDING TO HER movie star client and maybe her lover, Shelby's dealer was an ex-con by the name of Orlando Perez.

I'd read his rap sheet. He was a violent prick who'd had arrests for domestic abuse and various assault convictions on a number of occasions, ending with a three-year stretch at Chino for possession with intent. He'd been smart or lucky enough to stay out of jail since he'd graduated from that hell-hole in 2008.

These days, Perez lived with his wife and kids in a two-million-dollar faux Greek revival on Woodrow Wilson Drive. There were two cars in his driveway: a late-model Beemer and a black Escalade with gold-chain rims.

Del Rio had been shadowing Perez for the past forty-eight hours, monitoring his conversations with a parabolic dish the size of half a grapefruit and a Sennheiser MKE 2 lavalier mic. I didn't care about Private's expenses on this case.

According to Del Rio, Perez used a succession of boost phones to set up his impromptu drug deals, which took place in parking lots and on roadsides. His customers were executive types as well as models and starlets, who in all likelihood got discounts for favors provided in the front seat of Perez's SUV.

The front door of the house opened, and a pretty brunette carrying a baby and holding the hand of a toddler came out, got into the Beemer, and then drove right past us.

"The wifey-poo," said Del Rio with a smirk.

He put on his headset and told me that Perez was alone. He was on the phone with a disgruntled client named Butterfly, telling her to take a deep breath. He'd be there soon. He'd bring her what she needed.

"Okay, he's meeting Butterfly in the parking lot of the Holiday Inn on Cahuenga in twenty minutes," Rick said.

"No, he's not. Let's go."

We got out of the fleet car and walked up to the front door of the house. I rang the bell. Rang it again. Then I yelled, "Open up, Perez. You won ten million dollars from the Publishers Clearing House."

I'd just told Del Rio to go stand by the Escalade, when Perez suddenly opened the door.

He was barefoot, his shoulder-length bleached-white hair contrasting with his tanned skin and dark Fu Manchu mustache. A scar ran through the mustache, enhancing the frig-you look on his face.

Was his the last face Shelby Cushman had ever seen? It wouldn't have surprised me at all.

Had this son of a bitch killed her for getting behind in her payments? I showed Perez my badge, and mistaking us for cops, the scumbag hesitated.

"You need a fug-geen warrant, yo," said Orlando Perez, his face balling up like a fist, the scar going white.

Del Rio put his shoulder hard against the door, and we were in.

"See, we don't need a warrant," Rick said.

Chapter 79

ORLANDO PEREZ SHOUTED over the ambient music, "Get outta my house. Get outta here!"

Del Rio took his gun out of his belt and said, "Jack, I left my book in the car. The one on negotiation called *Getting to Yes*. Think you can get that for me?"

I said, "Let's wing it without the book."

"Yeah," Del Rio said. "Sure. We can do that. See how much we remember."

Perez's pupils were large, and he was having trouble focusing. "Hey!" he shouted at Del Rio's gun. "I said ged out."

I pulled the plug to the sound system out of the wall.

Del Rio said, "We're not cops. But after we have a talk, go ahead and call them."

The dealer grabbed a gun resting in the seat of a lounge chair and got the grip into his palm. He was bringing up the muzzle of the semiautomatic when I hit him at the knees and brought him down.

A burst of rounds went off. Blew past my ear and took out a lamp with a glass shade and a painting of a bullfighter over the mantel.

Del Rio kicked the gun out of Perez's hand, and I rolled the dealer over and put my knee into his back with feeling. Then I cuffed him with flex ties.

When I stood up, Del Rio handed me his gun. Then he got a two-hand hold on Perez and dragged him by his white hair and the waistband of his jeans across the polished marble floors, past the indoor pool shaped like a bong, and into a high-tech stainless-steel kitchen that was actually quite nice.

"Yowww-ow-owww, hey! What are you doing, yo? Cut the chit, will you?"

Del Rio hauled the dealer to his feet and shoved his face flat onto the stove, inches from the front burner.

"Why did you kill Shelby Cushman?" Rick shouted into the drug dealer's ear.

"I don't know no Shelby."

Del Rio twitched the dial on the stove. Blue flames leaped.

Perez said, "You don't know what kind of sunnabeech I am, mister."

Del Rio said, "Ditto," and turned up the heat. The dealer's white hair sizzled and burned and scorched the air.

"Yowww. Turn it *off*, mannn. Please, turn it off."

Del Rio grabbed Perez's collar and lifted his head off the stove. He asked him again, "Why did you kill Shelby?"

"I *didn't kill her!* She owed me a few grand. Like four. She woulda paid. She was a good lady. I liked Shelby—everybody liked Shelby."

"Let me tell you how this game is played," Del Rio said. "You keep lying and I'm going to put your face *on* the burner. Are we clear?"

Perez kicked and struggled, but he couldn't loosen Del Rio's grip. Del Rio dialed up the flames again. The heat singeing the fuse of Perez's mustache definitely got his attention.

I was a second away from pulling Rick off Perez when the dealer screamed, "Listen to me. *I didn't kill her.* Maybe I know who did."

Del Rio yanked Perez upright, spun him around, and said, "Keep it real, yo. Or you go back on the hot plate."

"I heard on the street. It was a hit man. For the Mob."

"His name?"

"I don't know that. How would I know that? Yowww," he yelled as Del Rio gripped a hank of white hair and forced Perez's face down onto the stove again.

"Monkey. His name is Monty! Something like that."

Del Rio had briefed me on known enforcers, and Bo Montgomery, aka Monty, was local, which put him right at the top of the list.

"Montgomery," I said to Del Rio.

Perez shouted, "That's him. Now, turn off the gas, maaan."

Del Rio pulled Perez away from the stove. He said, "Be *right,* yo. Or I'll be back to visit. I keep my promises, maaan."

Chapter 80

NOW WE HAD something, and Rick and I were both feeling it to the max. It was a twenty-five-minute drive from Perez's two-kilo manse to a hit man's horse farm in the Agoura Hills, north of Malibu.

The approach was a dusty, unpaved driveway through tall brown grass and trees marked with "No Trespassing" signs. The drive curled around a bluff, then ran straight to a shingled farmhouse, weathered to a silvery shade of gray.

There was a new barn behind the house and a paddock where a mule and three bay mustangs stood head to tail, swishing at flies under a tree. Beyond the paddock was a riding trail that climbed a gentle hill a quarter mile away.

Del Rio braked the car, and light glinting off glass made me look up.

I saw the dome shape of an Avigilon sixteen-megapixel camera mounted under the eaves of the house. I had been thinking of getting the same surveillance system for myself. It shot wide-angle high-res video in color and infrared.

A door hinge squealed, and a man stepped out of the house with an AK-47 in his arms and a gnarly dog at his side. The man was wiry, nothing remarkable to look at, which probably helped him in his work. The dog had a head the size of a large melon. It tensed and growled as we got out of the car.

I kept one eye on the dog as I introduced Del Rio and myself to Monty, faking a casualness I didn't feel. The man was a killer many times over. He was holding a weapon that could turn a person into a colander in seconds.

At the same time, I was hyperaware of my hair-trigger buddy standing beside me. Del Rio had a loaded gun stuck in the back of his waistband. He couldn't outdraw Monty, but that didn't mean he wouldn't try. Sweat formed on my upper lip.

Monty said, "What do you want?" His voice was high, almost boyish.

"I'm Jack Morgan, with Private. Shelby Cushman's husband is my client," I said. "We have no issues with you. I just need to know who wanted Shelby dead."

"I've heard of you, Mr. Morgan. I don't know any Cushmans."

I kept talking. "If the hit on Shelby was personal, if killing Shelby was a message for our client, we want to work that out."

Monty's thin lips hardly moved when he said, "I repeat, I don't know any Cushmans. And if I did know that Shelby always took a nap at four in the afternoon, it still wasn't personal, and I don't send messages. Now, back up slow so you don't scare the horses."

"Thanks, Monty, you're a real professional," I said. Then Del Rio and I walked away and got into the car.

I took the wheel. I backed out slowly, then drove along the driveway, dust billowing up behind us.

Chapter 81

I HAD BEEN working the Schoolgirl case hard—for the girls, for Justine, a little of both, and had finally gotten to sleep. The buzzing of the phone jerked me out of a dream. My heart was pumping so hard, I thought I'd bust a valve. I opened the phone, didn't even bother to let the caller speak.

I shouted, *"Not yet,"* then slammed the phone down on the table.

That bastard. I was so close to getting it. So close to figuring it out. *I almost had it. What was I missing about Afghanistan and that exploding helicopter?*

I dropped my head back onto the pillow. The dream was still vivid in my mind, and it played out like a movie on the blank screen of the ceiling.

The dream matched up with what I remembered of that day. I'd been standing at the ramp of the CH-46. I heard artillery popping from the fifty-cals as the helicopter burned. Men screamed.

Danny Young was on his back in the dark. His flight suit was soaked with his blood, so much of it, I couldn't see where he'd been hit.

I called his name. Then everything stopped. There was a sound in my ears, like static, and my vision blurred.

I tried, but I couldn't see anything. I couldn't get a clue what had just happened. I'd just lost a few seconds, though.

The action began again.

In life as in the dream, I had pulled Danny out of the air-craft, slung him over my shoulder, started to run with him across that burning battlefield.

I'd put him down safely and then—what?

I was flat on my back, and Danny was lying lifeless a few feet away. I had died and come back. With Del Rio's help.

I put a pillow over my face, and more images of Danny came to me as I lay in my soft bed.

Danny had been a dairy farmer, the son of a son of a son of a dairy farmer in a small town in Texas. He had enlisted in the Marines because he felt it was his duty. And also so that he could get the hell out of the barn. I'd done the same—to get free of my father.

There was something so open about that kid, so gee-whiz about everything, that I had to love him. He had no guile. And while he was mostly innocent, he was also very aware of words and of feelings.

I'd served with him for just six months before he died, but in those six months, he was the only one besides Del Rio I could talk to in the squadron. The only guy who didn't see me as privileged, just let me be myself.

I flashed ahead to meeting Danny's wife, Sheila, when I got back to the States. She had strawberry blond hair and gray eyes. I remembered sitting in a small dark parlor in their house. There was black fabric draped over the mirror. The small-scale furniture was uncomfortable and looked unused.

I told Sheila that I'd been with Danny when he died. I told her that he'd been unconscious. That he hadn't been in pain. That he was a brave man. That we'd all loved him. Every single word of that was true.

Sheila had clasped her hands across her distended stomach. She didn't sob, but the tears poured down her face.

"We're going to have another girl," she said.

The static filled my mind again. It was that blank in my memory that told me something was missing. Something else had happened. What was it? What didn't I know?

The damn telephone started to ring again.

Chapter 82

THE PHONE VIBRATED inside my fist. The faceplate read 7:04. Incoming call: T. Morgan.

I put the phone up to my ear, said to my brother, "Did you call here a minute ago?"

"I called last night. Didn't you get my message? My shrink wants to see us together. This morning at nine."

"Today? Are you kidding? I have a business, you know?"

"Sure. It used to be Tommy Senior's business," he said. "It's important, but hey, suit yourself."

Now I was sitting in a reception pod at Blue Skies Rehab Center, a pale blue windowless room with a wraparound ceramic tile mural of birds in flight and discrete groupings of streamlined Scandinavian furniture.

I was upset that I'd been summoned the morning of the meeting, but I'd be damned if I'd give Tommy any excuse to fail at recovery. With luck, I'd be in the office by 10:30. Schoolgirl was bubbling—and so was the NFL.

While I waited, I joined a conference call with one of our clients in the London office, then signed off as one of a half dozen doors down the hallway opened. A man stepped out and came toward me. He was lanky, gray-haired, wearing a yellow cardigan and pressed chinos, had reading glasses suspended from a chain around his neck.

He was also smiling. I stood to shake his hand, and he lurched and was literally thrown to the floor.

Suddenly everything was sliding sideways. I grabbed for my chair and fell into it, hard.

What the hell?

Light fixtures swung overhead, and shadows swooped over the pale carpeting. There was a roar, like wind—but there was no wind.

The floor rippled like the surface of a river.

I clutched the arms of my chair, which bucked as if it were alive and trying to shake me off.

The man in the yellow cardigan had covered the back of his head with his hands. The mural cracked up the center, and red flowers shot out of a vase like rockets. Glass shattered—and then the power went out.

A herd of people ran helter-skelter through reception, shrieking in the darkened room.

I hung on to the chair. It was as if I were paralyzed, but my terror was lashing around inside me like a downed power line in a storm. The room spun, and I was *there* again. The helicopter whirled in a death spiral, dropping out of the sky. I couldn't do anything to prevent the crash and all those deaths.

Chapter 83

I KNEW THAT the monstrous dog shaking the building like a rag was an earthquake. Had to be. But in the dark, as the chair jounced and the floor rolled in waves under my feet, I was clawed out of the present and hurled seven years back in time.

I was in the cockpit of the CH-46 when the surface-to-air missile tore through the cargo bay floor and took out the aft transmission. The sound as it blew through the cabin was like the howl of the world coming to an end.

As the helicopter whirled downward, I was pinned to the left side of my seat. I pulled the engines offline to reduce the violent right-hand rotation, but there was nothing I could do to reverse gravity.

I held on to the cyclic, my shoulders nearly ripping out of their sockets, and tried to keep the aircraft level.

I had a single thought, to land the bird in one piece, and

the machine was fighting me all the way. I held on to the stick, staring out through the dual tunnels of my night-vision goggles as the swirling abstract pattern of the ground came up to crash into us.

The landing gear tore up through the chin bubble by my feet as we hit. The force was stunning, sickening, and it jarred me through my bones—but the aircraft was intact.

I released my harness, reached over, and shook Rick's shoulder.

He turned and grabbed my arm, said, "Bumpy landing, Jack. Very fucking bumpy."

The gunner and the crew chief bailed out of the crew door behind me. Rick went between our two seats and followed them down the steps into the night.

I could have gotten out through my window, but I must have gone back to the cargo bay, because what I remember next was the sight of the ruined cabin, half of it ripped away by the missile. What remained was littered with dead Marines.

It was a horror show, the real thing.

Fourteen men who had been joking and cheering when we lifted off twenty minutes before were now broken and heaped against the left side of the cabin.

Danny Young was lying apart from the others, and he was soaked in blood. I felt for a pulse, but my hands were numb and shaking. I couldn't feel a thing.

I called Danny's name, but he didn't answer me. Were his eyelids flickering? I couldn't be sure.

I inched my way through the aircraft, pulling Danny after me. I had him over my shoulder when I heard someone shout my name. I turned and saw Corporal Jeffrey Albert lying toward the rear of the cabin, where he was weighed down by the bodies of the dead.

He was screaming in pain.

Fire had started in the cockpit. As the cabin brightened, my ability to see through the goggles washed out.

Jeff Albert twisted his head to see me. I made a life-and-death assessment. Jeff was not only pinned, his legs had broken during the crash and his bones had torn through his flight suit. I couldn't get him out by myself.

He screamed, *"Get me out of here, Captain. Don't leave me here to burn."*

"I'll be back," I shouted to Albert. "I'll be back with help. I'll be right back."

Albert shrieked, *"He's dead, Captain. Danny is dead. Please help me."*

Chapter 84

THE LIGHTS IN the rehab center reception room flickered then came back on, their white incandescence practically blinding me.

When I took in the scene, I saw that the walls had cracked like eggshells, and the carpet was littered with shards of plaster and glass. I was both at Blue Skies and in Afghanistan, memories still pouring into my head like gasoline streaming over hard desert ground.

Men ran toward me, phosphorescent green figures against the black of night. I put Danny Young down on the ground, and then—the great gaping hole opened up in my memory. I was there. And then I wasn't.

I was dead—and then I returned to life. For what reason, I had no idea.

There was intense and painful pressure on my chest, and Rick Del Rio was in my face. "Jack, you son of a bitch—"

He hadn't known I'd left Jeff Albert to die.

He hadn't known — and I hadn't either. I had been out of my mind, hallucinating that I was in a bar. I'd thrown a jab at Rick. Now I was remembering for the first time, falling down the hole in my memory toward searing mortification.

Everything I believed about myself melted before this terrible truth. I'd left a man behind. I'd promised him I would be back, but I had left him. I wished Rick hadn't brought me back to life.

I wished that I had stayed dead.

A voice called to me, "Jack. Jack, are you all right?"

Rick? Where the hell am I?

I stared at the gray-haired man, whose face was close to mine. Who was he? How did he know my name?

"I'm Brendan McGinty, Tommy's therapist. You were moaning. Where are you hurt?"

"I'm...okay. I just—"

I struggled to stand, and Dr. McGinty held out his hand to help me up. I clasped his forearm and pulled myself to my feet. People scurried past in pairs and groups.

McGinty was speaking in a soothing tone. "It's going to be all right. I'll call a doctor to look at you, Jack."

"No, I'm fine. I'm really fine."

McGinty said, "Tommy, we have to postpone our session. We'll reschedule."

I looked up and saw my brother standing only a few feet away. He said, "Hell, no. We don't have to cancel anything. Jack's been through firestorms on the dark side of the moon. A little quake isn't going to bother him. Right, Jacko?"

I wanted to get into the Lambo and jam the pedal down to

the floorboard. I wanted to drive until I fell asleep at the wheel. I wanted to do whatever it took to get away from the guilt and the unbearable pain of what I'd finally remembered. I had carried a friend who was dead out of a burning helicopter, and left another man behind.

"You are okay, aren't you, bro?" Tommy asked. "What the fuck. You're already here. You're a busy man, remember."

I was so dazed, I could hardly speak, but I got out a few words. "Let's do it," I said.

Chapter 85

THE WORLD OUTSIDE my head seemed insubstantial, as if the present could be a dream and my memories much more solid and alive in the now.

Sounds were irrelevant; the sirens shrilling outside on the highway, the blaring voice over the PA system, Tommy and Dr. McGinty talking together as they walked down the hallway with me trailing behind.

I ducked my head as I crossed the threshold into Dr. McGinty's office.

The room was small, and the quake had flung pictures and books across the hardwood floor. McGinty returned a floor lamp to its upright position and switched it on.

He said, "Jack, honestly. We can do this another time."

"I'm fine," I said. "Really. I'd like to have our talk now."

We cleared the center of the room and placed two identical wooden armchairs side by side across from McGinty's recliner. I felt Jeff Albert's presence eyeing me from a corner of the room as Tommy and I sat down in the chairs and McGinty got comfortable in his La-Z-Boy. It was a pretty crazy thought, but I wondered—*had Jeff Albert been calling me every day to tell me that I was dead?*

Tommy said, "I don't think California broke off the continent, at any rate."

We were dressed the same. White shirts, blue blazers over jeans. I wore loafers; Tommy wore moccasins. The smirk on his unshaven face made him look a little like the guy who stars on *Mad Men.*

The arrogance was completely unearned. The smug, invincible affect had come from my dad. Tommy was grounded in Tommy Sr.'s crap.

McGinty asked if either of us needed anything and then said, "Let's begin. Jack, we're hoping you can give us some additional insight into your father's personality."

Speak of the devil.

"How would you describe him?"

My father had been dead for over five years, but he would never really be dead to me. I said, "He was cruel. That was his best trait."

Dr. McGinty smiled, then asked, "Can you tell me more, Jack?"

"Oh, hell, volumes. He was abusive to my mom all the time. He pitted Tommy and me against each other for his amusement. He didn't stop until someone bled or cried. He was never wrong about anything—sports, human nature, the weather. He was a perfect godlike creature in his own mind."

The shrink nodded. "What we call in my business 'a real SOB.'" He looked to my brother. "Tommy, what do you think about your father?"

"Jack just sees it his way. *Jack* is never wrong either. Dad was trying to toughen us up," my brother said. The smirk was gone. I'd attacked something he had defended his entire life. "He didn't want the world to take advantage of us."

I barely listened as my brother excused my father's brutality. He said to Dr. McGinty, "Jack never gives him credit. Dad wanted us to succeed. He encouraged Jack to play football and to be good at it. Jack and I were black belts before we were thirteen. And when Jack became a Marine? Dad lit up when he talked about his son the war hero. He was really proud."

I was looking over Dr. McGinty's head, seeing Jeff Albert's face through my NVGs. I saw the fear and the agony, the broken bones coming through his pant legs. He was screaming, "Don't leave me here to burn!"

"What are you thinking right now?" McGinty asked me.

Images were firing off like fifty-caliber rounds. I had repressed the truth to protect myself. Now I had no place to hide. I wasn't who I'd thought I was.

I said, "This was a mistake. I don't belong here. I have to go."

Chapter 86

I GOT OUT of the chair, made for the door. I had my hand on the knob when Tommy called out, "Hey, Jack. Whatever it is, you should stay. Take my session, bro. Okay, Dr. McGinty?"

"Of course. Please, Jack. Sit down."

I didn't want to let the demon out. It was too big and still too raw. How could I tell a stranger what I'd managed to keep from myself all these years? How could I tell Tommy?

"This is a safe place," McGinty was saying.

McGinty was wrong. It wasn't safe. Dropping my guard with Tommy took more than courage. It was a high-risk bet with bad odds and an irretrievable downside. At the same time, the pressure to talk was building into a runaway need to admit what I'd done.

"I was flying a transport mission from Gardez to the base at Kandahar," I choked out. "I had fourteen Marines in the back. You can hear a screwdriver drop in the cargo bay of a CH-46, so when the missile came through the floor...the sound...of the aircraft being ripped up..."

I envisioned the dead Marines piled up against the left side of the cabin.

I forced myself to continue. I described the crash and the aftermath: staring into the cabin through my NVGs, seeing the dead men, my friend soaked in blood.

"I had Danny slung over my shoulder—a fireman's carry—and then Corporal Albert woke up. He begged me not to leave him there to burn. I already had Danny. I had to get him to safe ground. Albert was half-buried under the casualties. His legs were in pieces. I needed help to get him out of there. I promised him that I'd come back."

The words were stopping my ability to breathe.

"Are you all right, Jack?"

"Jeff Albert told me that Danny Young was dead."

"Do you think he was? How could Albert have even known?"

"I don't know. It was night....Danny didn't speak....I couldn't feel a pulse because my hands...were numb.

"The way we're briefed before each flight...is take someone out with you. You take out the most urgently wounded who are still alive first. If they're dead, they don't need to be rescued—everyone understands that.

"If Danny was dead, I saved a dead man and left a live man to burn up. I would've gone back."

There was a long pause until McGinty finally spoke again. "Why didn't you?"

"I died," I said.

Chapter 87

I HADN'T CRIED since I was a small boy, maybe four or five years old. I didn't cry when my father died, not even close. But my grief for having deserted Jeff Albert seemed unstoppable right now. I put my head in my arms, and the pain just flowed.

I heard Tommy explaining to Dr. McGinty that a chunk of debris had slammed into my flak jacket and that my heart had stopped. It had taken CPR to start my pump again.

As Tommy talked, I saw Rick Del Rio's face as if he were in the room. I heard him laughing, saying, "Jack, you son of a bitch, you're back." I heard the helicopter blow up and felt the scorching heat come in waves across the field.

The shrink said, "You were *dead*, Jack. Tell me what you could have done to save that man."

My mouth moved, but I couldn't speak. I stood up and so did Tommy. He put his arms around me and hugged me for the first time since we were ten. I cried onto his shoulder and he comforted me.

This was my brother. We'd shared a room from the time we were brought home from the hospital. I knew him as well as I knew myself; maybe I knew him better. I had to accept that underneath the enmity, Tommy and I still loved each other. It was a huge moment between the two of us.

I started to say it was good to be able to tell him what had happened to me, but he spoke first.

"Well, isn't this something? And Dad thought you were perfect. I guess he was wrong, brother Jack. Not perfect at all."

Tommy had suckered me. And now he was twisting the blade.

The anger was instant and overwhelming. I pushed him with all my strength, watched as he slammed into a bookcase and tumbled to the floor.

"What else do you need to know, Dr. McGinty?" I said. "I think you've heard enough."

Then I left the building.

Chapter 88

I FELT PRETTY bad now. I felt betrayed by my brother. I got on the freeway and drove north, just barely noting the highway signposts zipping by.

Speed gave me a feeling of escape, but my thoughts circled like a hawk on meth. I could run, but I couldn't hide from this terrible feeling of guilt about Jeff Albert. I knew that logically I shouldn't blame myself, but it didn't help one bit.

I took the off-ramp at Carrillo Street in Santa Barbara and got back on the 101, this time heading south back toward LA.

I put my phone into the holder and called Justine.

The sound of her voice over the speaker made tears come to my eyes. "Jack. Are you on the way into the office? I want to bring you up to date."

"Got time to have coffee with me?" I asked her. "I need to talk to you about something."

"Uh, okay," she said. "Meet you at Rose. Don't tell me you're going to share, Jack?"

"Hey, you never know. Stranger things have happened."

"Not true," she said. "Not with you."

Nothing bad had ever happened while I was having coffee with Justine. Also, I couldn't remember a time when she hadn't been there for me.

The Rose Café had once been a gas company dispatch office. It had multipaned windows and I beams overhead. There was an in-house bakery and tables the size of pizzas, all of them full. The place smelled like cinnamon-apple pancakes.

Justine was waiting at her favorite table in the back when I got there. She was wearing skinny black trousers and a pearl-colored blouse with a ruffle at the neckline. Her hair was cinched up in a ponytail with a pink band that matched her lipstick.

She smiled at me and put her handbag on the floor to free up the stool. I sat down and she asked me, "And where were you when the earth sneezed?"

It felt like old times to be with Justine at the Rose. We used to come to this place on Sunday mornings, read the paper, rate the bodybuilders who came in after their workouts at Gold's Gym. I'd seen Arnold here often, and Oliver Stone, whose studio was a couple of blocks away.

I told Justine that I had been at Blue Skies, and that there hadn't been any real damage. That was factually true but not entirely accurate.

I wanted to tell her the rest of it. I wanted her to help me put myself back together. I hoped she would read the trauma in my eyes.

"I was on Fairfax," she said. "I pulled into that strip mall off Olympic. Holy crap. Talk about a minute and a half lasting a lifetime."

She hardly stopped for breath. She put her briefcase on the table. Yearbooks came out, and Justine showed me a list of names and page numbers.

"I'm praying that I'm right about this feeling of mine, Jack. One of these kids could be our killer. I'm meeting with Christine Castiglia after this. She's the key to this; I swear she is."

Justine showed me pictures of teenage boys who matched Christine Castiglia's description of a kid who might have abducted Wendy Borman. I tried to stay focused, but my mind kept shooting back to Afghanistan. I saw Danny, his blood glowing green through my NVGs. Jeff Albert screamed in my mind, "Danny is *dead*."

"Are you all right?" Justine finally asked. "Is Tommy okay? Something happened, didn't it?"

"He's fine. But I..." My face got warm. "Some memory from the war shook loose. I want to tell you."

Justine closed the yearbook and looked at her watch. "Damn it, Jack. I have to go. I'm meeting Christine on Melrose in twenty minutes. If I'm not there, she'll bolt. Here's an idea. Come with me. We can talk on the way in the car."

"No, you go ahead," I said. "This can wait. Honest. Tommy's fine. I'm fine."

Justine snapped her briefcase closed and picked up her handbag. She stood and put her hand on my shoulder.

Our eyes locked. She smiled, and for a second I thought she was going to lean down and kiss me. But she didn't do that.

"Wish me luck," she said. "I'll need it with this girl."

I said, "Good luck." She said she'd see me later. Then I watched Justine through the multipaned windows as she walked up the street to her car and left me all alone.

It's what you deserve, Jack, I told myself.

Chapter 89

JUSTINE HAD BEEN seesawing for days between mindless optimism and gutless despair. If the e-mails Sci and Mo-bot had found on Jason Pilser's computer could be trusted, the Street Freeks were going for another kill in just days. They had to be stopped somehow.

She could just about picture their target: a teen girl who was either cocky or naive, but either way, vulnerable to being talked into a careless rendezvous, and then, possibly, her death.

Justine's head hurt thinking about it. She felt she was so close to the killer, but she knew she might fail anyway.

On the other hand, Christine Castiglia was a force for good. There was reason to believe that she could help Private get ahead of the killers before Monday, before another girl died.

Justine parked her car on the busy block on Melrose

where she and Christine had agreed to meet. She was ten minutes early.

Traffic was heavy, and the air quality was poor. Justine dialed up the air conditioner, then she took her BlackBerry out of her handbag and put it on the dash.

She scanned the street, saw kids in clumps, hanging out on the sidewalk.

None of them was Christine.

As noon passed, Justine had a bad thought that started to grow. Christine had defied her mother by asking for this meeting. It had been courageous to do that. But had the girl changed her mind? *Or had something happened to Christine?*

By twelve fifteen, Justine was sure of it.

At twelve thirty, she called Private and checked her voice mail. There was no message from Christine.

Justine tossed the phone back onto the dash. Her head-ache was making spidery inroads into both hemispheres of her brain.

She really wanted to talk to Jack. But there was a danger in seeing him outside the office. Coffee with him at the Rose Café had pulled hard on old feelings, made her wistful and sentimental about what they'd once had.

They had both been so stupid in the past. For her part, she'd thought she could get him to open up and tell her his feelings. But Jack apparently couldn't do that kind of inti-macy, and Justine couldn't do without it.

She'd bought him a mug with a happy face and lettering on it that read: "I'm fine. Really. How are you?" Jack had laughed and used the mug, but he still kept big parts of him-self locked away from her. He never saw why talking about his inner life was good for him. He didn't seem to need to do it.

Jack was gorgeous and he knew it. Women flattered him, flipped their hair, touched him, gave him their phone numbers. Jack was always modest about his good looks, probably because he could be.

She and Jack had fought, made up spectacularly, fought again, and when they broke up the third or fourth time, Jack had slept with an actress. So she and Bobby Petino had spent a memorable night dealing with their own purely sexual tension—and Jack had found out. Of course he had—Jack knew everybody's secrets.

She and Jack had another reconciliation, but both had brought so much past hurt to the party, the relationship could only fail. They'd broken up again a year ago, and now any thoughts of getting back together came with the knowledge of how the relationship would end. . . .

She was startled by a tap on the window.

Christine Castiglia, pale in a black hoodie and jeans, looked nervously up and down the street, then opened the car door and got inside.

"Dr. Smith, I had this idea?" Christine said. "We should go to the coffee shop where I saw those boys that time?"

Justine smiled at Christine. Hope spread its great, wide wings and soared. "What an excellent idea," Justine said.

Chapter 90

THIS WAS WHERE it had all started, wasn't it? All of the mur-ders so far.

Becki's House of Pie was a hole-in-the-wall eatery on Hyperion. It was gloomy, and it smelled of coffee and the dis-infectant a busboy was using to mop the floor. There was an electric clock on the wall above the cash register. It made a loud tick every time the second hand moved.

Justine wondered what the Schoolgirl killers were doing right now, at this very second.

"This is where we sat," Christine said, pointing to a red vinyl booth with a table scarred by decades of blue-plate specials.

A picture window alongside the booth faced onto the lunch hour traffic streaming up and down Hyperion. A motorcycle farted through a yellow light, the rider's fat ass slowly moving away.

Christine said, "I sat here. My mom sat there. I can still see it."

The waitress had bushy gray hair, a pinafore over her blue velvet dress, and a name tag reading "Becki." She looked as though she'd been in the house of pie for fifty years.

Justine ordered coffee, black. Christine asked for tuna salad, then said, "To be honest, Dr. Smith? I wouldn't want to get someone in trouble if I'm not sure."

"Don't worry about that, Christine. Your word alone can't hurt anyone. We'll still need proof. It's not that easy to convict somebody of murder."

"The van stopped in the middle of the road," Christine said, pointing to the cross street. "I looked away, and when I turned back? These two guys were swinging the blond girl into the van."

"Would you like to look at some pictures for me?"

"Sure. If it will help."

Justine got the three heavy yearbooks out of her briefcase, then pushed the short stack across the table to the girl.

Justine sipped her coffee and watched Christine scan the pages. The girl paused to examine not just the portraits, but the group and candid photos too. For a few long moments, she stared at a black-and-white group shot under a heading "The Staff of *The Wolverine*."

"What do you see?" Justine finally asked.

Christine stabbed the photo with a finger, pointing out a boy in a line with nine or ten other kids.

Then Christine exclaimed, "It's *him*."

Justine turned the book around and pulled it toward her.

The caption identified the yearbook staff and their

graduating classes. She checked the caption against the students' faces, then flipped to the portraits of the class of 2006.

The boy Christine had stabbed with her chewed-up fingernail had dark hair, a nose that could be called pointy, and ears that might be described as sticking out.

Suddenly Justine was so wired, she felt as if she could run electricity for all of East Los Angeles off her mood.

Was Christine's memory this good? Or was she just trying to please Justine like her mother had said she would?

Justine said, "Christine? It was nighttime, right? The van stopped for a minute, and the kids were moving. Are you sure this is the boy you saw?"

Christine was a bright girl, and she understood the potential problem instantly.

"I worried that I wouldn't be able to recognize him? But I do. Like I said the first time, Dr. Smith, I'll never forget his face."

"Okay, Christine. Great job. And now that face has a name. *This is Rudolph Crocker.*"

Chapter 91

IN THE BEGINNING, Justine had fought Sci's suggestion to install a high-tech dashboard computer in her Jaguar. It would mess up the look of the car, and also guaranteed that she'd never have a moment away from work.

Sci had won the battle using undeniable logic, and now Justine silently thanked him. The little box, with its seven-inch touch screen, connected up with Private's international network and forensic databases. It also did engine diagnostics, had a rear-obstacle-detection system, and played CDs.

Ingenious little box.

Justine punched Rudolph Crocker's name into a search engine. As the compact computer brain searched the Internet, the screen filled with a list of men named Rudolph Crocker. There were Rudolph Crockers in many states and in diverse professions: doctors, lawyers, firemen, a handyman, a pool boy, and an underwear model in Chicago.

There were no Rudolph Crockers with a criminal record, but there were three men with that name in greater Los Angeles.

The first had been born in Sun Valley in 1956 and worked as a schoolteacher in Santa Cruz until his early retirement in '07.

The second Crocker on the list was an equities analyst at a brokerage firm called Wilshire Pacific Partners.

Justine tapped the keyboard, and the firm's website came up on her screen.

There was a tab, "Who We Are," and Justine clicked on it and scrolled down the list of personnel, which displayed bios and thumbnail portraits.

Rudolph Crocker was the seventh party down.

Justine stared at the small picture. She had to be sure that this slick business-style portrait matched the one in an old yearbook—but it was undeniable. Indisputable. This Crocker was the same one who had graduated from Gateway Prep in '06.

Justine called the office. Her calls to Jack, Sci, and Mo-bot went straight to voice mail. She knew everyone was working flat-out. Sci and Mo were immersed in the computer angle of the Schoolgirl case. Jack, Cruz, and Del Rio were working the NFL fix and Shelby Cushman's murder.

The Wendy Borman connection was Justine's brainstorm, and she had to take it to the end. Sci had isolated two male DNA samples from Wendy Borman's clothing. The samples didn't match anyone on file, living or dead, so she would have to collect a DNA sample from Crocker for comparison.

And she'd have to do it herself.

Or would she?

An idea bloomed. She happened to know someone who was completely up to speed on the case and as motivated to catch the Schoolgirl killer as she was.

Unfortunately, this person happened to hate her guts.

Chapter 92

JUSTINE HAD BEEN aware of Lieutenant Nora Cronin for years. Cronin had five years in homicide and was known to be an honest cop. She would've had a big future, but back-talking her superiors had stunted her career. Also, her weight problem probably didn't help, especially not here in LA.

Bobby Petino, however, thought Cronin was the real deal and a winner. He had talked her up to Chief Fescoe, who had assigned Cronin to the Schoolgirl case, reporting directly to him.

Justine knew that Cronin had worked hard on the case since Kayla Brooks was strangled two years ago, and that she was conceivably more frustrated than Justine. Cronin had more at stake too. The Schoolgirl case was her number one job.

After parking her car on Martel, a narrow road in West Hollywood, Justine walked a dozen yards to where Nora

Cronin was lying on her stomach, peering underneath an ancient Ford junker parked at the curb.

"Hey, Nora, it's me," Justine said.

"Oh, happy day," Cronin muttered. She came out from under the car with a knife in her gloved hand. She gave the knife to a uniform, saying, "Edison, bag this, tag it, take it to the lab."

"Yes, ma'am, Nora, ma'am. Forthwith."

Cronin stripped off her latex gloves and scowled at Justine. "So what's the deal, Justine? I hear you and Bobby are kaput, and you didn't even tell me. I have to wonder: Are you still even working the Schoolgirl case?"

"Private is under contract to the *city*. We're doing this for free. No billable hours."

Justine waited for Cronin's next crack, but it didn't come. Cronin put a hand on her hip and said, "Is your air conditioner working?"

The two women sat in the Jag with the air on high while Justine briefed Nora on Christine Castiglia.

"In 2006, Castiglia saw two kids toss a girl who looked like Wendy Borman into a black van. An hour ago, she identified one of them. I think Wendy Borman might have been the first schoolgirl in the spree."

"I know about that Castiglia girl. Kid was eleven at the time, right? Her mother put up a firewall to keep the cops away from her. You saying you trust her five years later to make a positive ID?"

"Not entirely, no. I got Borman's clothes out of evidence, ran them at our lab. The DNA is good," Justine said to Cronin. "Two male single-source samples. But no bells went off in the database."

"So what do you want from me? I'm a little lost here."

"We have reason to believe that another murder is going down in two days."

"Oh, really? But you can't tell me how you know this, right? So, I repeat, what do you want from me?"

"Christine Castiglia saw a Gateway Prep decal on the kidnap van," Justine said. She tapped buttons on the dashboard computer and called up the photo of Rudolph Crocker's face.

"This is the guy Christine Castiglia ID'd. Name is Rudolph Crocker. He graduated from Gateway in 2006. Now he's a suit at a brokerage house. Christine is sure he's the one she saw."

"Uh-huh. Now what, Justine?"

"So, I've got a suspect over here," Justine said, holding up one hand. "And I've got a DNA sample over here." She held up the other hand. "If we can put this hand and this hand together, we might just put a bloody psychopath out of business."

"Saying I want to do it, I'd have to know everything you know," Cronin said. "None of this 'We have reason to believe' crap. You hold anything back from me, I quit."

"Of course."

"I don't answer to you."

"No, you don't. And you can't bring anyone from LAPD into this without my okay. Okay?"

"Yeah," said Nora.

She was smiling now. It was probably the first time Justine had seen a smile from her. "I'm gonna take a lotta crap for working with you. After all the names I've called you."

Justine nodded. "Deal?"

"Deal." They slapped high fives in the frigid air.

"We're going to make a great team," said Justine.

"Let's not get ahead of ourselves," said Nora Cronin. "I still don't particularly like you."

Justine finally smiled. "Oh, you will."

Chapter 93

I WAS HEADING into the office, stuck in a swamp of traffic on Pico, when Mo-bot called me from the tech center.

"Five minutes ago, our friends at the LAX Marriott made a call to a bottling plant in Reno asking for a donation to the State Troopers' Widows Fund," she said, her voice trilling with excitement. "The plant is owned by none other than Anthony Marzullo. Happy, Jack?"

"Good catch, Mo. That's excellent. But you know what I really want."

"To hear the sound of coins changing hands?" Mo laughed. "After the call to Nevada, Victor Spano called Kenny Owen on his mobile. They're meeting at the Beverly Hills Hotel. Bungalow four this afternoon."

Mo had been tapping into Kenny Owen's and Lance Richter's phones since they'd arrived in LA in advance of tomorrow's game. We already knew that the professional handicappers expected the Titans to crush the Raiders by three touchdowns. And we knew that if the two refs could skew the calls, could make a seventeen-point spread hold up, tens of millions in illegal bets would slide over to the Marzullos' side of the ledger.

But Uncle Fred and his associates would want more than idle chitchat and suspicion. They'd need proof.

I called Del Rio, met him at the garage, and swapped my car for one of our Honda CR-Vs. The Honda was black with tinted windows, outfitted with cutting-edge wireless electronics.

I drove myself and my wingman to Sunset, pulled the car under the porte cochere at the entrance to the Beverly Hills Hotel, and dropped Del Rio off.

He pulled down the bill of his cap and adjusted his camera bag as he entered the hotel. Once he was inside, I looped around Sunset and parked on Crescent Drive, a hundred yards and a stucco wall away from the pretty white cottage in the lush garden surrounding the hotel.

Del Rio kept me posted through his lapel mic as he planted the pin cams, one at the bungalow's front door and another at the patio, and stuck three more "spider eyes" on windows facing into the three rooms.

A long twelve minutes later, Del Rio was back in the CR-V, and the microcameras were streaming wireless AV to our laptops.

The only things moving inside the bungalow were dust motes wafting upward in columns of sunlight.

For all of his volatility, Del Rio could sit on a tail for ten hours without having to take a leak. I was still suffering mental whiplash from the earthquake and the devastating memory it had dislodged. After a half hour of staring at sunbeams, I had to say something or I was going to explode.

"Rick. Did you take a look at Danny Young when I brought him out of the helicopter?"

"Huh? Yeah. Why?"

My voice was flat as I told him about my morning. I was a dead man talking, but I got to the point. I didn't need to add color commentary. Del Rio had been there.

"So let me get this straight," Del Rio said when I'd finished. "You're beating yourself up for leaving Jeff Albert in the Phrog and trying to save Danny Young? What about the other guys? We took a missile, Jack. And you landed the goddamn aircraft."

"Do you remember Albert?"

"Sure. He was a good kid. They were all good kids. Jack, you were just a kid yourself."

"I think Danny Young was dead when I pulled him out."

Del Rio stared at me for a few seconds before he said, "Danny's blood was still pumping out of his chest when I got to you. He died on the ground. The helicopter blew up, Jack. If you'd gone back in, Danny Young, Jeff Albert, and *you* would have died.

"And nobody could've brought you back."

Del Rio was right. Danny's blood had been splashing on my shoes. He had been alive. I had brought him out *alive.*

I almost felt fully alive myself.

Neither of us spoke again until two men came up the bungalow's front walk.

One was Victor Spano. The other was a short man in a good suit. The guy in the suit put a key card into the slot and opened the door to Bungalow 4.

I put my arms up like a football referee.

"Touchdown!"

Chapter 94

I HAD BIG NEWS, but not necessarily good news, to tell.

It was dark when I pulled up to my uncle's huge Italianate manse in Oakland. I parked at the top of the circular drive and trotted up the walkway.

Fred's second wife, Lois, came to the door and was joined by my boisterous eleven-year-old cousin, Brian, who tackled my thighs like the All-American linebacker for Southern Cal he was sure he was going to be one day.

I rolled around and groaned in fake pain as Brian whooped and did a white-boy sack dance in the foyer. My little cousin Jackie stooped down and patted my head as if I were a golden retriever.

"Brian is a big fat brat, Jack. Are you hurt bad?"

I winked at her and told her I was okay, and she pulled my nose.

"Did you eat, Jack?" Uncle Fred asked, giving me a hand up, then throwing an arm across my shoulders.

"I wouldn't say no to coffee," I said.

"How about coffee and a slice of banana cream pie?"

"Sold."

I grabbed a chair at the dining table, and the kids pelted me with questions—about the earthquake, if I'd nailed any bad guys lately, the fastest I'd ever driven my car.

As soon as I answered one question, they loaded up and fired again.

Normally, I'd have grabbed one kid under each arm, taken them into the media room, and watched a Spider-Man or a Batman movie, but tonight I was thinking of the time, how little of it was left before the Sunday schedule of games, one game in particular.

I caught my uncle's eye and patted my breast pocket. He nodded and said to Lois, "I'm going to steal Jack for a few minutes."

I followed Fred to his study, a beautiful mahogany-paneled room with two walls of trophy cases and a sixty-eight-inch flat-screen hung like a trophy over the fireplace.

"I'm going to drink," Fred said.

"I'll have what you're having."

Fred poured J&B over rocks, and I shoved the flash drive into his video setup. I gave him the desk chair so he could have the better angle. Fred Kreutzer was a complicated man. I couldn't guess at how he would react to the unfortunate movie I had to show him.

His high-def screen was first-rate, a perfect match for our NASA-grade cameras.

We began to see images captured from outside the Beverly Hills Hotel bungalow, looking in.

A red light winked on a telephone.

A man in a suit, his back to the camera, picked up the receiver, punched in some numbers, and collected a message.

Behind him, Victor Spano took a Heineken out of the fridge and turned on the television.

I took the remote control off Fred's desk and sped the action forward, then slowed it as the man in the suit turned his face for his close-up.

It was Anthony Marzullo, the third-generation boss of the Chicago Mob bearing his family name.

On camera, he said to Spano, "Get the door."

Spano did, and two men walked in: Kenny Owen, referee and crew chief with twenty-five years of experience on the field, and Lance Richter, a sharp young line judge who clearly saw that his financial future lay in queering the game, not playing by the rules.

My uncle Fred drew in a breath, then let out a string of curses.

Onscreen, hands were shaken, and the refs filled seats opposite a man who had taken on the heretofore impossible task of corrupting modern-day pro football.

"There can be no mistakes," said Marzullo. He smiled without moving the top of his face. "As per usual, here's twenty percent down. The rest you get tomorrow night. No more than seventeen points. Understand? If you have to call the game on account of the sun's in your eyes, that's good enough. Whatever it takes to hold the spread."

Richter said, "We understand, and we know what's at stake." He reached for a fat stack of banded hundreds.

"Do you?" Marzullo said, putting his hand over Richter's.

"Yes, sir. It'll happen just like you want. It's not a problem. Whatever it takes."

Owen slapped his packet against his thigh before pocketing the cash.

I stopped the video and turned to my uncle.

The poor guy looked as though he'd taken a wrecking ball to the gut. Actually, I remembered the look from my father's trial, a combination of terrible shame and sadness.

"It's pretty bold," I said. "This isn't just a case of one ambitious mobster and a couple of crooked refs. It's much bigger. The Marzullos are moving in on the Noccias' territory."

"I never thought Kenny Owen would take a nickel that didn't belong to him," said Fred. "I know his wife and I've met his kids. One plays ball at Ohio State."

"The tape is good," I said. "It'll hold up in court."

"I've got some calls to make," Fred said. "I'll get back to you in the morning, let you know what we're going to do. You did a good job for us, Jack."

"Yeah, well, I'm sorry, Uncle Fred. I couldn't be sorrier."

"Yeah," Fred said. "Tomorrow'll be worse."

Chapter 95

IT WAS PAST midnight when I finally got to Colleen's house.

I was wrung out, and I needed Colleen's cool hand on my forehead. I wanted to listen to the musical sound of her brogue and fall asleep with her body curled around mine.

She came to the door in a camisole and a pair of panties the size of an afterthought. Her hair was bunched loosely on top of her head. She smelled wonderful, like pink roses with sugar on top.

"I'm sorry, but the inn is closed," she said. "There's a Days Inn down the road a piece."

"Colleen, I should have called first."

"Come in, Jack."

She opened the door and stood on her toes to kiss me. Then she leaned in and pressed her hips against me for the couple of seconds it took to get me hard.

She ran her hand across the front of my pants, then took my hand in hers and led me to her bedroom. Filtered moonlight was coming through the curtains as Colleen stepped into a pair of high-heeled shoes.

"Want to watch the telly?" she asked. "Or is it something else you have in mind?"

"What's on?" I said, and grinned.

So did Colleen.

Chapter 96

I PUT MY hands on the straps of her camisole and pulled them down onto her shoulders. No farther than that. Just a tease.

Colleen kept smiling as she unbuckled my belt and stripped off my clothes. Then she sat me down, took off my shoes and socks, and pushed me back onto her bed.

"God, I do love that body," she said. "I do. God save me."

This wasn't what I had expected when I rang her doorbell, but there I was, naked on flowered sheets, watching Colleen tug the clips out of her hair. That curtain of fragrant black silk fell around her shoulders, covering, then revealing her breasts.

She bent over me, hair tickling my face, and she kissed me deeply and for a long time. It was glorious. She slid into the bed and wriggled against me, her cool skin sliding across mine, pulling away, then pressing against me.

I had my hands around her narrow hips—felt a prick of high heels at the small of my back—and then I was inside her.

My mind emptied, thoughts of sleep having burned away completely. Love poured in and filled my heart, love and gratitude and ecstasy and then, after maybe ten minutes of this, release—for both of us. I moved off Colleen's body and sank into the bed.

The sweat began to dry on my skin, and unbelievably, Colleen began to cry.

I felt a flash of regret. I couldn't take any more this day, not another thing, but the feeling dissolved, replaced by shame and then compassion for Colleen.

I gathered her into my arms and held her as she sobbed quietly against my chest. "Colleen, what is it?"

She shook her head no.

"Sweetie, tell me what it is. I want to hear it. I'm right here."

Colleen struggled out of my arms. Shoes flew, banged into the corner. The bathroom door opened, and I heard water running. Minutes later, Colleen came out in a long sleep shirt and got into the bed.

"I've made a right fool of meself," she said.

"Talk to me. Please."

She lay on her back, staring up at the ceiling. I put my hand across her belly.

"It's hard, Jack. This—leaves me so sad sometimes. I see you at midnight some random nights. I work with you at the office. And in between?"

"I'm sorry."

I couldn't say that things would change. We were smack up against the wall, and I had to tell the truth.

"This is all I've got, Colleen. I can't move in. I can't marry you. This has to stop."

"You don't love me, do you, Jack?"

I sighed. Colleen hugged me as I stroked her hair. "I do. But not the way you need."

I felt as heartsick as she felt, and then I had to disengage from her embrace.

"Stay, Jack. I'm okay now. It's Sunday morning. A bright new day."

"I've got to go home and get some sleep. I'm working today.... This NFL thing is about to blow. My uncle is depending on me. I gave him my promise."

"I see."

I gathered my clothes from the floor and dressed in the dark. Colleen was staring at the ceiling when I kissed her good-bye.

"You're not a bad person, Jack. You've always been honest with me. You're always straight. Have a good day for yourself, now."

Chapter 97

COLLEEN WAS STILL on my mind when Del Rio and I met Fred in the stadium parking lot at noon.

Horns blared without mercy. Motorcycles sputtered and roared as they came through the gates. Cars and trucks streamed across asphalt. Fans of all ages wearing Raiders T-shirts—some with their faces painted silver and black, a select few in Darth Raider costumes—were having tailgate parties, cooking burgers and steaks and getting bombed.

The home team was going to play, and the fans always dared to hope that by some miracle their glory days would return, that the Raiders would triumph—and if they didn't, it was still a good day for a party.

I looked across to the owners' lot, saw Fred lock his car and start toward the entrance. He was wearing his favorite warm-up jacket, Dockers, and orthopedic shoes. His thinning hair was neatly combed. I thought that he looked older than he had a week ago, like he'd suffered a great loss, which I guess he had.

I called Fred's name, and he looked up, changed course.

He shook hands with Del Rio, clapped my shoulder, and led us through the crowd toward a side door beyond the lines.

"Thanks for coming, Jack, Rick. I appreciate it."

He flashed his ID at one of the security guards, said, "They're with me," and a door opened into a tunnel fit for a remake of the Mean Joe Greene commercial.

For one bright green instant, I saw the field, the stands filling on all sides, and then we took a sharp left and headed down beneath the stadium.

Doors opened and closed along the underground hallway. Stadium personnel called out to Fred, and he acknowledged them with a wave and a smile—but my stomach clenched thinking about what was going to happen in the next few minutes.

"Let's get it over with," Fred said. "This is going to be tough, really bad, Jack."

He put his key into a lock and stood back to let me and Del Rio pass in front of him into his office.

I was surprised to see Evan Newman and David Dix sitting around Fred's desk. Two men I didn't recognize sat on a sofa at the rear of the room. They were wearing black-and-white stripes. Their expressions were grim.

Fred introduced the men as Skip Stefero and Marty Matlaga, then said, "Jack, you got the pictures? You and Rick, come with me. Everyone else, we'll be back in a couple of minutes. If we're not, bust in."

Private

Rick and I followed Fred a short distance to a door marked "Officials."

Fred knocked twice, and without waiting for a response, turned the knob and pushed the door open.

The echo of conversation and the rattle of lockers opening and closing stopped dead as the three of us stepped inside.

Chapter 98

THE REFS WERE in various states of undress and they were all looking at us. Fred calmly said, "Kenny, Lance, I need to see you both for a moment."

Kenny Owen was buttoning his black-and-white-striped shirt. He put his foot on a bench and tied a shoelace.

"Outside," Fred said. "I mean *now*."

Lance Richter's sunburned complexion paled, but he and Kenny Owen went through the door, and Fred closed it behind them.

We five formed a huddle a dozen yards away from the refs' locker room. Fred said, "There's no easy way. We can do this hard or we can do it *harder*."

"What are you talking about, Fred?" Owen asked, playing dumb and doing it rather well.

"We've got the whole revolting fix on tape, you pathetic

assholes. Jack, show them the pictures you took at the Beverly Hills."

I had printed stills from the video of Owen and Richter's meeting with Anthony Marzullo, had them in an envelope inside my breast pocket.

I took out the pictures, sorted through them, and put the money shot right on top.

Richter saw the photo of him and Owen holding stacks of money, sitting across a coffee table from the boss of the Chicago Mob.

I smelled urine, saw the front of Richter's pants get wet. He blurted, "I had to go along with it. It was go along with Kenny or lose my job."

Owen snarled. "You pussy."

Fred went on, "Don't waste time giving me bull, Richter. I don't care why anyway."

"This was the first time," Owen said. "Have a heart, Fred. You can't make money working this job."

"Ken. Did you hear me say I had it on tape? Marzullo says, 'Here's twenty percent down. As per usual.' Listen to me. Newman and Dix are in my office. Dix would like to take you out to the desert and shoot you both. He'd do it too. Newman wants to run for Congress. He'd like to have you arrested right now, which would partially protect the NFL's reputation—and destroy the game.

"I see it differently, and my partners trust my instincts. If you've got any brains at all, these are your options. Now *listen*."

The two refs stared unblinkingly as Fred continued.

"Plan A. You go back into the locker room, say that you were seen having dinner with a couple of players, you can't say who. That's a league violation, with a termination penalty.

"Here's Plan B. I take our video of you accepting a payoff from Marzullo to the commissioner. The integrity of the game goes under the microscope. All the games you officiated in your depraved little lives will be examined.

"You'll be arrested and charged with criminal conspiracy, and the story will be news across the country overnight and for years to come.

"The Marzullos will be charged with racketeering, and your lives won't be worth a hangnail either in jail or out.

"Frankly, I wouldn't bet a buck on your lives right now. You've got three hours at the most to disappear. When the Marzullos don't see you on the field, the word's gonna go out. When the game doesn't go the way the Marzullos expect, you're marked men. I don't think your bodies will ever be found."

Kenny Owen's eyes were huge and wet. He paraphrased what Fred had fed him. "We had dinner with some players, but I can't say who because it wasn't their fault. It was stupid. We went for the free steak and broke the rules. Please accept our resignation."

Fred said, "Empty your lockers and get the hell out of here. *Run.*"

Ten minutes later, Fred, Newman, and Dix marched the new refs into the officials' locker room. As predicted, the Titans hammered the Raiders, 52 to 21, beating the spread by 14.

Private

I took the video back to Private and locked it in the vault where a lot of other secrets were kept. If Fred ever needed it, I'd have it for him.

But I kept the still shots of Spano, Marzullo, and the refs in my pocket. I had a clever idea. But I couldn't tell anyone about it yet.

Chapter 99

IT WAS THREE FIFTY on that same Sunday afternoon.

Justine and Nora Cronin had been parked outside Rudolph Crocker's white stucco three-story apartment building on Via Marina since eight in the morning. The two of them weren't exactly friends yet, but no blows had been struck either.

Justine had clipped a "little ears" parabolic dish to the window of the car. She and Nora had listened to Crocker's morning bathroom noises and later *Meet the Press,* accompanied by Crocker's running, ranting commentary.

At a few minutes before two, Crocker had left the building in shorts and a T-shirt, and Nora and Justine got their first live view of the twenty-three-year-old who might have murdered more than a dozen girls.

"Doesn't look like much," Nora grumbled.

"He isn't. He's just scum, Nora."

Crocker went for a run up Admiralty Way, with Justine and Nora following behind him at a safe distance in one of Private's standard-issue gray Crown Victorias.

After returning home, Crocker took a shower, singing "Unbreak My Heart" off-key but with meaning. He watched CNN's *Your Money*, and then everything inside his front-facing apartment went quiet. Justine guessed that Crocker might have been working on his computer. Or maybe he'd gone back to sleep.

"Is he in for the frickin' night?" Nora fretted. "I thought this guy needed excitement."

"Lean back. Close your eyes," Justine said. "If he is, then so are we."

"I can't catnap in a car. You?"

"How do you like your coffee? There's a deli at the corner. I'm buying."

At just after five, Crocker emerged from his apartment building again, this time in a smart blue blazer over a pink shirt, gray slacks, and loafers that looked like they cost a lot.

He walked to a late-model blue Sienna minivan parked at the end of Bora Bora and got inside. He backed out smoothly, then turned up Via Marina.

Justine was a professional stalker and she was good at it. She followed Crocker's van, staying two to three car lengths behind him.

She almost lost him when a light changed, but Justine gunned the engine and blew through the light.

"Son of a bitch," Cronin murmured. "Did he make us?"

"Don't know," said Justine. "We'll find out soon."

They entered Westwood on Westwood Boulevard and

cruised onto Hilgard. They saw Crocker pull into a driveway, leave his keys and van with a valet, then take the stairs into the lobby of the W Hotel.

The bar, located at the corner of the building, was visible through the plate glass windows on two sides.

"He's going to the Whiskey Blue," Justine said. "It's a pickup joint for richy singles. Perfect for our purposes, really."

Their agreed-upon mission was narrow and very precise. They weren't going to confront Rudolph Crocker. They weren't going to arrest him. They didn't even want to meet his eyes, though Justine wouldn't have minded scratching them out.

They just needed a smear of saliva, a microscopic sample of skin cells, a hair, or a flake of dandruff. That was all it would take.

Easier said than done, though.

"How do I look?" Nora asked Justine.

"Adorable. Use this."

Justine took a lipstick out of her bag and handed it to Nora while watching the door Rudolph Crocker had just entered. He was still in there.

"Let your hair down," Nora said. "Shake it out. Open a few buttons."

Justine did it and said, "Let's go. Let's meet the devil."

Nora slammed the door, showed her badge to the valet, and said, "Our car stays right here at the curb. Police business."

Justine gave the kid a ten, then followed Nora up the stairs.

"I get it," said the kid. "Good cop, bad cop."

Nora turned to him and laughed out loud. "No, this is fat cop, skinny cop!"

Chapter 100

"A GOOD LAUGH always helps," Justine said as they entered the bar.

Since Justine had last been at the Whiskey Blue, it had undergone a modern makeover. The lounge was swathed in earthy neutrals; there were angular couches in chocolate and umber, and soft lighting over the bar. Techno music pounded out of the speakers, making real conversation impossible.

The place was jammed with young execs and wannabes savoring the remains of the weekend. Still a chance to score. Girls with great hair and tight clothing, breasts squeezed up to their collarbones, laughed into the faces of young guys obviously on their way up in the world. Every other one of them seemed to have dark hair and very white teeth; most wore sunglasses.

Justine felt an unnerving sense of urgency. This was it, all she had. Rudolph Crocker had to be their guy, and he was here.

For too long she'd been working this case as though the murdered girls were her own children. It had been months of frustration and grief, hearing the indelible cries of the girls' parents etched into her mind like the grooves of an old-fashioned vinyl record.

She and Nora had given themselves a difficult but critical task. If they pulled it off, they might shut down a heinous fucking killer—but there were so many ways this could go wrong.

Chapter 101

JUSTINE SIGNALED to Nora with her eyes, and they inched and edged through the crowd.

When they got to the bar, Justine said to a big, bluff twenty-something red-faced guy wearing a shirt that matched his complexion, "Mind if I slip in there and order a drink?"

"What are you having?" said the guy, checking her out from the neck down.

"My girlfriend and I, we're together."

The large guy looked at Nora, then quickly back at Justine. This time, her eyes. He sneered, but he backed away.

Justine nabbed a stool, put a hand around Nora's arm, and pulled her close. She leaned in and whispered, "Got a clear view of him?"

"Yeah. Crocker's asking for a refill. The bartender just took away his glass."

The bartender was in his early thirties, sandy hair

thinning in front. He was buffed and looked bored, had the name Buddy appliquéd on his shirt.

"What can I get for you ladies?"

"Pinot Grigio," said Justine.

"Perrier," said Nora. There was a jostling movement at Justine's back, someone bumping into her.

"What the . . . ?"

"Don't look now. Crocker's got company," said Nora. "Skinny guy, hair down over his eyes. Looks like a total geek."

"I can't hear what they're saying," Justine said.

"Doesn't matter," said Cronin. "As long as we can see them we're cool."

The bartender put their drinks on the bar. Justine paid with a twenty, told Buddy to keep the change. The bartender palmed the bill, took a bowl of nuts out from under the ledge, and placed it in front of her.

Justine lifted her eyes and watched Crocker in the mirror behind the bar.

He had the stand-out ears, the memorable nose. The rest of the picture was just un-freaking-believable: how could a guy this ordinary be vying with legendary psychos for a top spot in the killer lineup?

The busboy brought a rack of clean glasses to the back bar, and the bartender took a few orders. Crocker's friend had a beer from the tap, and the two of them talked without looking around.

Justine dropped her eyes when Crocker signaled to the waiter for the check. She watched him sign it, then both men got off their stools and left the bar.

Buddy moved to clear away the glasses, and Nora slapped her badge down on the bar in a fraction of an instant.

"Don't touch the glassware," she said to Buddy. "I need it. It's evidence."

"Evidence of what?" the bartender asked.

"I think that pretty girl over there is looking for another drink," Justine said to Buddy. "Why don't you go give one to her."

Nora and Justine each wrapped a paper napkin around a glass: the one belonging to Crocker and the one belonging to his friend.

Only when they were out of the bar, sitting together again in the Crown Vic, did they allow themselves to smile.

Justine opened her phone and tapped in some numbers.

"Sci. Can you meet us at the lab in twenty minutes? I think we've got something good."

Chapter 102

AS YOGI BERRA would have said, it was "déjà vu all over again." Rick was sitting beside me in the Cessna. We landed at the Las Vegas airport at dusk and rented a car.

Then we drove out past the sandy lots of stillborn subdivisions that had gone silent in '08. Eventually, a gray wall appeared, blocking the view of the gated community from the street.

We stopped at Carmine Noccia's front gate.

Rick pressed the button, and a voice answered, then someone buzzed us in. We crossed the bridge over a man-made recirculating river that could only have existed in Las Vegas, or maybe Orlando. We continued past the spotlit stables and came into the forecourt with its island of date palms outside the massive oak door.

Squint your eyes and you were in Barcelona or Morocco.

The Noccia goon we'd last seen wearing a red shirt was now in a tight black pullover and leather-like jeans.

He opened the door for us, then took Rick's gun and mine and put them on top of that double-wide gun safe masquerading as a Moorish armoire in the hallway.

The goon took the lead as he had before: through the billiards room, filled with the clacking of colored clay balls, to the great room where Carmine Noccia sat in his leather chair.

This time Noccia wasn't reading. He had his eyes on the ginormous screen over the fireplace, watching a rerun of the Titans' flat-out massacre of the Raiders a few hours ago.

He shut off the TV and, as before, offered us seats without shaking our hands.

I was feeling heady.

On the one hand, we'd been warned off by Carmine Noccia and his "family," and they had good reason to dislike us. I'd snubbed his lawyers, beaten up his guys at Glenda Treat's whorehouse, and I'd been disrespectful to Carmine's father, the don.

Now I was back with Del Rio, my loosely wrapped bodyguard buddy, wanting to make a deal. Took some nerve. I had asked Rick to keep his mouth shut, his eyes open, and his ass on the sofa. He'd said, "Yeah, boss," and I could only hope that he'd firmly chained his loose cannon to the deck.

The pool outside the glass doors reflected waving bars of light across Noccia's face, making his expression unreadable.

Would he tell me what I wanted to know? I sure hoped so.

"What is it now, Morgan?"

"You saw the game?"

"Call that a game? More like a turkey shoot."

"I've brought something to show you."

I took the packet of still shots out of my pocket and handed them to Carmine Noccia.

He took the photos with his cool, manicured hand and flipped through them. His eyebrows lifted minutely as he recognized the people in the pictures and realized what they were doing and what it meant to his business.

"How did you come by these photos? If you don't mind me asking."

"I shot them myself. But here's what matters. The game was rigged, and it's been going on for a while. If we hadn't intervened, money was going to keep hemorrhaging out of the bookie joints, and you might have bled to death.

"Instead, the Marzullos got it in the teeth. It should set them back for a while. Keep them out of sports betting on the national level. That's what I think. What do you think?"

Carmine put the pictures down on the table between us. He leaned back in his chair and watched my face. I watched his.

I tried to imagine what he was thinking. Did he believe that I'd done something this enormous that actually benefited him? Was he mapping out a war against the Marzullos? Or was he simply composing a way to tell his father how narrowly they'd avoided a calamity that could have sunk a very important component of the family business?

No words were spoken for a long time. Time expanded beyond the beveled glass windows in the great room, out past the man-made paradise and into the desert.

Private

As I've said, Del Rio is a patient man when he wants to be. I needn't have worried, because he was showing me what he'd proven many times as my copilot in Afghanistan. He was waiting, watching and waiting.

Carmine Noccia finally blinked.

"Tell me what you want," he said.

Chapter 103

CARMINE NOCCIA had asked me what I wanted. It was like a genie granting one of those fairy-tale wishes—you just have to be careful not to wish for a sausage on the end of your nose.

"I've shown good faith," I said. "I cleaned up a mess you didn't know you had. I want your father to know what we did. Here's my point in all of this. You're not going anywhere and neither are we. Let's accept the reality of that."

"You want détente. Peace between our operations. Stay out of one another's way."

"Pretty much. And I want to know who put out a hit on Shelby Cushman."

Noccia smiled. It was a small smile, but it seemed real. "No better friend. No worse enemy," he said.

I'd been expecting him to say anything, *anything* but that.

The words Noccia had just spoken were what the Marines say about themselves.

No better friend. No worse enemy.

Like Del Rio and me, Carmine Noccia had been in the Corps.

"Can I get you boys something to drink?" he said. "Or maybe you'll be my guests for dinner? We can talk while we eat."

"Thanks very much for the offer, but it's late. And I'm flying."

Noccia nodded, got up from his chair, and asked me and Del Rio to follow him into the billiards room. He said to the men around the table, "Go outside, guys. Take a break."

The room emptied quickly. There was a score counter over the billiards table, but Noccia walked past it to the chalkboard that hung on the wall. It appeared to be the long-running tally of winning games.

Noccia picked up an eraser from the tray below the board and wiped out some phone numbers that had been written in the corner.

His back was to me as he spoke. "We have a partner in a number of construction projects: a hotel in Nevada, a couple of malls in LA and San Diego. This partner came to us with a request," said Noccia. "We had no choice except to honor it."

I was mesmerized as he began to write his partner's name with a square of blue pool chalk. At first I didn't get it. I thought maybe he was going to draw a diagram from the partner to the man who had hired the hit.

But that's not what happened.

Carmine Noccia scratched letters onto the slate and said, "This is who contracted the hit on your friend Shelby Cushman."

When he was sure that I had seen what he'd written, he spat on the eraser and rubbed the name out.

He put the eraser down and walked me and Del Rio to the door, where he said good night.

And he shook my hand.

Chapter 104

IT WAS PAST midnight again, and I was back in LA. I had told Del Rio I'd see him in the morning, and he looked at me like he was a dad who'd just put his small son on a school bus for the first time.

"I'll be okay," I said.

But would I? Rick was still watching me as I got into my Lambo and strapped myself in. I got on the 10 East and then took the exit toward Sunset.

If I'd been driving a Volkswagen, I could've gone faster. It was the downside of owning a fast car. It alerted every cop in the state and every good-doin' citizen with a cell phone.

My mind was flying out in front of my hood, and still I stayed within the speed limits, finally slowing down and stopping at the entrance to the Chateau Marmont Hotel.

I took the elevator from the parking garage without seeing

anyone, and pressed the button for Andy's floor. I stood outside his door and used my cell phone to call him.

The phone rang and rang and rang. Finally, he answered.

"Jack? What's wrong? It's one in the morning."

"Everything's wrong. I'm right outside your door. Open up."

Andy was wearing the same pajamas he'd worn the last time I saw him. Crumpled silk, wide maroon stripes interspersed with thin black lines.

The room smelled like flatulence and the garlic bread sitting on the coffee table.

"You don't look so good," Andy said.

"I just flew in from Vegas," I told him. "Then I drove here."

"Sit down, Jack."

I stood.

"I spent some quality time with Carmine Noccia. I was at his house."

Andy looked into my face. There was no fear in his eyes.

How could he not have thought that I would find out? Had he underestimated how I would react? Or was Andy a far cooler customer than I'd ever known? This was not how I thought of my fraternity brother, my close friend since we were little kids.

I said in a voice that was ringing with shock, "Carmine told me about your request, that you were the one who asked him to have Shelby killed. How could you have done that? Tell me something I can believe."

Andy's face fell and his knees caved. I watched him drop to the floor, then I grabbed him up roughly, two steely hands at his shoulders, and threw him into an armchair that almost went over.

He was sobbing now, but I'd seen this embarrassing and pathetic act before.

"Come on, Andy. Really pour it on, you fuck."

"She was a *whore,* Jack. You told me so yourself, but I already knew that. She was doing every perversion with every scumbag with a buck. And I had to find out about it from some lowlife greaser who didn't know or care that Shelby was my wife."

"There are divorce courts," I said, but I was thinking of Shelby, seeing her face, remembering the belly laughs at the Improv, how she'd been a rock for me and maybe my salvation right after I'd come back from the war.

It killed me that she'd gone into whatever drug hell had made her fall so far. And then I thought about how I had introduced her to a man who had paid to have her murdered. If I hadn't introduced them, Shelby would still be alive. I had loved her, and I had trusted him. And I missed her badly.

How could Andy have done that to Shelby? How could anybody want to kill Shelby? She was gentle and kind and she made us all laugh—she made *me* laugh.

Andy's weeping was infuriating. The last time he'd sobbed his heart out, I'd felt his grief. Now there was no hiding it from myself: I'd been perfectly played. And my friend had done it to me.

I didn't know Andy Cushman anymore.

I said, "For a bean counter, you're a damned fine actor. Maybe overplaying it a touch right now."

The sobbing stopped, and Andy sobered. "Please, Jack.

You don't understand what it was like living in the same house with her. Knowing what she was doing: the junk, the men. I had to do it—but I couldn't do it myself. I did love her, Jack. I honestly did. Please. Don't tell the police."

"Don't worry about it. I won't call the cops. You're a client, you shit."

"And a friend?"

The pleading look just enraged me more.

By way of an answer, I punched him in the face. His chair fell back, and when he was down, I yanked him up by his hair, kicked him everywhere: legs, kidneys, ribs. I poured a three-hundred-dollar bottle of Scotch over his head. I couldn't think of anything else to say, nothing else I could do without actually killing him.

Andy Cushman, my former client, my former *friend,* was still crying when I left his suite.

Chapter 105

DR. SCI CAME spinning around the corner to Justine's office, grabbed the doorjamb, and leaned straight out as if he were a flag in a gale.

It was ten after ten in the morning, and he'd been working in the lab with Justine's two bar glasses all night.

Justine placed her palms flat on her desk and searched Sci's baby face. He was a scientist, so even if the news was bad, his expression could read happy: happy that he'd solved a problem.

"Tell me something good," Justine said. "Put a smile on my face, boy wonder."

"I've got good news and I've got bad news," Sci said.

Justine put her face in her hands. "Bad news first," she said.

"The *good* news is that I have isolated the unknown male's DNA. It matches the DNA we found in Wendy Borman's clothing."

"That's the good news?" Justine said. "We only got a forensic hit off that male DNA."

"Yep, he's still unknown. But you saw him. He's alive and well and living in LA."

"Listen, Sci, good news would be that you've got a positive match to Rudolph Crocker. I was sitting right next to him in the bar. I wrapped up his glass like I was swaddling a baby chick. His DNA has to be on that glass."

Sci let go of the doorjamb, came into the office, and sat in the chair across from Justine. He jammed his flip-flops up against the side of her desk. His yellow print aloha shirt picked up the blond streaks in his hair. It made him look like he had just wandered in from a surf shop in Venice Beach.

"The problem isn't that Rudolph Crocker's DNA isn't on that glass. It's that what I got was allele soup. So while I can't exclude him from the sample, I can't positively match his DNA to the DNA we found on Wendy Borman's shirt. I'm sorry, Justine. The sample is crap."

"Wait a minute. Wait a *minute*. Can you run the test again, try to isolate his DNA somehow—"

Sci watched Justine try to twist the result he'd given her into hope. If he could do it for her, he would.

"—can't you?"

"No. If I were to guess what happened," said Sci, "the barkeep was out of clean glasses. He rinsed out a dirty one in the sink and gave it to Crocker. New glasses came after that, and the barkeep gave a clean glass to the unknown male. Plausible?"

"I can't get another sample from Crocker," Justine said. "Not in time."

"If you can't find what you want on the street, go into his house and take it," said Sci.

"You don't really mean break into his house. . . . Oh. You're saying get a search warrant."

"If that's your best shot."

Shit, Justine thought. She dialed Bobby's number. She knew it by heart, of course.

Chapter 106

JUSTINE SIGHED, then swiveled her chair toward the windows and away from Sci. She lowered her face as she spoke urgently to Petino.

"Bobby. Sci says we can't *exclude* Rudolph Crocker's DNA from the sample. That means he could have been one of the psychos who kidnapped Wendy Borman.

"Right, Bob," Justine continued into the phone. "The sample is contaminated, but Crocker is *included* as one of many possibilities—

"Yes, that's true. Crocker is one of many possible contributors, so I need a search warrant—

"Are you serious? I only need to go into his apartment for one second and get his toothbrush—

"Thanks for your time, and thanks for nothing, Bob. Whatever happens is on you."

Justine banged down the receiver, spun around, and said to Sci, "He says even if he could strong-arm a judge, the evidence would be inadmissible. I don't care about the *case* right now. I want to stop this freak from *killing* someone tonight."

Sci's phone buzzed on his hip. He glanced at it and said to Justine, "I'll be downstairs if you need me."

Sci took the stairs to the basement lab. He found Mo-bot in her druid cave of an office, incense burning. It smelled like perfumed garbage to him.

Mo didn't look up from the computer. She said, "Morbid has hijacked a screen name and launched a text message to the target."

Sci rolled a chair up to Mo's desk and studied the screen. The stealth program they'd created was awfully good. It could hack calls wirelessly once the outgoing number was plugged in — but it also picked up chatter.

"Highlight Morbid and Lady D," Sci said. "Let's make it easier for us." He pulled his cell phone off his belt and called Jack.

"Morbid's making small talk with the target," he told Jack. "The little fuck is using the handle Lulu218. His text to her says 'C U after school.' Doesn't say where."

Sci said to Mo, "Can you get a better fix on Morbid's location? . . . Jack, he's in West Hollywood. That's all I can tell you right now. We'll track the pings until we can refine his location."

"Can't you trace him?" Jack asked.

"Nope," Sci said to Jack. "We can't intercept the call, and that poor girl will be dead before the cops can get a court order."

"I'm working on it!" Jack practically shouted.

Sci said, "Okay. We'll keep trying," then disconnected from the call to Jack.

"Text Lady D," Sci said to Mo.

"I tried. We're blocked. She's being so careful, poor lamb. She knows there's a killer out there, so she lets in the wolf wearing her girlfriend's screen name—and she locks us out."

Chapter 107

LIEUTENANT NORA CRONIN sped up Figueroa, jerked the wheel to the right, and double-parked in front of the obscure five-story white building that housed Private and its many secrets. Justine walked out of the glass front doors at a smart clip, got into the squad car, and buckled in.

"Pisses me off," Justine said.

"You know, even though Bobby's a complete prick, you gotta give him points here, Justine, because he's right. We don't have probable cause."

"Crocker and his buddy are going to kill someone tonight, another girl. That's my 'probable cause,' damn it."

The car radio sputtered: a hit-and-run on Cahuenga and Santa Monica Boulevard.

Nora dialed down the volume and said, "I say we hit Rudolph Crocker's office unannounced. You stand there looking like you look. Like a prosecutor with a stick up your ass. I badge Crocker, ask him nicely to come downtown. He's not under arrest; we just need his help with a case we're working on. Good-citizen kinda thing. Say he could have witnessed a crime."

"Okay," Justine said. "He comes in. Now he's in the box. You say he was identified driving past the street where Borman was kidnapped five years ago."

"Sure. That could work. Maybe he gets nervous and says something incriminating. Or maybe he leaves his DNA on a Coke can," Nora said. "Maybe coming into the station throws him off. So he cancels the kill tonight, and then, partner, we've bought more time, at least."

Justine nodded. "He works on Wilshire, near Fairfax. At ten forty a.m. he should be there."

Nora hit the gas and drove for fifteen minutes up Wilshire, located the address easily, and parked. Then she and Justine entered the chilly office building with a vivid barn-sized Frank Stella construction in the lobby.

Nora badged the blade-thin receptionist at the long green marble desk on the second floor. She asked to see Rudolph Crocker.

The receptionist said, "Mr. Crocker isn't in. He's taking a vacation day."

"Fuck!" Nora said, and banged her fist on the desk.

Back in the squad car, Nora drove toward Crocker's apartment building. "If he's not home, we wait for him like last time," she said to Justine.

"Or why don't you put out an APB on his stinking minivan?"

Nora said, "Fine. Good call, Justine."

Nora gave dispatch Crocker's name, said that he was driving a late-model blue Toyota Sienna minivan, and requested an all-points bulletin on the vehicle. "I want that van," she said, "in connection with the Schoolgirl murders."

"Watch. He'll be parked right outside his apartment," Nora said to Justine.

But the blue van wasn't in sight, and the doorman said that Crocker had left the building early that morning, around seven, and no, he had no idea when Crocker would be back.

Nora and Justine settled down in the squad car parked across from Crocker's apartment building. Nora continued with her litany of "fuck this" and "fuck that." More than four hours later, Nora got the call from dispatch.

"Lieutenant, that blue Sienna van is in Silver Lake. It was last seen heading north on Alvarado. Our unit was traveling south, then lost him in the turnaround."

Nora barked, "Tell all units to find that van, Sergeant. I want the driver pulled over under any pretext and held until I get there. The suspect may be armed and dangerous. He's our primary in a series of homicides."

Chapter 108

"JACK," MO-BOT SAID in a voice that was unusually tame for her, "so you can keep this straight, we don't know the real names of any of these people."

It was almost four thirty Monday afternoon. I was driving a fleet car, Cruz was riding shotgun beside me, and I was talking to Mo-bot, who was back at the office.

I put Mo on speakerphone so Emilio could hear this too.

She said, "'Morbid' is texting the unknown target, 'Lady D,' with a name he hijacked off her phone. It's a friend of hers."

"Gotcha."

"So Morbid just texted: 'I got something big to tell you. Can you meet me at Slommo's.'"

"What's Slommo's?" I asked Mo.

Cruz said, "I know it. Newsstand on Vermont."

Mo jumped back in. "Lady D texted again. 'I can't girlfren.

I'm cookin tonite. Goin shoppin.' Morbid writes back: 'This is major. I need to meet you at the store.'"

"*What* store?" I asked.

"Jack, you know everything I know. Uh-oh. The target says 'OK. C u in 15.' She disconnected the call."

"Got a location, Mo? On either party?"

"Morbid is on Montrose, closing in on Glendale. That's as close as I can make it. Wait, Morbid's signal is moving. Heading north.

"Jack, he stopped on Glendale. He's either at a light or, no, his speed tells me he's now on foot."

Cruz was cracking his knuckles obsessively. He said, "There's a Ralph's Supermarket on Glendale. What are we looking for?"

"Justine said he's white, skinny. Early twenties."

"We're on our way," I told Mo-bot. I felt like I was back in combat, like I had a second chance for everything to turn out right.

Chapter 109

EAMON FITZHUGH, aka Morbid, spotted Graciella Gomez standing outside Ralph's Supermarket.

The pretty girl was wearing denim short-shorts and one of those baby-doll tops, a pink one. He came across the parking lot toward her, his hands thrust into the pockets of his jeans, his head down, hair covering his eyes, which were definitely lusting for this little doll face.

"Lady D" didn't look up. Why would she? She was waiting for her girlfriend Lulu Fernandez to meet her and tell her some major news.

Morbid watched Graciella looking at her wristwatch, and then he walked right up to her, called her by her nickname. This is where he had to be a good actor, which he was. That was why he was on point.

"Gracie?"

"Yes?"

A little shy. "I'm Lulu's friend. I'm Fitz."

"Yeah? I never heard her saying she knows any Fritz."

"It's been our secret so far. Forget about that. Lulu sent me to meet you because she has to go to the hospital. She's in trouble."

"What? That's not right. What happened to her?"

"Look. Okay, she's pregnant with my kid. She told me to tell you she's spotting and she could lose the baby." Fitzhugh teared up. "It's your decision. She really needs you, though."

"You know what? You're bullshitting me, man. She woulda told me she was hooking up with a white boy, 'specially one as old as you."

"Don't you understand English? I said she needs help."

The girl's face stretched in anger. She screamed, "You *liar*. Get away from me." She backed up into a train of shopping carts, stumbled, righted herself, tried to run.

Fitzhugh caught up with her easily. He grabbed her arm, dragged her to a halt, and held her firm. "Stop, Gracie, you moron. Stop that. I'm for real, okay? Look—I'll let you go."

The girl was almost buying it. He was going to tell her that Lulu was waiting in the van, but he never got to say another word.

There was a stunning blow to his ribs. He fell back, looked up at the slick Mexican guy who had thrown him to the ground and was now yanking his arms behind his back, practically wrenching his right shoulder out of the socket. Fitzhugh screamed.

"What are you trying to do to this girl, you little prick? What's your name?" Cruz said. "I'm talking to you!"

Cruz bent down, grabbed the kid's wallet out of the back

of his jeans, and handed it to Jack. Then he said to the guy on the ground, "Where's Rudolph Crocker?"

"I don't know any Rudolph Crocker. Let me go or I'll yell for the police."

"Don't sweat it, Mr. Fitzhugh. The police are already on the way. I called them for you."

Chapter 110

JUSTINE GRIPPED THE armrest tightly with her right hand, held her phone with the other, and shouted to Jack over the sirens. "I'm with Nora Cronin. We've located Crocker's van a block from Ralph's. The van is pinned in by black-and-whites.... Jack, I'll call you back. This thing could blow up right now."

Nora braked in the street, and she and Justine jumped out of the squad car. One of a half dozen uniforms came up to Nora.

"LT, here's the thing. He was already parked when we located him. As soon as we pulled up, he put his hands on his head. His doors are locked and he won't get out."

"He's refusing to get out of the vehicle?"

"Right. Who does that? He must have something locked in there. Dope, maybe. Or hot electronics. Guns. He can't go anywhere, though."

Justine looked through the windshield at the young white guy with the wire-rim glasses. He looked out at her, seeming oddly calm.

It was definitely Crocker, the savage sonofabitch psycho. She knew his face from the yearbook, and from seeing him yesterday in the Whiskey Blue. For the past two years, every couple of months he'd lured and killed young women who'd fallen for whatever story he and his partner had concocted.

Justine knew the names of the victims and all about their promising, too-short lives, all thirteen of them. She hated Crocker. And she was also afraid.

Neither she nor the LAPD had anything substantial on Crocker except for a five-year-old ID from a minor who might not even testify.

Justine edged forward until she was close enough to Crocker to see that his nostrils were blanched, his eyebrows hitched up, and that he had a smile on his face.

It was almost like he was excited and just daring someone to shoot him.

What was this? A bid for suicide by cop?

That would not do. *Would not do.*

Justine went back to Nora's car and took the ASP baton from where it rested on the console. She returned to where Nora held her gun with both hands, the muzzle pointed at Crocker through the closed driver-side window.

"Get out of the car," Nora shouted again to Crocker. "This is the last time I'm telling you. Get out. Keep your hands where I can see them."

Crocker shouted back, "I'm not armed. I don't really think you're going to shoot me."

Justine knew her anger was calling the shots here, but she didn't care. She flicked the ASP down and out, the sound of it like racking a shotgun. The heavy six-inch metal bar extended to become a sixteen-inch nightstick.

Justine said, "Stand back, Nora."

Holding the ASP like a bat, she swung it at the Sienna's driver-side window. Crocker ducked too late. Glass shattered.

Then Justine swung and hit the glass again.

Nora gaped at Justine, then stuck her hand through the broken window and unlocked the door. She holstered her weapon and dragged Crocker out of his seat and down onto the pavement.

As the lanky young man tumbled to the ground, guns came out all around.

Nora barked, "On your stomach, hands on your head." Blood streamed down Crocker's face.

Justine felt sudden fear. If she was wrong about Crocker, there were going to be lawsuits, big ones. Crocker would sue the city for false arrest, police brutality, assault on his person and property. At the same time, he would sue her personally, and because she wasn't rich, he'd sue Private.

But right now it didn't matter. Nothing mattered except this stone-cold killer stretched out on the asphalt.

"Rudolph Crocker, we're arresting you for interfering with police," Nora said.

"I didn't interfere with anything. I was sitting in my car, minding my own business."

"Save it for the judge," said Nora.

"Man, are you going to look dumb," said Crocker.

Chapter 111

CRUZ AND I reached Justine within minutes of her call. The four-lane roadway was jammed to the sidewalks. Traffic cops were rerouting the rush hour surge, and the two southbound lanes were cordoned off with squad cars.

Cruz and I abandoned our car and walked through the cordon. I counted eight cruisers, twenty uniforms, and assorted other cops surrounding Nora Cronin, who had her small foot on the neck of a man who was lying facedown on the ground. Cronin was reading him his rights.

Justine stood a couple of yards away, wearing an expression I'd have to call rapt. She barely glanced at Cruz and me, kept her eyes on Cronin as the lieutenant grabbed the guy up off the ground and got him to his feet.

"I want to call my lawyer," said the guy with the glasses.

"Call all the lawyers you want, asshole," Nora said.

Four cops piled on and threw the guy across the hood of a

squad car and cuffed him behind his back. The guy looked benign and, more than that, unworried.

I said to Justine, "That's Crocker?"

She looked up at me, said, "Yeah, that's him. Did he kill anyone? I don't know. Maybe someone will get us that warrant now so we can collect his freakin' DNA."

News choppers materialized overhead. A BMW, a Ford sedan, and a TV satellite van came up the street.

Chief Michael Fescoe got out of the Ford. I couldn't believe he was here already.

DA Bobby Petino got out of the BMW.

The two of them converged, talked briefly, then came over to where Cruz and I stood with Justine.

"What happened to you?" Bobby said to Justine.

She looked down, saw blood streaks from her elbow to her wrist. "It's not mine," she said. "It's Crocker's."

Her face flamed — *but why?*

She turned away from Bobby as Fescoe said to me, "The one Cruz assaulted. Eamon Fitzhugh. What happened to him?"

I said, "In brief, we learned that he and Crocker were going to commit a murder tonight. Nothing we could verify. We tailed Fitzhugh, caught him getting into something hinky with a fifteen-year-old in the parking lot at Ralph's."

"He's at the hospital, dislocated shoulder and contusions, shouting about police brutality," Fescoe said.

Cruz said, "He was going to kill that girl —"

"So you say," Fescoe interjected.

"So I say," said Cruz. "All I did was tackle him with conviction. He's a bantamweight."

Fescoe's eyes were wild with anger when he looked at me. "Jack, this is crap. You've got unnamed sources. Putting guys in the hospital. Arrests without cause. I want you in my office in half an hour. Bring Cruz and Smith. If this disaster isn't explained to my satisfaction, I will be pulling your license."

As he walked off, I asked Justine, "You say that blood is *Crocker's?*"

She nodded. "Yep."

There was shattered glass all over the seat of the Sienna. Before the uniform could tell me not to, I put on a latex glove, picked up a few shards with blood on them, and folded the pieces into another glove. I handed the impromptu evidence bag to Justine along with the keys to my car.

"Get this to the lab, pronto. I'll meet you in Fescoe's office. Should be fun."

Justine didn't exactly smile, but her look softened. "Thanks, Jack."

Chapter 112

CHIEF MICHAEL FESCOE'S office smelled of yesterday's lunch.

The blinds over the interior glass walls were opened halfway so that Fescoe could see the squad room. The smudged windows peered onto Los Angeles Street, where cars rushed by like phantoms in the dark.

The tension in the room was electric and not in a good or positive way.

There wasn't a person sitting there who could say with confidence that as a result of today's operations, he or she wouldn't be sued or fired or jailed—or all three.

As Private's sole proprietor, I would be the first to face the firing squad. I was just a contractor. Private would be blamed for everything in the first round. We were guilty of using electronics that would be illegal except that laws against this advanced technique for remote wiretaps hadn't even been written yet.

On our say-so and at our urging, Lieutenant Nora Cronin had arrested a man who'd been injured by one of our operatives during the arrest, and our evidence against Rudolph Crocker was based solely on the five-year-old memory of a teenage girl who might not be willing to testify.

True, Fitzhugh had left DNA on the clothes of the murder victim five years before, but DNA on an ankle sock wasn't proof that he had killed her.

If we didn't prove a connection between Crocker and Fitzhugh and the deaths of any of the schoolgirls from Borman through Esperanza, their lawyers would get them out of jail free.

Petino and Fescoe both had a lot at stake, but the police chief in particular had his cajones in a waffle iron. One of his cops was involved. As Fescoe uncapped his coffee container, Petino paced at the back of the room. Because of his relationship with Justine, he'd brought Private to Fescoe and had vouched for us all. If we went down, Bobby Petino would never eat lunch in this town again—let alone become governor of the state.

People took their seats. Nora Cronin sat between Fescoe and Justine. Justine sat to my right, Cruz to my left.

"I want to go over all of it," Fescoe said. "But keep it simple. Justine, you first. Let's cut through all the bullshit—at least inside this office."

Justine used her most professional voice, but I knew her well enough to see and hear her fears. She held it together as she told Fescoe about Christine Castiglia, the witness to

Wendy Borman's abduction, a claim that had been borne out by the results from our lab.

"Two single-source DNA samples were recovered from Wendy's clothing," she said. "One of those samples absolutely matches Eamon Fitzhugh. The other sample doesn't match anyone *yet*. But from Castiglia's eyewitness report, Rudolph Crocker was the second boy who hustled Wendy Borman into the van."

Fescoe asked how Wendy Borman linked up with the Schoolgirl killings, and that's where it got dicey. I jumped in eventually and explained that the MOs were similar if not identical. "We think Wendy Borman was the first victim."

"If not the first victim, certainly an early one," said Justine.

I explained that Crocker and Fitzhugh hadn't made any substantial mistakes until Fitzhugh recruited Jason Pilser, possibly to raise the stakes of the game.

"We intercepted Pilser's electronic footprints. This bastard was bragging to his virtual friends about a club he was inducted into called the Street Freeks. And that the Street Freeks were doing killings in real life."

"You're losing me a little bit," said Fescoe.

"You asked for the simple version, Mickey. The point here is that we intercepted messages from Crocker to Pilser, and again from Crocker to Fitzhugh, describing a plan for them to kill another girl tonight. The girl he named was the girl Fitzhugh was talking to when Cruz brought him down."

"I see dots all over the place and zero connections," said Fescoe. Storm clouds were forming in his eyes. "Everything you've told me is either circumstantial or inadmissible or too damn obscure to convince a jury of our inferiors. I want *murder weapons*. I want *forensics* that match up. I want *eyewitnesses* who weren't eleven years old or who didn't jump or get pushed off their terraces to their deaths.

"Do you people understand me? Beri Hunt is going to represent Crocker. If we don't button this up, this case will never even go to trial."

"You have to keep Crocker and Fitzhugh apart," I said. "We need a little time to run Crocker's DNA against Wendy Borman's clothes."

I turned to Bobby Petino, who was still pacing a rut in Fescoe's carpet behind me.

"We need search warrants for Crocker's and Fitzhugh's homes and offices, Bobby. You think you can help us out? Don't let these two walk."

Chapter 113

NORA EASED INTO Crocker's apartment with her gun in hand, turned on the lights, slapped the warrant down on the hall table, then checked off what she saw in the one-bedroom apartment.

No visible computer in the main room.

Windows closed.

Air conditioning on.

Apparently no one home.

"Don't be sorry, Justine," Nora said over her shoulder, answering Justine's apology, delivered on the way up in the elevator. "*I'm* not the one going down. I can't speak for you, but seems like little Nora is the low man on the totem pole. I'm just your whatchacallit. Pawn. *Clear,*" she said.

Justine entered the apartment and followed Nora into the kitchenette, the bedroom, the bath.

Nora cleared all the rooms and closets, then put her gun away.

"Nobody here but us chickens. You take the bedroom and the bathroom," Nora said. "Shout if you find anything."

Justine stood in the bedroom doorway, studying the place. The room definitely showed an active brain. It was painted dark blue and had woodwork in different neon colors—pink, green, yellow—and orange baseboards and moldings. There was a California King platform bed for the young killer.

His books covered the full range of human knowledge, from arts and sciences to politics and ecology. His nightstand held a flashlight, an unopened box of rubbers, ChapStick, TV remote control, batteries.

There was a desk, and Justine went to it. No computer on the surface. The drawer was locked.

She took a pair of scissors out of the pencil cup and pried the lock as quickly as a B and E artist could. That was probably illegal, but what the crap? She'd bashed in his car window. That had to be worse.

Crocker's desk drawer was a disappointment, though. Six Krugerrands in an empty paper clip box. A baggie with some loose dope and rolling papers. The rest was office supplies. Not even any photographs.

Justine closed the drawer, went to the dresser, and opened every drawer.

She was looking for evidence of heinous crimes or the slightest memorabilia of those crimes: newspaper clippings or a notebook with handwritten notes or souvenirs. *Anything.*

Crocker took souvenirs from his victims, but unlike many trophy hunters, he had hidden them, then sent snarky, nose-thumbing e-mails to the mayor that led to the whistle-clean artifacts that proved nothing.

Surely, with all his pride in his success, Crocker would have kept *something*. Or was he just too damned smart?

Nora came into the room, and she and Justine flipped the mattress, revealing a clean box spring, no pockets cut into the fabric.

Nora said, "I never met any guys this clean."

Justine went to the closet, reached up, and tugged on the light pull, a doodad attached to a chain.

Crocker had six dark suits, six sport jackets, and several blue shirts, all hanging from hangers. Shoes were lined up neatly under the clothes. She checked pockets and felt inside shoes. And the longer she searched, the greater was the cold feeling of defeat.

Had Christine been wrong about Crocker? Was that possible?

Had Justine forced the girl to create false memories? Justine reached up to turn off the closet light, and that's when *it* clicked.

Crocker, that fool. He'd never expected anyone to look for it. Why would they? It had happened five years ago.

Justine shouted for Nora, and she appeared almost instantly.

Justine's heart was doing a happy dance, and her blood was pounding so hard in her ears she could barely hear her own voice when she said, "Nora. Tell me I'm not seeing things. Tell me I'm not making this up."

Chapter 114

JUSTINE LEANED BACK against the wall of "the box" and watched Nora Cronin doing her fearless, practiced interrogation.

Across the table from Nora sat Rudolph Crocker. He had sutures in a couple of places on his face, but otherwise he looked almost happy, as if he were enjoying the hell out of being the center of attention.

When he looked at Justine, he grinned as if to say, "You're in trouble, lady. Look who I got on my side: Beri Hunt, criminal-defense attorney to the stars."

Beri Hunt looked the way she looked on TV: early forties, short dark hair, and porcelain white skin. Her suit was of fine summer-weight gray wool, and she wore a strand of gray Pacific island pearls at her throat.

Hunt had already told Nora and her superiors up the line

that yes, they could get away with holding Crocker for interfering with the police. But as soon as Crocker was arraigned on this little misdemeanor, bail would be posted and her client would be out. At the same time, she'd be preparing lawsuits that would bring everyone involved in the arrest down. She'd smiled nicely as she said this.

Nora said, "Mr. Crocker, I apologize again for the injuries you sustained, but you understand, we thought you had a gun in the front seat."

"Right. But I *didn't* have a gun, and we're going to sue you for unlawfully assaulting me, right, Beri? We're going for millions."

"Rudy, let the lieutenant talk. We're just listening to what she has to say."

"It's Rude," said Crocker. "My nickname."

"You also understand, don't you, Mr. Crocker," Nora continued as if Rude hadn't spoken, "that once we were inside that van, we saw some very disturbing decor."

"Nothing in that van is admissible," said the attorney. "My client was not armed. And you had no cause to search the vehicle. What else have you got?"

"Let's talk about the van, okay, Ms. Hunt? It was lined with construction-grade black plastic, and the toolbox we found inside there was full of electrodes and clamps. So we've gotta ask what those tools were for.

"Any reasonable person, especially one who has seen the bodies of thirteen dead girls and has seen how they were killed, might think that the van was lined with plastic so as not to get any bodily fluids on the interior when your client tortured and killed another young girl."

"I just like to keep the van in mint condition for resale," Crocker said, but his smile was gone, at least temporarily.

"Don't say anything," Hunt said. "This detective is firing blanks in the dark."

"Well, I have some live ammo now," said Nora. "And it's getting nice and bright in here."

She opened the folder in front of her and turned the top sheet around so that Hunt and Crocker could see the report from Private's lab.

Hunt put on her glasses. "This is a DNA analysis," she said.

"That's correct," said Nora Cronin. "You don't have to answer any questions, Mr. Crocker, because I'm not asking a question. I'm letting your attorney know what we have so she can defend you from the charges we will be making against you.

"This report positively matches your DNA to the DNA found on Wendy Borman's shirt."

"I'm sorry," said Hunt. "Who is Wendy Borman?"

"Tell her, Mr. Crocker. Never mind. I'll do it. In 2006, a seventeen-year-old girl named Wendy Borman was Tasered on the street. After that, Mr. Crocker held her under the arms and his friend Mr. Fitzhugh took her by the ankles, and they swung her into a van.

"A day later, Wendy Borman turned up dead. Her clothing was properly stored, and the DNA left behind on her socks and her shirt was matched conclusively to Mr. Fitzhugh and to your dirtbag client.

"The kidnapping of Wendy Borman was witnessed," Nora continued. "The witness can positively identify your client, and she will testify."

Private

The lawyer said, "Do you have any proof that my client had anything to do with her death, Lieutenant? Touching and killing are two different things entirely."

Nora turned to Justine and said, "Dr. Smith. Want to clue Ms. Hunt in?"

Chapter 115

JUSTINE SAT DOWN at the table next to Nora, across from Crocker and his famous attorney. It felt like her pulse was beating in the low hundreds, but she thought she had her game face under control. She'd been looking forward to this.

She opened the folder and took out the wonderful photo of Wendy Borman standing between her two parents, taller than both of them, arms around their shoulders.

Wendy had been more than just beautiful. She'd looked like she was all set to win at life.

The pendant hanging from Wendy's necklace was circled with a marker pen, and Justine produced a close-up of that pendant.

It was an unusual gold star, almost like a starfish, with the points waving at the ends. It looked custom-made, one of a kind, and it was. The jeweler in Santa Monica was still in business and could identify the piece.

354

The lawyer stared at the picture, then looked up with a question on her face.

Justine reached into her jacket pocket and pulled out a small glassine bag with Wendy Borman's necklace inside.

"Your client was using this *as a light pull*, Ms. Hunt," she said. "Mr. Crocker's fingerprints are on it—and so is Ms. Borman's blood. It's engraved on the back: 'To Wendy with Love, M and D.'

"I photographed this charm hanging in Mr. Crocker's closet. Lieutenant Cronin witnessed it. We've got more than enough to hold your client on suspicion of murder while we negotiate with Mr. Fitzhugh."

"I want to speak with my client in private," Hunt said.

"Great. Do that," said Nora. "A couple of things you should know. We obtained a warrant for Mr. Crocker's office computer and it's being strip-searched right now. We've already found incriminating e-mails between Mr. Crocker and Mr. Fitzhugh saying where and when each of the thirteen girls was killed."

Justine watched Crocker go from Cool Dude Rude to a kid who was about to shit his shorts.

"Something else you should both know," Nora went on. "Mr. Fitzhugh is in the hospital under police protection. He hasn't seen a lawyer, but we've explained to him what we've just explained to Mr. Crocker. Ms. Hunt, you know the drill.

"You can take a chance with a jury. Or. You have a very small window of time to get ahead of this before Mr. Fitzhugh flips on your client and makes his own deal."

"I saw Mr. Fitzhugh this morning at the hospital," Justine

said. "He understands that picking up a fifteen-year-old girl with intent to kill isn't going to play well with a jury.

"Professionally speaking, I don't think Mr. Fitzhugh has the stomach to wait on death row for the needle. He's a sensitive and very logical person. And logically, that's too much stress for him. Frankly, he's on the verge of cracking wide open. If he hasn't already."

Justine felt a little giddiness lifting her voice, but it didn't matter, so she went on. "The district attorney wants to try both of you," Justine said to Crocker. "But Michael Fescoe, my good friend and chief of police, wants to keep things simple. The first confession wins.

"So you decide," Justine said, clasping her hands on the table in front of her. "Who gets life? Who gets death? Right now, it's up to you, Rude."

Chapter 116

JUSTINE FELT WIRED and almost high as she left her office for the meeting at city hall. She touched up her lipstick, took the elevator down to the street, and got into the backseat of the fleet car.

Jack was at the wheel, Cruz in the passenger seat.

"You okay, Justine?" Cruz asked her.

"Yeah. Why do you ask? Because the mayor wants to see us *now* and didn't say *why*? Or because my brain has been permanently polluted by a serial killer?"

"Tell him, Justine," Jack said with a big smile. "I haven't had a chance."

Cruz turned his head and grinned at her. "Yeah, Justine, tell me everything."

"So okay. After Crocker fires his attorney, he tells us about killing Wendy Borman in this grandiose, halfway laughing, private-school voice of his."

"Here's a quote, Emilio," Justine went on. "'It was a *game*, and I want *credit*. Why else would I have done all this planning and, *you know*, execution?'"

Cruz whistled. "You've got to be kidding me. He actually said that?"

"He was shooting for the top slot," Jack said. "Or the bottom—depends on how you look at it."

"Exactly. 'Rude' wants to be known as the most atrocious piece-of-crap serial killer in his 'age bracket' in the history of LA," Justine said.

"Like it or not, I guess he's going to have to share that honor with Fitzhugh. As for the fourteen victims we knew about? Crocker *hints* maybe there are more. He may even have some information for us on Jason Pilser's so-called suicide. Then he asks to speak to the DA."

Jack picked up the story from there. Justine put her head back and closed her eyes as Jack told Cruz that Bobby Petino had made a deal with Crocker: no death penalty for a full confession to the other killings, whatever number there were.

After that, Bobby had left the interrogation room as cool as ice. He didn't *care* why the kid was a psycho-killer.

But Justine had to understand why these privileged kids had become monsters. Crocker and Fitzhugh reminded Justine of Nathan Leopold and Richard Loeb, another pair of brilliant teenagers who killed a schoolmate in the early 1900s, to see if they could get away with it. Smart as they thought they were, they made a rookie mistake and were sent to prison for life. It came out later that those boys had had an acted-out but unacknowledged homosexual attachment.

Crocker and Fitzhugh had tortured their female victims, but none of the girls had been sexually assaulted. Were Crocker and Fitzhugh Leopold and Loeb all over again?

There were more questions than answers about the nature of their psychoses, and many different bags to choose from: genetic predisposition, trauma, brain physiology, and the ever popular "who the hell knows, because we're all different, right?"

As a potential witness against him, Justine couldn't spend any more time with Crocker, but she wished she could. That reptile would have told her anything she wanted to know — as long as it was about him.

Jack pulled into the garage behind city hall, opened the door for Justine, and gave her a hand.

Justine got to her feet, lowered her sunglasses, and said, "I'm just warning you, Jack. If the mayor tries to kick our butts for roughing up those bastards, I'm gonna kick back."

Chapter 117

MAYOR THOMAS HEFFERON was a wiry man with thick gray hair and a hanging left arm from an injury he'd taken in Desert Storm. Chief Fescoe, at a muscular six-three, looked like a bodyguard standing next to him, but Hefferon could handle himself just fine.

Hefferon motioned all of us—Justine, Cruz, Fescoe, Petino, Cronin, and myself—to join him at the glass conference table with its long view of the skyline.

He said, "I'm glad all of you could make it on such short notice. Chief Fescoe has news."

Fescoe folded his hands on the table. "Eamon Fitzhugh made a deal with Bobby and confessed to his part in killing Wendy Borman. We've got his computer at the lab now. Turns out this sick SOB must have obsessive-compulsive disorder," the police chief said. "He saved every file, every text message back to 2006. It's going to take weeks to figure out the wireless eavesdropping program he used to bait the victims. That freak is kind of a genius, I've been told."

Justine said, "That's interesting, Mickey. Crocker thinks of *himself* as the genius. He calls Fitzhugh a tool."

Cronin said, "Both of them are tools. So that's it, huh? I get my life back after two years? Hey, now I don't know what to do with myself."

After the laughter stopped, Hefferon said, "You folks did a tremendous job. Chief, it took guts to bring Private in on the case. Jack, hope to see you again.

"Justine, Nora, all those hours, and years, more than paid off. You too, Emilio. I hear you scared the snot out of Fitzhugh. Fact is, LA is a safer place because of your dedication. Thank you."

Damn, but that thanks felt good. Whatever brain chemical it released made my whole body happy. No amount of money could compare to the high of taking out the trash and slamming down the lid, knowing it was nailed shut for good.

We were sipping champagne and joking around as we had our pictures taken with the mayor, when my phone signaled me from my inside breast pocket.

It was a voice mail message transferred from my office phone and marked "urgent." The caller was a Michael Donahue.

I knew the name but couldn't place it—then it came to me like a punch to the face. Donahue was the owner of the Irish pub Colleen frequented.

I hit a button, listened to Donahue speaking gravely in his heavy Irish brogue. I replayed the message so I could be sure of what he had said.

"Jack. It's bad. Colleen is at Glendale Memorial Hospital. Room four eleven. You need to come there quickly."

Chapter 118

I TORE UP the freeway north, heading toward the hospital.

I tried to reach Donahue, but my calls went straight to voice mail.

I was scared, preoccupied, and the exit came up too fast.

I twisted the wheel hard and lost control. The car fishtailed, came to a stop, and stalled out five inches from a concrete divider.

Horns honked as freeway traffic flashed by me at seventy. My hands shook as I restarted the engine and finally made it safely down the off-ramp. Jeez, I'd almost totaled my car, and maybe myself.

Twenty-five minutes after getting Donahue's call, I bulled my way through the lobby of Glendale Memorial and stabbed the elevator button until the doors opened and then closed behind me.

By some kind of blind bloodhound instinct, I found Colleen's room on the first try.

I strong-armed the swinging door, and Donahue got up from the bedside chair, came toward me, and shook my hand.

"Take it easy on her, Jack. She's not well."

"What happened?"

"I'll leave the two of you alone."

Colleen's cheeks were flushed. Her hair was damp at her temples. The white cotton blankets covered her to her chin.

She looked very small in the bed, like a feverish child.

I took Mike's vacated chair, leaned over, and touched her shoulder. I was scared for her. She'd never been sick since I'd met her. Not a day.

"Colleen. It's Jack."

She opened her blue eyes and nodded when she saw me.

"Are you okay? What happened?" I asked.

Medication dragged at her voice. "I'm going home."

"What are you saying? To Dublin?"

A terrible thought came to me—like a balled fist to the gut. "Were you pregnant? Did you lose the baby?"

Colleen's blank expression became a smile. She laughed and then she was swept up in a kind of hysteria that turned to sobs. She put her hands up by her cheeks, and I saw shocking white bands of gauze and tape binding her wrists.

The gauze was striped with bright blood, which was seeping through.

What had she *done?*

"I told Mike not to call you. I'm mortified for you to see me like this.... I'll be all right. Please go, Jack. I'm fine now."

"What were you thinking, Colleen?"

I thought back over the past weeks and months. I hadn't noticed that Colleen was depressed. How had I missed it? What the hell was wrong with me sometimes?

"I was completely daft," she said. "I just hurt so much. You don't have to tell me again. I know it's over."

"Colleen. Oh, Colleen," I whispered.

She closed her eyes, and shame washed over me. Guilt and shame. I did care about Colleen, but she cared more. It had been selfish of me to stay with her for so long, when I knew we'd gone as far as we could go. I'd hurt this woman—and she'd done *this* to herself. What a terrible thing.

I don't know how long the silence between us lasted. Maybe it was only a minute, but it was time enough to think about what Colleen meant to me and to try to imagine a future for the two of us. It was sad, but I just couldn't see it.

"At least you won't be having to listen to my queer way of talkin'," she said.

"Don't you know that I love to listen to your voice?"

"You were good to me, Jack. *Always*. I won't forget that."

"Damn it, Molloy. I want you to be happy."

She nodded, tears slipping down her cheeks.

"You too," she said. "I want that for you too."

Neither of us said another word.

I kissed her good-bye, then I walked out, and I knew I would never see Colleen again, and that was my loss.

I had let another good woman get away, hadn't I? What the hell was wrong with me?

Chapter 119

I HAD PLANNED a "wrap party" at the Pacific Dining Car to thank the guys in the lab as well as the primaries on the Schoolgirl case for a job extremely well done.

After seeing Colleen, I couldn't celebrate and I couldn't fake it.

I phoned Sci, told him I had a family emergency, and asked him to stand in for me as host. Then I did the unthinkable. I turned off my phone.

I drove to Forest Lawn, an old and sprawling cemetery where dozens of celebrities were buried. My sweet mom was buried there too.

She'd been taken down by a previously undiagnosed heart disease during the heat and ugliness of my father's trial. It was a sharp, unexpected ending to an unfulfilled life. Maybe it was my mother and father's bad relationship that kept me away from marriage.

Private

I took off my jacket and sat on the grass near her simple stone, engraved with hands folded in prayer above an inscription: "Sandra Kreutzer Morgan is with God."

A lawn mower hummed in the distance, and I saw the flash of Mylar balloons, probably hovering over the grave of some poor child buried nearby.

I didn't talk to my mother's bones or her spirit. I didn't even pray until just before I left.

But I thought about the good times we'd had together: the rare picnics, a few tailgate parties after football games, watching Peter Sellers movies with her on late-night TV. She had probably seen *The Pink Panther* a hundred times. So had I. So had Tommy.

I grinned thinking about that, and after a while I rolled my jacket into a pillow and lay down. I got mesmerized by the slow shifting of the oak leaves in the branches overhead.

And then I fell off the planet for a while.

I must have slept long and deep, because I was awakened by a groundskeeper shaking my arm, saying, "Sir, we're closing. You have to leave, sir."

I touched Mom's stone, found my car, and as the horse knows the way to carry the sleigh, my car seemed to drive itself to a pretty carriage house I knew well in the flats of Beverly Hills.

I parked on Wetherly, a tidy residential block, and sat for a while just looking at Justine's small, beautiful house. I turned my phone back on and tapped in her number.

Justine answered on the first ring. "Jack. What was this family emergency?" she asked. "You missed the party."

"Colleen is going back to Dublin," I said. "We talked it

over. After that I went out to Forest Lawn. I needed time to think."

"Are you okay?"

"Sure."

"'Sure,' he says," Justine said, tweaking me. "Well, I've had to do some mental reorganization of my own. See, um, Bobby dumped me to go back to his wife. Too bad for Bobby, though; she didn't want him anymore."

I wanted to comfort Justine, and at the same time I was happy to hear this breaking news. Justine was too good for Bobby Petino, or to get tainted by the smudge and stink of California politics.

I wondered where Justine was right now. I pictured her in a chaise in her study, or lying in bed with the TV turned down, a glass of wine in her hand. My emotional pull toward her was almost a physical force.

"What are you doing right now?" I asked.

"Why?"

"I could come over," I said. "Just for a while."

There was a deep pause that I filled with hope.

"Jack, we both know that would be a bad idea," Justine said. "Why don't you just get a good night's sleep, and I'll see you tomorrow."

I was saying her name when she disconnected the line. I watched the lights go off in her house, one by one.

And then I drove to my home alone.

Epilogue

IT'S A WRAP

Chapter 120

OUT-OF-WORK actor Parker Dalton knocked on the door of Suite 34 at the Chateau Marmont.

He held the folding massage table by its handle, reset his cap with his other hand, and waited on the dark print carpet for Mr. Cushman to invite him in for his daily rub.

Dalton loved this job, actually. Stars had always stayed at the Chateau, and some of them actually lived here several months at a time. The sightings of Drew Barrymore, Cameron Diaz, Matthew Perry, and others made fantastic entries on Dalton's blog and always gave him hope for his own career.

Mr. Cushman was no star, but he was a celebrity, what with his wife having been murdered and the killer still on the loose.

Dalton had tweeted about his sessions with Mr. Cushman,

and his friends and innumerable friends of friends begged for more tweets, more details, more snarky observations.

When Mr. Cushman didn't come to the door, Dalton phoned his room on the direct line. He heard the phone ring inside the suite, and when Mr. Cushman didn't pick up, he considered his options.

Should he leave—or call the front desk?

It wasn't exactly rare for Mr. Cushman to be semidrunk when Dalton arrived. But maybe there had been an accident. Maybe he had fallen in the shower.

Dalton finally called the desk, and within minutes the day manager came up, a tall blond guy with a rockin' build and the name "Mr. Straus" on the tag on his vest. Straus questioned Dalton briefly and then opened the door to Cushman's suite.

Dalton stood at the threshold and called out, "Mr. Cushman." When there was no answer, he followed Straus into the large suite.

The spare 1930s-style furniture was undisturbed. Bottles and glasses littered the tabletops, garbage spilled out of trash cans, and white curtains billowed over the unmade bed.

"I don't see Mr. Cushman anywhere," said Dalton.

"No kidding," said Straus.

Dalton watched Straus open the closet doors—and he saw his opportunity to snoop. What did Mr. Cushman wear when he wasn't naked or in his pajamas?

The closet was empty and so were the dresser drawers.

The bathroom, with its wonderful period black-and-white tiles, was a mess: medicine cabinet open, just a used razor and a bottle of aspirin inside, towels all over the floor.

"Man, looks like he checked out without telling me," said Parker Dalton.

"Christ," said the manager, beginning to shake his head. "He didn't check out. He bolted."

"Are you calling the police?"

"Be serious. This is the Chateau Marmont."

Parker Dalton was tweeting before he left the legendary and, some said, haunted hotel. *Oh, man, what a tale he had to tell.* By the end of the day, twenty thousand nosy people would know that Andy Cushman had stiffed the hotel and scampered away.

Chapter 121

IT WAS LATE afternoon when Del Rio turned off Lobo Canyon and parked his gray Land Rover off Lobo Vista Road.

The sky was as gray as the car, as gray as his clothes, camouflage he didn't need because this was such a desolate spot.

Del Rio was thinking about Jack as he took his Remington 700, fitted with a ten-power scope, from the rear of the car.

He walked off-road, taking a deer path up an incline through the scrub.

The rise got steeper, and when the trail bore to the right, Del Rio broke a new path through the weeds, grabbing onto grasses and coyote brush and pulling himself up the hillside in places where his shoes slid on the slope.

When he reached the plateau, he took in the view of the farmhouse seventy-five yards below him, with its sun-bleached outbuildings and stretch of terrain that looked like a rumpled and dusty carpet had been tossed over the hills.

Del Rio assumed a prone position with the muzzle of the gun extended over the edge of the bluff.

Forty minutes crawled by before the back door of the farmhouse opened—and the man he was waiting for came out with a dog, a handsome Rhodesian ridgeback.

The guy had a rolling walk, wore a plaid shirt, jeans, a brown brimmed hat. He chained the dog to the porch post, patted its head, then picked up a bridle and saddle from a railing before heading to the paddock.

The guy with the hat saddled up a bay mare and rode it out to a bridle path that led into the hills, where trouble was waiting for him.

Del Rio lined up his shot where two lines of plaid intersected and squeezed the trigger.

The mare's ears went back, and Del Rio saw the hole appear in the rider's shirt just as the horse rounded a bend.

Del Rio stood and saw that the rider was still sitting upright, until, as if in slow motion, he tipped to the left and fell to the ground.

The mare stepped off the trail, dragging the rider by one boot until he fell free. Then the horse stopped and grazed on the dry grass.

Del Rio picked up his shell casing, put it in his shirt pocket, and walked down the bluff at a right angle to the trail.

When he reached the hit man's body, he checked for a pulse. There was none.

He kicked the contract killer a couple times in the side to be sure he was dead, then said, "Hey, Bo Montgomery, you scum. Shelby didn't see it coming either."

Del Rio wiped down his gun with his shirttails and tossed it over the cliff, saw it bounce and get lost in the miles of unbroken scrub.

He polished the casing and hurled it after the gun, watched it disappear.

One shot. One kill.

Job done. Very professional. Very Private.

Very personal too, thought Del Rio.

Jack had loved Shelby—and he loved Jack.

Chapter 122

ALL OF OUR major cases were closed at the moment. At least that was true in the Los Angeles office.

London, Frankfurt, Chicago, and New York were busy, and they were fighting a war in Presti's office in Rome—which was good for the bottom line, though I didn't much care about that.

Our morning meeting in the war room had turned into an ad hoc, standing-room-only, hip-hip-hooray bash. Mo dished up cheesecake, Sci topped up coffee mugs with a jug-size bottle of Bailey's, and Cruz stood close enough to Sci's lab assistant Karen to see down her neckline and into her shoes.

Pressured into saying a few words, Justine took the floor and spoke three syllables: *"We got 'em."*

The group broke into whooping applause.

Just then, the door opened, and my new assistant, Cody Dawes, slipped in and made his way toward me.

"A Jeanette Colton showed up without an appointment, Jack. She's in reception. What should I do?"

"I'll bring her up to my office," I said. "Get in here, Cody. Get to know people. That's the most important part of your job here."

"Your phones."

"This is why we have voice mail."

I left the war room and found Jeanette Colton sitting off to the side of the reception desk. The last time I'd seen her, she was neatly coiffed and contained, telling me how she and her tennis star husband and the couple down the street wanted to swap partners.

I'd referred her to my old friend Haywood Prentiss, thinking it was too bad we couldn't take the assignment.

As I closed the distance between us, I could see that something was terribly wrong with Jeanette Colton. There was a fresh handprint on her left cheek, and both eyes were swollen and turning black.

Her hand felt like a hook when she grabbed my arm and held on.

"Jack, I have to talk to you. I'm sorry I just showed up like this."

"Jesus, what the hell happened? Let's go upstairs to my office."

Her face twisted, and she started to cry. Suddenly she looked like a little girl.

"I did a bad thing," Jeanette Colton sputtered as we got into the elevator. "I ran Lars over with his Rolls."

"You did what?"

"I ran him down, backed over him too."

"You killed him?"

She shook her head no. "He was swearing at me when I left. I called an ambulance, but I didn't wait for it to come. I need your help, Jack. I need the best."

We got out of the elevator and headed toward my office, lickety-split. Scratch that about all our major cases being solved.

"I'll help you any way I can," I said, opening my door and stepping aside to let Jeanette walk into my office ahead of me.

The door yawned open, and both Jeanette Colton and I did a double take. My twin was sitting in my chair, moccasins up on my desk, a smirk on his face.

Why was he here?

What new load of garbage was he going to dump on me now?

"How is it going in the hero business?" Tommy said. "No need for tears, fair damsel in distress. Jack will straighten everything out for you."

Chapter 123

"I JUST NEED a minute, bro," Tommy said. "And then I'll get out of your way."

I asked Jeanette Colton to take a seat next to Cody's desk and said I'd be right back. Thirty seconds. I closed the door behind me.

"Start talking," I said.

"It's more like show-and-tell," Tommy said, handing me a document from inside a blue folder.

"Get away from my desk," I said.

Tommy snickered, got up, and took a seat in the side chair as I sat down at my desk and unfolded the legal document. I saw Tommy's name *and my dad's*.

I looked at my brother and said, "Cut to the chase, will you, Junior? My client is in trouble."

"She'll be just fine. I can tell. Anyway, happy to boil it

down, twinster. I finished rehab with flying colors and mentioned it to Dad's lawyer. I got big news. And I mean *big*."

"Dad wasn't our real father? That's a relief."

Tommy laughed. "Oh, he was our real father, all right. And since I successfully completed treatment, I inherit a bunch of money. Fifteen million, Jack. Same as you, I think."

I controlled my expression, but I was shocked. Knowing my father like I did, I figured he was running a Jack-versus-Tommy competition from the grave. The old man was sneaky even in death. Why else hadn't he told me that he'd put money away for Tommy too?

"You know what I'm going to do with my inheritance, Jack? I'm going to expand Private Security. We're going to go global. I have Dad's name, and I think he would want me to whip you. Private Security is going to be bigger and better than Private Investigations. You can count on it."

"Good for you, Tommy. I wish you and your business much success."

I stood up, showing him the door without taking a step. "Thanks for stopping by. Don't let the door hit you on your way out."

But Tommy wasn't done. His smirk broadened.

"I have something else for you," he said. He took a slip of paper out of his breast pocket and handed it over.

It was a check for $600,000, made out to me.

"We're even now, Jack," he said.

And then he stood and made a gun with his forefinger and thumb, pointed at me.

"You're *dead*, Jack."

He said it with an eerie bleat, and I understood that he was imitating the sound his voice had made all those times it came through the electronic gizmo used to disguise it. Seeing his face as he said "You're dead" had an even more chilling effect than hearing a mechanical voice over the phone. It was that much more real.

This was my brother; this was my twin.

He hated me so much that he'd been secretly tormenting me for years.

I didn't flinch even though he'd hurt me. I said, "So it has been you, Junior, calling me all this time. I asked you if you were calling, and you lied. And like all the other times I gave you the benefit of the doubt, you turned it back on me.

"I won't trust you again, not ever. And by the way, bro. I'm not dead. No way. No how. Not yet."

Tommy said nothing. His grin was wooden as he left my office. My womb mate, my sworn enemy, my daily death threat caller headed down the winding nautilus shell staircase and out of sight. I hoped I'd never see him or hear his voice again.

Fat chance of that.

I went out and got Jeanette Colton. "My evil twin," I explained.

Chapter 124

I WOKE UP the next morning in accord with my own circadian rhythms.

For a change, I wasn't torn out of a nightmare. The phone hadn't rung. The surf was up behind my house, and the sound of crashing waves was coming through the open windows. Nice.

Even nicer, Justine was lying next to me.

I turned to look at her gorgeous face and saw that she was watching me and smiling. I was filled with complete love for this woman.

She put her arms around my neck and pulled me close to her.

"The music of the surf," she said. "I've always loved this house."

"This house has always loved *you*."

We were on our sides, facing each other. I pulled her thigh

over my hip and suddenly we were immersed in a deep kiss, the sound of our breathing overwhelming the rush of the waves.

I didn't think I could wait another moment—when the goddamned phone rang on the table.

Tommy. I reached for the phone, planning to blast him to hell. Then I read the caller ID. It wasn't Tommy—and *still* I had to take the call.

"Jack Morgan," I said, panting a little.

Carmine Noccia's tone was casual, but his message was deadly serious.

"Sorry, Jack, but I've got bad news for you. Andy Cushman was involved in a one-car accident up the coast. He met a turn in the road head-on and went over a cliff near Marin. The car burned right the hell up. There were no skid marks. I think maybe his brakes failed."

"You're sure it was Andy?" I asked. I was having a little trouble talking, and breathing.

"Oh, yeah. It was him. One of my guys saw it happen. We were keeping an eye on him, you know. Hey. You have a good weekend."

I closed the phone but hung on to it for a moment. I thought about my new silent partner, Carmine Noccia. Never a better friend. Never a worse enemy.

And I thought about how my feelings for Andy had changed once I knew he'd had Shelby murdered.

Andy had been my closest friend. I'd stood up for him at his wedding. I had expected to be godfather to Andy's kids, or at least hang out with him when we were old, jetting around to golf courses, swapping memories, laughing our faces off.

And now Andy was dead. I knew I would feel something later, but for now I felt nothing for him.

Nothing at all.

I got out of bed and opened the sliders. Then I hauled back and hurled the phone as far as I could. Far. When the phone hit the waves, I closed the doors and locked them. I went back to Justine.

Could she read my face? Sure.

Could she read my mind? Probably.

"Who was that?" she asked.

"It doesn't matter."

She ran her hands down my sides and up my back. "You okay, Jack?"

"I'm fine," I said, moving her long dark hair away from her face. "It's time for a new phone, a new phone number."

"Surprise me sometime, okay? Can you do that? Tell me what you're actually thinking."

"I'm thinking we were in the middle of something really good," I said.

"I remember."

I pulled Justine close, snugged her thigh over my hip. I kissed her again and got lost in the wonder of her. It was good, exactly where I wanted to be. I could tell her anything, and I did.

"Andy's dead," I whispered against Justine's cheek.

COMING IN AUGUST 2010

Don't Blink

James Patterson
& Howard Roughan

James Patterson delivers the scariest mafia thriller since *The Godfather* – all-out mob war, and one man caught in the crossfire.

New York's Lombardo's Steak House is famous for three reasons – the menu, the clientele, and now the gruesome murder of an infamous mob lawyer. Effortlessly, the assassin slips through the police's fingers, and his absence sparks a blaze of accusations about who ordered the hit.

Seated at a nearby table, reporter Nick Daniels is conducting a once-in-a-lifetime interview with a legendary baseball bad-boy. Shocked and shaken, he doesn't realise that he's accidentally captured a key piece of evidence. Ensnared in the city's most sensational crime in years, Nick investigates for a story of his own. Back off – *or die* – is the clear message as he closes in on the facts. Heedless, and perhaps in love, Nick endures humiliation, threats, violence, and worse in a thriller that overturns every expectation and finishes with the kind of flourish only James Patterson knows.

Century · London

Read on for a sneak preview of

Don't Blink

One

LOMBARDO'S STEAKHOUSE on Manhattan's Upper East Side was justly famous for two things, two specialties of the house. The first was its double thick, artery-clogging, forty-six ounce porterhouse, the mere sight of which could give a vegan an apoplectic seizure.

The second claim to fame was its clientele.

Simply put, Lombardo's Steakhouse was paparazzi heaven. From A-list actors to all-star pro athletes, CEOs to supermodels, rap stars to poet laureates—anyone who was anyone could be spotted at Lombardo's, whether they were brokering deals or just looking and acting fabulous.

Zagat, the ubiquitous red bible of dining guides, said it best. *"Get ready to rub elbows and egos with the jet set because Lombardo's is definitely the place to see and be seen."*

Unless you were Bruno Torenzi, that is.

He was the man who was about to make Lombardo's

Steakhouse renowned for something else. Something terrible, just unbelievably awful.

And no one seemed to notice him . . . until it was too late . . . until the deed was almost done.

Of course, that was the idea, wasn't it? In his black, three-button Ermenegildo Zegna suit and dark-tinted sunglasses, Bruno Torenzi could have been anybody. He could have been *everybody*.

Besides, it was lunch. Broad daylight, for Christ's sake.

For something this sick and depraved to go down you would have at least thought night-time. Hell, make that a full moon with a full chorus of wolves howling.

"Can I help you, sir?" inquired the hostess, Tiffany, the one person who did manage to notice Torenzi if only because it was her job. She was a young and stunning blonde from the Midwest, with perfect porcelain skin, who could turn more heads than a chiropractor.

But it was if she didn't even exist.

Torenzi didn't stop, didn't even glance her way when she spoke to him. He just waltzed right by her, cool as a cabana.

Screw it, thought the busy hostess, letting him go. The restaurant was packed as always, and he certainly looked like he belonged. There were other customers arriving, getting in her face as only New Yorkers can. Surely, this guy was meeting up with someone who was already seated.

She was right about that much.

Table chatter, clanking silverware, the iconic jazz of John Coltrane filtering down from the recessed ceiling speakers—they all combined to fill the mahogany-paneled dining room of Lombardo's with a continuous loop of the most pleasant sort of white noise.

Torenzi heard none of it.

He'd been hired because of his discipline, his unyielding focus. In his mind there was only one other person in the busy restaurant. Just one.

Thirty feet . . .

Torenzi had spotted the table in the far right corner. A special table, no doubt about that. For a very special customer.

Twenty feet . . .

He cut sharply over to another aisle, the heels of his black wingtips clicking against the polished wood flooring like a metronome in three-quarter time.

Ten feet . . .

Torenzi leveled his stare on the bald and unabashedly overweight man seated alone with his back to the wall. The picture he'd been handed could stay tucked in his pocket. There was no need to double check the image.

This was him, for sure. Vincent Marcozza.

The man who had less than a minute to live.

Two

VINCENT MARCOZZA—weighing in at three hundred pounds plus—glanced up from what remained of his blood-rare porterhouse steak, stuffed baked potato, and a gaudy portion of onion strings. Even sitting still the guy looked woefully out of breath and very close to a coronary.

"Can I help you?" asked Marcozza. His raised-on-the-streets-of-Brooklyn tone, however, suggested otherwise. It was more like, *Hey, pal, what the hell are you staring at? I'm eating here.*

Torenzi stood motionless, measuring the important man. He took his sweet time answering. Finally, in a thick Italian accent he announced, "I have a message from Eddie."

This amused Marcozza for some reason. His pasty complexion spiked red as he laughed, his neck fat jiggling like a Jell-O mold. "A message from Eddie, huh? Hell, I should've known. You look like one of Eddie's guys."

He lifted the napkin from his lap, wiping the oily cow juice from the corners of his mouth. "So what is it, boy? Spit it out."

Torenzi glanced to his left and right as if to point out how close the nearby tables were. They were too close. *Capeesh?*

Marcozza nodded. Then he motioned his uninvited lunch visitor forward. "For my ears only, huh?" he said before breaking into another neck-jiggling laugh. "This oughta be good. It's a joke, right? Let's hear it."

Over on the far wall a waiter stood tiptoe on a chair, erasing the Chilean sea bass special from a large chalkboard. Hustling by him, a busboy and his gray bucket carried the remains of a table for four. And at the bar, a waitress loaded up her tray with a glass of Pinot Noir, a vodka tonic, and two dry martinis with almond-stuffed olives.

Torenzi stepped slowly to Marcozza's side. Placing his left hand firmly on the table he unclenched his right fist tucked neatly behind his back. The cold steel handle of a scalpel fell promptly and rather gracefully from his sleeve.

Then, leaning in, Torenzi whispered three words, and only three. "Justice is blind."

Marcozza squinted. Then he frowned. He was about to ask what the hell that was supposed to mean?

But he never got the chance.

Three

IN A HELLISH BLUR, Bruno Torenzi whipped his arm around, plunging the scalpel deep into the puffy fold above Marcozza's left eye. With a good butcher's precision and hard speed, he cut clockwise around the orbital socket. Three, six, nine, midnight . . . The blade moved so fast the blood didn't have time to bleed.

"*ARRRGH!*" was a pretty good approximation of the sound Marcozza made.

He screamed in agony as the entire restaurant turned. *Now* everyone noticed Bruno Torenzi. He was the one carving the eye out of that fat man's face—like a pumpkin!

"*ARRRRRRGH!*"

Torenzi was outweighed by over a hundred pounds but it didn't matter. He'd positioned himself perfectly, his rigid choke hold keeping Marcozza's head dead still while the rest of his body violently jerked and thrashed. What was premeditated murder if not calculated leverage?

Squish!

Scooped out like a melon ball, Marcozza's left eye fell to the white linen tablecloth before rolling to a stop.

Next came the right eye. *Slice, slice, slice* . . . Beautiful handiwork to be sure.

But the right eye didn't pop out like the left one. Instead, it dangled, held by the stubborn red vessel of the optic nerve.

Torenzi smiled and flicked his wrist. He was almost finished here, so hold the applause.

Snip!

Marcozza's right eye, with a gooey tail of flesh and vein, careened off the bread plate and fell to the floor.

Blood, finally catching up to the moment, now gushed from Marcozza's empty eye sockets. In medical terms, his ophthalmic artery had been severed from his internal carotid artery, the high-pressure mainline to the brain. In layman's terms, it was just a god-awful, horrifying and disgusting mess.

A few tables away, a woman wearing everything Chanel fainted, passing out cold, while another threw up all over her tiramisu.

As for Torenzi, he simply tucked the scalpel into the breast pocket of his Zegna suit before heading toward the kitchen to exit through the back door—back into broad daylight.

But before he did, he leaned down again to repeat his message into Marcozza's chubby ear as he lay hunched over the table dying a slow, mean death.

"Justice is blind."

We support

I'm proud to support the National Literacy Trust, an independent charity that changes lives through literacy.

Did you know that millions of people in the UK struggle to read and write? This means children are less likely to succeed at school and less likely to develop into confident and happy teenagers. Literacy difficulties will limit their opportunities throughout adult life.

The National Literacy Trust passionately believes that everyone has a right to the reading, writing, speaking and listening skills they need to fulfil their own and, ultimately, the nation's potential.

My own son didn't used to enjoy reading which was why I started writing children's books – reading for pleasure is an essential way to encourage children to pick up a book. The National Literacy Trust is dedicated to delivering exciting initiatives to encourage people to read and to help raise literacy levels. To find out more about the great work that they do visit their website at www.literacytrust.org.uk.

James Patterson